WHAT IT TAKES

DR. J GIRARD JR.

The final approval for this literary material is granted by the author.

First printing

This is a work of fiction. Names, characters, businesses, places, events and incidents are either the products of the author's imagination or used in a fictitious manner. Any resemblance to actual persons, living or dead, or actual events is purely coincidental.

ISBN: 978-1-61296-802-5
PUBLISHED BY BLACK ROSE WRITING
www.blackrosewriting.com

Printed in the United States of America
Suggested retail price $18.95

What it Takes is printed in Cambria

To my wife, Tara, who stood by me every step of the way.

What it Takes

CHAPTER 1

"They all think they're worth more than they bring in, you know," the large man in a dark suit exclaimed. "They think because they're the ones on the field that they're the most important part of the organization. Even if they go oh-for-five with four strikeouts or give up seven runs in two and a third innings, they think they're better than the rest of us. Don't they know we're the ones who pay their checks every week, do all the marketing, convince the fans they're even worth seeing? And all they do at the end of every season, no matter how poorly it turns out, is ask for more money! It's insane!"

The large man talking was "Big Eddy" Dillinger, business tycoon of the Midwest. His remarks were made to a mostly uninterested group of similar entrepreneurs, all "friends" of his from over the past twenty years.

Big Eddy appeared enormous at the table of four in the small yet elegant downtown Chicago restaurant. His dark suit was well tailored for his broad shoulders and large torso. Big Eddy's gelatinous neck hung over the tight collar of his button down shirt, despite the first button being unfastened and his silk tie loosened.

His fat face was reddened even more than usual, hot from the words he spoke about today's baseball players. His thin hair flopped from side to side as he gestured from one lunch partner to the next, attempting to convince just one of them of his implausible points.

Dillinger was the owner of the Chicago Cubs and had been ever since the Ricketts family sold the Cubs to him in 2021. He had bought the team as an investment more than anything, the Ricketts desperate to sell after the strike of 2020 made baseball the least profitable it had been in over five decades.

For the last three years all he had seen was an even steeper decline in the fan base of the north side lovable losers. Dillinger had done everything he thought possible to try to get fans into the seats of the once entertaining Cubs, but he found that nothing, outside perhaps winning, would make his investment worthwhile.

"These guys are nobodies now. It's not like the old days when players were heralded for their home runs and sub-three ERA's! Ever since they were uncovered as drug-enhanced, money-crazed buffoons, the public has practically made them pariahs!" Big Eddy continued.

"Let's remember the owners are largely to blame for the disheartened fans, Eddy," countered Stan Maverick, an old business partner of Dillinger's and avid fan of baseball. "It wasn't just the players who were to blame for the strike."

Maverick was a thin man in an expensive, old-fashioned grey suit. He was almost seventy and had been part of Dillinger's circle for some time now. He enjoyed the same monetary success that all the men present had had, and he had a knack for being the only one to repeatedly stand up to Dillinger's ridiculous accusations.

Maverick was sensible and reserved, an antithesis to his counterpart, and he often caused Dillinger to act even more rashly than the corpulent man usually did.

"Sure, Stan," Eddy acquiesced, "but the players were the ones taking the drugs and demanding all the money! Us owners were just protecting our investments, like all businessmen do!"

"'Us owners', he says, like he was one during the strike!" Scott Pryzbilla stated to the chuckles of the others. "You weren't an owner then! In fact, you even capitalized on that strike to fleece the Ricketts out of the Cubs! Don't try to be a martyr for some principles you never sacrificed. And leave the players alone. It takes a tremendous amount of skill to be in the position they're in. The majors are tough!"

"Oh, sure, defend my players, the ones who haven't been to the playoffs in seven years!" quipped Dillinger. "These guys haven't finished better than fifth place in the last five seasons!"

The Chicago Cubs had been on one of their many infamous losing streaks. Only one World Series championship in over 100 years. The Ricketts family had put together a formidable team, but after the Cubs won it in 2016, they were only able to make it to the playoffs once more after bad injuries to two of their star players left them losing confidence and their elite status. The Cubs lost a large core of their prospects and found themselves falling to the back of the division once again. The Cubs had once more wasted a talented group and the Ricketts found themselves losers once again.

After the uncovering of the second steroid era in 2019, many who had been holding on to their beloved pastime finally gave up. When the owners had to cut the salaries of their players because of decreased revenue, a player's strike cut short the 2020 season. The remaining fans were thoroughly devastated.

All across the U.S. baseball fell further behind football and it was now only the fifth most watched sport in America.

Chicago was even worse off than the rest. Once their beloved World Series team lost their best players and fell in the division almost as quickly as they had ascended, their fans couldn't bear to watch their team become the lovable losers again. The Cubs went from the third most watched team in baseball to the fifteenth in just three years.

America was giving up on baseball, and congruently Chicago was giving up on its Cubbies.

"Maybe it's because their owner doesn't know the first thing about how to run a ball club!" joked Stan, causing laughs around the table and rousing Dillinger further.

"Shows what you know, you ignoramus!" Eddy shot back. "I don't run the club. The General Manager does! That's what I pay him for, and a terrible disappointment he's been. That's not my fault!"

"We know, Big Eddy. It's everybody's fault but yours," Stan answered. "Can't you admit you just got in over your head on this one? We understand how good an opportunity it seemed to own the Cubs, but it didn't pan out. Baseball has had it. It'll be a surprise if the MLB lasts another decade."

"Right," Dillinger snapped back, "and it's all because of the players not performing and tricking the public with their steroids and whatnot! These prima donnas have cost America its pastime and me a lot of money!"

"Fine," Pryzbilla stated calmly. "I'll give you the steroids as a reason for baseball's decline, but stop trying to tell us these guys are no good! I'd like to see you try to hit a ninety mile per hour fastball!"

"Not my strong point, Scottie," Dillinger answered. "But it doesn't make them any better. Everyone has seen the downturn in the players over the last five years. Where have you been?"

Dillinger had a point. The players collectively displayed quite a dip in their performance after the second steroid era. At the time of the uncovering of the scandal, more and more fans and media were speculating about the use of new performance enhancing drugs, the ones that there was no detection for. The pressure had so enveloped the commissioner that he decided to fully invest in a test to reveal the deception the players were forging.

After paying some of the nation's most talented scientists, the commissioner discovered the use of the new steroids in over forty percent of the players. The information caused speculation that all the players were doing it, and the fans began to abandon their beloved teams.

Fines, suspensions, and even complete dismissals were put in place, taking a large portion of the most talented players out of the game. Those who did come back were forced to play without their routine enhancements, causing a decline in their performance. Every misplay was now amplified by the jaded fan base, and players continued to show flaws which were no longer accepted by demanding customers.

"Downturn, fine," Maverick stated, rejoining the argument, "but it doesn't mean they're no good! These players are still the best in the world and are right to demand the salaries they receive. You think you should profit over them? By the looks of that steak in front of you, not to mention the gut I've seen enlarging, you're certainly not starving!"

Dillinger shot him a sharp, derisive look as the others laughed at the quip. Maverick had gone too far and his calm demeanor while doing so only enraged Dillinger further. He was not going to let Maverick win this one.

"OK, then let's take an example, shall we?" Dillinger posited, calming himself for the benefit of his argument. "Casey Earl, Chicago Cubs second baseman last year. His average was .204 for the season with three home runs and twenty-four RBIs. Barely hits his weight and then has the nerve to say he wants two million to play for me next year! Two million for a guy who almost was below the Mendoza Line?"

The Mendoza Line was a term derived from an old Pittsburgh Pirates shortstop, Mario Mendoza, whose lifetime batting average was .215. He was known as a defensive specialist, but his poor average made people ponder the minimum a player needed to hit—despite his defensive prowess—to be considered acceptable in the majors. The number .200

was the rounded off average that stuck, and those players who hit below it were rarely back the following season.

"Yeah, but he's the best defensive player in the league, and he hit .250 the year before," Maverick defended.

"And his OBP was almost .300 last year," Pryzbilla added.

"Oh come on!" Dillinger interjected. "You guys are just arguing with me to argue! How can you defend this guy? .204? Really? Anyone could hit that!"

"Please, Eddy! Anyone? You think you could hit .200 against major league pitching?"

Maverick had capitalized on the clumsy comment of Dillinger, who now realized he had gone overboard.

"Well, not me, of course. I'm an old man! But if you take some healthy twenty year old and give him the same training as these coddled superstars, I'm sure he could hit over .200!"

"No way," Pryzbilla stated. "You're crazy!"

"Do you know how hard it is to hit a major league pitcher, Eddy?" Maverick added. "These guys are the best in the world! They would make ordinary people look silly! "

"Not if those ordinary people had the proper training, Stan. You don't know the game like I do! I work with these guys, I watch them up close! Believe me, they're not as special as you think! I could find you a guy right now who, with the same instruction, could hit .200. I'm telling you. I work with them. You just don't know because you aren't there like I am."

Now anger from the rest of the group began to rouse up around the table. They knew there was no way Big Eddy was right, but he had trumped them by claiming he knew better by way of his position with the Cubs.

No one could think of a quick way to prove him wrong, and all were silent while trying to discover a way to do it. They became even more irritated when they saw Dillinger revel in their moment of awkward silence, his smile gloating and obnoxious.

"Yeah?" Maverick said, finally breaking the quiet. "You think you won the argument because you know we can't prove you wrong and you have this 'inside information' that none of us do."

"Well, maybe that's the case, Stan," Dillinger exulted. "Not my fault the facts favor my opinion."

"Then prove it, Dillinger," Maverick challenged. "Put your money where your mouth is!"

"And how can I do that?" Dillinger chuckled. "It's impossible!"

The group was again silenced, trying to think of a way to quiet their outspoken lunch partner.

"What about having a fan day where they can hit live pitching?" Pryzbilla asked. "We can watch them play and see if there is someone who can hit the professional pitchers well."

"That's not even close to what we're talking about, Scottie," Dillinger responded. "How can you assess what a person's average is just hitting a pitcher a few times? No comparison."

"Well, I was just trying to come up with something is all."

"Big Eddy's right," Maverick said, "the only way we could really test this is by getting someone who could go through the exact same warm-ups, training, and spring ball as the regular players. Then he would have to play a whole season to get a clear understanding of what his average was. It's impossible."

Dillinger smiled again, this time more covertly, knowing he had won. There was no situation he could contemplate that would give some guy off the street the opportunity Stan described.

Finally the fourth member of their party, the soft-spoken billionaire Ted Callahan, who at this point had been enjoying the conversation, decided to enter the debate.

"Why is it impossible?" Callahan asked. "Big Eddy is the owner of the team. He can do whatever he wants, even if that means pulling some nobody off the streets and making him a Chicago Cub."

"Well sure, Ted, I *could* do it, but how would I justify it? It doesn't make any business sense to get all the Cubs fans mad at me just to prove a point."

"Just tell them you're giving a commoner a shot at playing in the big leagues," Callahan answered coolly. "You can tell them you're trying to get the average person back in the game by showing one lucky fan what it means to be in the majors. You know, it's like a contest. People all over would be talking about it."

"Well, maybe at first," responded Dillinger nervously, feeling the back of his neck get hot, "but after a short time people will get mad at me for bringing in an unskilled player to their beloved Cubbies. It would be hurting their chances for winning too much. People won't stand for that!"

"But you said that some unskilled player could come in and hit the same average as Casey Earl!" said Pryzbilla. "If you're right, it wouldn't be much of a downgrade at all!"

"Besides," chimed in Maverick, "your team is no good anyway! They'll be picked to finish dead last again. No one can claim you ruined their chances because of it."

"Not logically, Stan," Dillinger replied, "but you know how these Cubs fans are! Eternal optimists! Every year they think they can win it all, despite their misery at the end of each failed season. They won't stand for it, I tell you!"

"Aw, forget it," Maverick answered dejectedly. "We all know Eddy is wrong and this would prove it. He'll say anything he can to avoid the opportunity to make himself look stupid. This argument is ridiculous and a waste of time."

"You're the one who's lucky it can't be done, Stan!" shouted back Dillinger, now angered by Maverick calling him out. "This whole ridiculous scenario would prove I'm right! And you'd be out a whole lot of money when I won!"

Maverick stared into Dillinger's eyes and knew he had him. Big Eddy was too riled up to back down now, as long as there was a substantial amount of money put on the line. The question was, would Dillinger actually go through with such a process to prove himself and win a bet? It would be the most talked about event in the city, the Chicago Cubs with a player nobody ever heard of, never went through the system, maybe never even played baseball before! It was tempting to Maverick to be part of such an operation

"Like ten million?" replied Maverick calmly.

"Ten million dollars?" Dillinger awkwardly stammered.

"No, ten million spaghetti noodles, you jackass! Of course ten million dollars! You pick the man right now, and he plays next season for the Chicago Cubs. If he finishes the season over .200, with at least 300 at bats, I give you ten million dollars. If he hits below the Mendoza Line, you pay me. What do you say, pal?"

Maverick emphasized the last word while staring daringly into his partner's eyes and holding out an outstretched hand to seal the deal. The challenge scared Dillinger, but he was too deep now.

The other two at the table eagerly waited his response, knowing the public implications of a Dillinger acceptance to the craziest and most exciting bet they had ever witnessed. The whole table started to feel that maybe Dillinger was actually going to say yes and take the bet. Their anticipation, while only seconds long, seemed to last the whole afternoon.

"Done!" Big Eddy called out, grabbing the hand of Maverick's to confirm. All eyes, including Stan Maverick's, were wide with surprise at the culmination of the escalating debate. Big Eddy Dillinger looked proud and haughty, knowing his courage had dazzled his lunch partners. The time for regret would be later, but the liquor induced honor was all his at the moment, and he relished it.

"You said I pick him, Stan," Dillinger added, giving everyone at the table reason to believe he could actually win this bet.

"Well sure, Eddy," Maverick responded, now seemingly the nervous one, "but you said any guy could do it, remember?"

"Maybe so, but I'm putting my reputation, my investment, and an extra ten million on the line. You said I get to pick him, and I'll take any advantage I can get!"

"OK, but I said you pick him right now, meaning out of the people in the restaurant. Take a look around, Eddy, who do you like?"

Big Eddy looked around the rather small restaurant and only saw seven tables with guests, all of them in suits and skirts. The establishment, Ruby's, was an expensive one, and it was midday on a Tuesday. Only businessmen and women were having lunch now, and it was hard for Eddy to find a single person under the age of forty.

Maverick and the others looked around, too, and realized the paucity of potentials Big Eddy was faced with. They all smiled, again confident Dillinger had lost before it all began.

Just then the front door opened. Everyone at Eddy's table had become aware of every movement in the restaurant and they all swung their heads toward the sound, but only saw on older couple enter the establishment.

Dillinger furrowed his brow in disappointment.

"We haven't got all day, Eddy," Maverick stated, irritating Dillinger further.

"Calm down! It's my pick and I'd be wise to do it deliberately," replied Dillinger, his eyes scanning the room again as he tried to buy more time.

"The reason I'm where I am today is because of my ability to assess such a situation, you know."

The other three at the table groaned and rolled their eyes at more of Eddy's arrogant dribble that they had been hearing for years. Pryzbilla was about to remark when they heard the door open again. This time was different.

All turned to see a thin boy in his twenties, dressed in a cheap pair of pants and a short-sleeved button down shirt, walk through the door. He was going to the front counter for what appeared to be a take out order.

Big Eddy smiled.

"You, son!" Dillinger shouted out across the restaurant, oblivious to the sudden silence of the other patrons.

Everyone, including the boy, looked to the large owner of the Chicago Cubs, and the boy saw him staring right at him. After turning around to make sure there wasn't someone behind him, the boy pointed to himself.

"Me, sir?"

"Yes, you! Come over here, please."

The whole restaurant, especially those at Dillinger's table, sized up the young man as he approached the table slowly. Fear could be seen in the boy's eyes, not knowing who this man was or what he was about to propose. The young man got to four feet from the table and instinctively stopped.

"You wanted to speak to me, sir?"

"Yes," answered Dillinger, smiling as if he was making a business proposition to the stranger. "What's your name?"

"Um, Jake. Jacob Riley."

"How old are you, Jacob Riley?"

"Twenty-four, sir."

"Jake, have you ever played baseball?"

"You can't ask him that!" Maverick shouted out.

"I can ask him whatever I want, Stan. You told me I can pick him, and you didn't restrict the questioning! Son, have you ever played baseball before?"

"Well, yes sir, I have," replied the boy sheepishly. "Little league and then a couple years in high school."

The young man was built well. Although thin, his frame was athletic and wiry. He appeared coordinated and Dillinger assumed he wasn't going to find better at this time.

"What position did you play, son?"

"Well, mostly second base."

Dillinger smiled. Earl's position. This was all working out better than he could have hoped. Maybe this bet wasn't as hopeless as he was fearing. The others looked excitedly at the boy and then at Big Eddy.

"Well, Jacob Riley, how would you like to play for the Chicago Cubs?"

CHAPTER 2

Jacob Riley was born a Cubs fan.

His neighborhood was middle class and on the north side of Chicago. When springtime hit, everyone was on the streets talking about the Cubbies, and Jake's family was no exception. His father took him to his first game at Wrigley Field. Jake was in awe of the beloved stadium and he had watched in delight as his favorite player, Kerry Wood, pitched in relief of a Cubs win.

The event became cemented in his mind and he was a die-hard Cubs fan for life.

Jake was a thin boy with strong limbs. He had pale blue eyes and thick, wavy brown hair. His face was masculine with strong cheek bones and a prominent chin. He walked freely and easily, his balance and coordination superb. When people met Jake, they were struck with his presence, although that quickly disappeared when he spoke with his customary timid apprehensiveness.

Jake had the looks of a warrior, but the spirit of a field mouse and he was often taken advantage of because of it.

Jacob Riley was a typical young man with atypical capabilities. He was intelligent and intuitive and able to devise new ways to do the most common of tasks. In school he was always at the top of his class. Jake's peers looked to him for answers to the difficult problems they faced, whether in the classroom or in the complex life of an adolescent.

Jacob often impressed his instructors and his coaches. He not only solved the quandaries at hand but, if given ample time, he would figure out a better way to accomplish them. For these reasons he was looked at as the student most likely to succeed and sculpt the world to his liking.

Unfortunately, the praise Jake received from others was not imitated internally. He thought colleagues exaggerated his accomplishments and potential. Although Jake knew he had a knack for figuring out certain predicaments, never did he see his ability as a precursor to actual life. He worried that when the time came to really produce, he might come up short. It was easy for him to remember the few times he had failed and hard to recall the many times he had succeeded.

This central feeling of ineptitude plagued Jake throughout his young life. Although an excellent athlete, he limited himself to one sport, baseball. He was a standout in little league and had played well his first couple years of high school. When it was time to try out for varsity, he worried it would be difficult to make the team because only about half the players on his sophomore team would be picked their junior year. The coaches were excited to see him try out, as they had already realized his solid defense at second base and his excellent contact at the plate, but Jake convinced them, and himself, that he had to concentrate on his studies in order to get into a good college.

He immersed himself in his books while his friends continued on the team.

Even college worried the bright young Jacob Riley. His grades in school were excellent and he did very well on his SATs, but when it came time to apply, he was worried about being rejected from the bigger schools in the area such as the University of Chicago and Northwestern. Instead he chose a small liberal arts school, Benedictine University, in the suburbs of Chicago.

His peers wondered why he hadn't tried to get accepted into the more competitive programs in the state, but they didn't question him. Jake was always his own person and his decisions were difficult to dispute.

Jake studied biology and worked hard at getting into medical school. His grades put him at the top of his class and his science GPA was a smidge under perfect. He belonged to all the pertinent pre-med clubs and purposely joined student government as a resume builder. He studied throughout the summer of his sophomore year for the MCATs, the necessary pretest for medical school.

He scored high on the exam and had great recommendation letters to send to the medical schools in the area. His applications were complete and he awaited responses from the eight schools he applied to. However, something suddenly came up which changed his mind about his comfort in medicine.

He had heard about how difficult medical school was and he learned of a neighborhood friend who had recently failed out of Rush medical school. It was horribly embarrassing for the boy and his family, who had flaunted his early successes only to be humbled by his later failure. That scenario worried Jake to the point of exasperation and he pulled his application from all eight schools, saddening his family and friends. Nothing they said or did could convince him otherwise. Their concern only further alienated Jake from his potential.

Jake had all the tools, but he was too frightened to use them.

After college Jake had a resume crowded with distinction and a future devoid of spectacle. He spent so much time and energy trying to attain a position in medical school that he was left in the cold when he turned his back on it. He lived with his parents and found a job at Northwestern Hospital in one of the medical laboratories. The pay was low and his position lower, but he was able to use his scientific mind and skills and that made him feel better about the biology degree he had worked so hard for. He was well liked in the lab and found he fit in, an important factor in the happiness of Jacob.

He even felt he could make a career out of research. That is, if it wasn't for Angie.

Angie was a thin woman of twenty-three with dark, Asian skin and a pretty smile. She had been Jake's girlfriend for over three years. They had met in Jake's third year of college when both were attending Benedictine. Angie found Jacob attractive both in his looks and his capabilities, but the real hook was his demeanor. She quickly learned of his fears and inhibitions and found it easy to use these attributes against him. The controlling girl saw Jake as the perfect guy for her to mold.

Without Jake realizing it, Angie controlled his life from the beginning of their relationship and her stronghold never weakened. She was instrumental in his decision not to attend medical school, assuring him he was not ready for such a task. She also discouraged him from the sports he enjoyed playing in his free time, demanding he spend all his non-study time with her.

Jake enjoyed having a girl in his life and at first saw Angie's personality only as a minor inconvenience. After he was thoroughly invested in the relationship, he began to hold in to himself his annoyance at her habits. He was non-confrontational and feared angering her. He thought it better to just listen and agree than to strike up an argument he was sure he would lose.

Angie often griped about Jake's laboratory position. It was not one of high prominence nor did it pay enough to allow the two to move in together, let alone get married. She made sure he knew she did not approve, and Jake was always reassuring her it was only temporary. He was considering graduate schools and nursing programs, but he was having a hard time deciding what he would want to do as a career. Everything paled in comparison to medicine.

He would bring up his decision not to apply to medical schools as a possible mistake, but it would only lead to a prolonged argument with Angie. Jake learned to hold in his true desires in order to not rock the boat.

Angie wanted Jake to succeed, but for many reasons feared medical school. She feared the commitment. Angie had heard how dedicated the medical students and residents had to be and how hard it was on their families. She did not want that. Angie also feared Jake doing well and building his confidence. If that happened, she was worried he would find someone else to share his life with. She couldn't bear the thought of Jake leaving her. Angie loved him, or at least loved the way she felt controlling him.

Jake's parents were in direct opposition to Angie. They were fearful of their son wasting his talents because of the trepidation he had about success. They saw their intelligent young boy living with them after college because his job didn't pay enough to get him his own place. They had their own surreal aspirations for Jake, which they knew were unfair, but that they couldn't conceal.

They continuously tried to get him to apply to medical schools, or even graduate schools, so he could further his education and open more doors for himself. They knew his potential but also were aware of the power of their adversary, Angie. They didn't want to be like her and tell Jake what to do, but they didn't know any other way as Jake seemed to listen to Angie too often. The conflict was hard on the Riley family, especially on Jacob.

Because Jake was being pulled in opposite directions, he stayed stagnant. He was more worried about upsetting others than in doing what he felt best for himself. He pondered future possibilities to himself and considered applying to different programs without doing much research into anything.

He continued his work at Northwestern and had now been there for over two years. He found his research somewhat dull, but tried to think of it as doing good for society and as sharpening his scientific mind for some future expedition.

His outer life was terrible, but comfortable. Therefore he tried not to meddle too much. Anything he did outside of the present would cause controversy either with Angie or with his parents and didn't seem worth it. He was willing to stay lifeless and apathetic as long as he didn't have to worry about anxiety. He assumed he would continue to work at the lab until Angie complained enough about it and suggested something else.

Jake worked with a team of seven researchers. Two were the physicians who ran the lab and were rarely present. There was one post-doctorate worker trying to obtain enough information for a thesis. Then there were the four lab rats, doing the work of the other three and collecting next to nothing in return.

The job was a good one for those looking to move on because it offered research experience and a chance to publish. Once one's name was on a publication, the chances of getting into medical school or graduate school increased. There was also the probability that the physicians who ran the project would write recommendation letters for the workers as a thank you for working so hard under such poor conditions.

Jacob would congregate with the other three workers and discuss their projects over lunch. This was a time for him to be himself. These friends had no preconceived thoughts of him and didn't judge him for what he was doing, at least not yet. They were all in the same position and could relate to Jake because of it.

He enjoyed his time at work because of these friends and he shielded them from Angie in order to continue to have time in which he felt he was in control. Jake might not have openly admitted it, but he craved a life which he had authority over.

The other three did wonder about Jake. They were all attempting to get into medical school, but had found it difficult. After numerous rejections they had decided to find a job in which they could make some money and increase their chances of acceptance. They all came together at Northwestern and were hopeful for their futures because of it.

Jake, on the other hand, had never been turned down by any

programs and had remained interested in medicine. They didn't see why he continued to work at the lab without applying to school. Not knowing his past, they assumed he wanted to get in but for some reason couldn't.

All these questions on their part finally led to a discussion over lunch.

"I just got out my last application," stated Bryan, a two-year lab tech and good friend of Jake. "It took me all night!"

"How many is that this year?" asked Jeff, the most seasoned tech of the four.

"Thirteen. Two more than last year."

"How much did it cost you?"

"Six hundred and eighty-fve dollars. Like I have that kind of money to spend on applications! I better get in this year."

This was the third time Bryan had been applying. The first two years he was hopeful and only applied to seven and nine schools, respectively. Now he was starting to worry he wouldn't get in to any medical institution and he decided to apply to as many as he could afford.

"That's a week's pay," stated Deb, not even looking up from her lunch. "I couldn't afford that."

"How many did you apply to, Deb?" Bryan asked the only female member of the group.

"Five. Same as last year, but I gave up on Michigan State and added CCOM. I think I can get in there."

"Well, I hope so," Jeff stated indefinitely. "We all need to get in soon or we'll go crazy working here."

They all paused, hoping Jake would add something to the conversation and give them a clue about his thoughts on school. They had never dared ask him. Nobody wanted to be the one to make him share something uncomfortable, but the group was getting tired of speaking of medical schools every day without Jake saying a word, as if he didn't even care what they were doing.

After a minute of silence, Jeff finally inquired.

"What about you, Jake? Any plans for next year?"

Jake didn't turn his head towards Jeff as one would when asked a question he was comfortable with. Instead he put down his sandwich and peered forward as he answered.

"You mean besides this dump?"

"Yeah," Jeff answered, relieved by the levity. "Are you applying anywhere?"

"Not everyone has aspirations of bigger and better things, you know," Jake announced stoically.

"Well, I know, but I just wondered if you wanted to keep working here or, you know, do something else."

"I don't know," Jake responded somberly. "I think I'll probably continue on here for a while. I'm still not sure I know what I want to do."

"No offense," Deb replied offensively, "but I could never plan on coming back to this place. If I don't get in anywhere, I guess I'll continue working here only because I know the place and am confident it helps my med school application, but it pains me to think that I might have to be here at this time next year."

"That's only because you want to be somewhere else," Bryan responded defensively. "If you weren't trying to get into school, this would be fine."

"You don't have to get snappy," Deb countered, "Jake's the one who called this place a dump. I'm agreeing with him!"

"Yeah, but you make it seem like he's stuck here just because we have different ideas of what we want to do with our lives! This is a very honorable place to work, all the research we do for the good of science while getting paid next to nothing for it. There's no reason to scorn Jake's choice."

"I'm not scorning anything!" Deb started, but she was suddenly cut off by Jake.

"OK, OK, OK," he interrupted, stopping the argument for the time being. "You can stop now. I'm not offended, although Bryan has a good point."

The two debaters looked away from each other while their red faces started to cool.

"I know you all want to know what my thoughts are, what my aspirations are," Jake started again. "I know I'm always silent when you talk about your med school applications and where you want to go, and there's a good reason for that. I really don't know what I want to do. I thought I wanted to go to medical school, but I pulled my applications at the last minute because I wasn't sure I have what it takes to be a doctor. It's not that I didn't think I could get in. I got a 33 on the MCAT's."

The other three's eyes widened. A 33! That meant Jake was in the top five percent of those who took the test and as long as his GPA wasn't below a 3.2, he could probably get in somewhere. None of them knew he had even wanted to get into medical school and now they all learned he could have easily done it if he applied.

Bryan felt his pity for Jake turn to a touch of jealousy.

"Now I'm working here and not sure what I want for my future," Jake continued. "Maybe it's medicine, but I don't want to jump into it without being sure. Maybe graduate school is better for me, I don't know. I'll take my time while I figure it out. In the meantime, I like being here."

"You can do whatever you want, Jake," answered Deb, some flirtation in her voice. She realized she suddenly had adulation for her colleague, the thought of a 33 still running through her mind.

"Well, it's nice to know you have medical school in your back pocket if nothing else works out," stated Jeff.

"How's that?" asked Jake, annoyed by the assumption.

"Come on, Jake! A 33? You know how desirable you'll be to the schools? I wish I had cracked 30. If I had, I wouldn't be sitting here talking to you guys. I'd be in at Rush right now!"

"It's not just about the MCAT, Jeff," Jake replied. "They look at GPA, student activities, and that's just to get the interview. Once you interview, who knows who they'll take."

"That's not true," Bryan interjected. "Even before they interview you, they know if they like you or not. You can lose your acceptance if you do poorly, but most people who can answer questions well will get in if their application is good enough. I'm sure you would be fine, Jake."

"Maybe," Jake answered hesitantly, "but even so I have to know it is what I want to do. Medical school costs about a hundred and seventy-five thousand dollars over four years. That doesn't even count living expenses. The average medical student comes out of school almost two hundred and fifty thousand dollars in debt. Then, for at least three years, you have residency which pays under fifty thousand dollars per year for eighty hours of work a week. I'm not sure that's the kind of financial commitment I want to jump into without being sure."

"It is something you have to be positive of," Deb affirmed. "My brother went to school with someone who dropped out after his second year and he was over a hundred thousand dollars in debt and making next to nothing. That sounds awful."

"Hey, I hate to break things up," Jeff interrupted, looking at his phone, "but the docs just texted me. They need us to pick up their lunch."

"Again?" Deb whined. "We just did this yesterday! Whose turn is it to go?"

"Jeff went yesterday, so I guess it's mine," Jake answered. "No problem, I'm almost done here. I'll see you guys later."

Jake got up and finished his sandwich while walking back to the lab. The two doctors he worked for would occasionally forget their techs were not their assistants and ask them to run out for coffee, lunch, etc. No one had the courage to tell them no because they all were looking for a recommendation letter. Jake didn't mind the task as he was able to get off campus and out into the city for an hour.

He stepped into the lab and saw the doctors waiting for him.

"Jake, you here to pick up lunch?" Dr. Mendelson asked as soon as he arrived.

"Yep. Where do you need me to go?"

"Ruby's on Halsted. You know where it is?"

"Sure, Dr. Mendelson. I'll be right back."

"It's already paid for. You just have to pick it up," the old doctor added as Jake exited the lab.

The restaurant was high end, one Jake would never enter for himself. He ate there once with his parents and found the food wonderful. Not having had to pay for it was even better. The walk was only fifteen minutes, so Jake knew he'd be back quickly.

He enjoyed walking the busy streets of the city on a workday. There were thousands of people on the streets moving in every direction. The pedestrians were so busy trying to get here or there it was a perfect opportunity to people watch. Jake loved looking at Chicago's citizens, wondering if he was looking at a restaurant worker or a business tycoon. No one noticed if he stared at them for too long, a different circumstance than the usual. Jake took every advantage of it.

He made it to Ruby's quickly. When he entered, he didn't notice anything outside the ordinary. He turned to the counter to ask about the pick up order, but no one was available. He figured someone would be by quickly to help him and he turned to look at the crowd. He expected he could again look at the people without a soul noticing him. This time he was mistaken. There was a table of men in business suits peering at him.

Jake was uneasy, sure they had to be looking at something else, but fearful he was the object they gazed upon.

Then he heard it. The raspy voice from the large man in the dark business suit that he would hear a thousand times more over the next year.

"You, son!"

Jake froze.

CHAPTER 3

Jake fumbled through the rest of the afternoon in a state of distraction.

He had already been looked at with disapproval by his bosses for coming back late with their lunch and he still had quite a few things to do before he was able to get out for the day, but he could only concentrate on the conversation he had with Mr. Dillinger at Ruby's.

The thoughts of playing baseball for the Chicago Cubs overwhelmed his attention and his holding in the information only worsened the situation. He found the last few hours of the workday the most difficult he had ever experienced.

Mr. Dillinger had offered him a chance to play baseball for one year in the major leagues. The situation was unprecedented. Jake understood that. What he couldn't understand was the angle of his benefactor. The explanation given to him in the forty-five-minute conversation he had was that the Cubs were looking to involve a common spectator in the game. The front office wanted to give the fans a chance to experience the game from the inside and use only one liaison to do it. Jake was offered the opportunity to be that liaison. He would be followed by specific media set up by Dillinger to ask him how the training went, how difficult the process was, etc. Other fans would then be able to listen in and attempt to understand the game through the eyes of Jake.

Jake was suspicious. It was hard to guess the intent of Dillinger while offered such a surreal opportunity, but Jake attempted to anyway. He couldn't help wonder why the other members of the table were commenting on the way Dillinger was explaining the situation. It was almost as if they had suspected Dillinger of something sinister and were trying to keep him in concordance with some rule set which was out of place for such a state of affairs.

There appeared to be another motive for the offer, too, some scheme that was not yet uncovered, and Jake had a bad feeling about it.

On the other hand, the excitement was inconceivable and almost unbearable. To play for the Chicago Cubs was the dream of every young baseball fan in Chicago. However, that dream seemed to disappear once Jake gave up on his high school baseball career. Admittedly he had thought about it often as a kid and had once hoped he would succeed enough to somehow one day play professionally, but that dream was held by so many that it was not thought of as realistic. Now he was given the opportunity without any diligence or sacrifice of his own. Or was there?

Maybe it was Jake's anxious nature or maybe it was his ability to thoroughly assess a situation in its entirety, but Jake saw the downfalls of this potential adventure before most would.

Although it would be exciting to meet the Cubs players, get a chance to play in real games at Wrigley Field, and possibly feel adoration from the fans, there would be pitfalls, too. The fan base might not accept him into his role. After all, he would certainly be a detriment to the team, never playing above the level of high school. This would make the team itself worse and perhaps the fans would resent him for it.

Also, the players would probably despise him for such a promotion without going through the same process they had to. He would be taking over for a player who was more deserving of the spot than he and the other players might ostracize him for it, regardless of whether he was to blame.

Those two combinations, along with the probability of his struggling immensely in the majors, could lead to a miserable seven months.

Despite his apprehension, he realized he'd be a fool not to accept the offer. He was given the chance of a lifetime and if he didn't take it, somebody else would. He also knew his parents and his friends would push him into doing it and would be excited about cheering for Jake.

The one he wasn't sure of was Angie. She was fickle and it was sometimes difficult to judge how she would react to a new situation. She might be excited about the opportunity or she might completely despise the thought of it. What Jake was sure of was that her idea of him playing major league baseball might be the deciding factor for him of whether he did it or not. He knew she had that power over him and he was tired of fighting it.

He would just have to see what she thought.

When Jake returned home from work, it was difficult to hold back the news from his parents. He tried to act normally and asked when dinner would be ready. His mother was busy in the kitchen and answered him without suspicion, but his father quickly picked up on the difference in his son.

"How was work today, Jake?" he asked, suspiciously.

"Just fine, dad," Jake replied with a smile. "Same old stuff, day in and day out, you know."

"Nothing special then?"

Jake couldn't help but grin as he tried to be nonchalant. "No, why?"

"Come on, what happened?" his dad asked boisterously. "You can't hide things from your old man!"

"OK, OK," Jake said bashfully, "I'll tell you. But it has to be kept between us for now. And I want mom to hear. Let's wait for dinner."

"Nonsense!" said his father impatiently. "Loretta! Get in here!"

Justin Riley, Jacob's father, was a pleasant man about five feet, ten inches tall. He had a plain face, now wrinkled and worn as he entered his late fifties. He appeared much older than fifty-nine, but was always jovial, no matter how uncomfortable it made him. Justin was confident, sometimes overly so, and he always fit in to any group he entered.

Jacob had few of his father's qualities.

Loretta Riley was a tall, thin woman with bright blue eyes like her son's. She was beautiful and, unlike her husband, seemed much younger than her actual fifty plus years. She was lissome and, despite her being a reclusive homemaker, was quite confident and intrepid when out with her family.

Her appearance was that of a woman who looked so much younger than her husband that others often wondered if she was instead with her father. Jacob had noticed this in people they met and it always left him uncomfortable.

"What is it, Justin? I'm in the middle of making dinner!" Loretta's shrill yet accomplished voice called out.

"Our boy has some news for us, exciting news, I believe!"

"Oh?" Jacob's mother asked, turning to him with an inquisitive face.

"Well, dad usually gets worked up over nothing," Jake started, "but today he is right. We better sit down."

They sat together in the family room, Jacob on the arm chair facing his parents, who sat at a skewed angle to him on the couch. The two were on the edge of the sofa, pushed up against each other, waiting eagerly for the news.

"Well, this is kind of crazy, but it all happened when I was getting lunch for the doctors today at Ruby's. They asked me to pick it up for them, and when I got there, this table of businessmen were staring at me. I didn't recognize them, but then one of them, a large fellow, called out to me. I couldn't believe he was talking to me, but I went over to the table anyway. You'll never guess who it was!"

"Who?" called out his father, barely able to contain himself.

"Edward Dillinger!"

"Big Eddy Dillinger?" his father replied, eyes wide with excitement as Jacob nodded in affirmation.

"Who's this now?" his mother interrupted, confused. "I've never heard of him."

"He's the business tycoon!" Justin answered her. "The owner of the Chicago Cubs!"

"Oh, the big annoying one who is always shooting off his mouth about something inane?"

"Yes, mother, that's the one."

"So what did he want with you, son?" his father asked, all his attention to Jacob's story.

"Well, like I said, it's crazy. You probably won't even believe it. I couldn't believe it myself! I'm still wondering if..."

"Come on!" interrupted his father again, too eager to hear anything but the electrifying news. "Out with it!"

"OK, sorry," said Jake, smiling at his father's youthfulness. "He wants me to play baseball for the Chicago Cubs."

Silence.

Jacob's parents were like two ash statues he had remembered seeing in Pompeii years before. They were motionless, yet stunned, waiting for the punch line, he assumed.

Finally, his father turned to gauge his wife's expression. When she was unperturbed by his movement, he turned back to his son and broke the silence.

"You're obviously joking, right? I mean, why would he ask you to play baseball professionally? He doesn't even know you, does he? What was his motivation to do such a thing? This is a joke, right?"

"One question at a time, dad!" Jake called out defensively. "I'll tell you the whole story!"

Jake told his family everything. They hung on every word and felt as if they were in a dream. Jake spoke excitedly and quickly, explaining every detail, sometimes in the wrong order, which caused him to have to stop, think, and correct himself numerous times. When the story was over, the Riley parents both flopped back on the couch in unison, emotionally drained from the roller coaster that had really just begun.

"This is all so amazing," his mother answered. "What are you going to do?"

"What do you mean what is he going to do?" Justin answered quickly, disallowing his son any opinion on the matter. "He's going to play for the Cubbies! How can he pass up an opportunity like that!" The old man turned to his son for affirmation. "Right, Jake?"

The look on Jacob's face showed he wasn't as convinced as his father had hoped he would be. Jake stood up uneasily and walked around the room, faking that he was in thought while his family knew he was in doubt. They had seen this disposition in their son many times before and recognized it well. His mother was understanding, but his father was concerned Jake was going to again throw away a great opportunity because of his fear of failure.

"You know," Jake started sheepishly, "I'm not sure I trust Mr. Dillinger. It's kind of hard to believe he would want me to play second base for a major league team just as a promotion, isn't it? There has never been anything like this done before that I know of, and it seems like it would really cause some displeasure from the fans. Imagine if they turn on me because of it! That's a lot of pressure. You know there's no way I'm going to be able to help the team. I'm no baseball player!"

"Some of that is true," stammered Mr. Riley while in thought, "but not all of it. I agree the fans will not like this. Mr. Dillinger obviously is trying some publicity stunt to get fans in the seats and I think it will backfire on him. However, it doesn't change the opportunity you have in front of you! Sure, it's going to be hard, but you'll get the hang of it! You were always a great hitter and fielder in high school. I'm still not sure why you gave up on it. You have a great eye and use all of the field. Once you get used to the timing, I bet you can contribute to some extent."

"Dad, that was against sixteen-year-old pitchers who could barely throw seventy miles an hour! These are professionals! All they've done for the last twenty years has revolved around how to make it in the big leagues! I haven't played for over seven years. I can't compete with them!"

"That's not exactly true, Jake," his father answered. "You played in that hardball league just a few years ago. Some of those guys were good, and you always played well."

"OK, I could hit some guys who probably never even played college ball, but that doesn't mean I can hit the pros!"

"No, but I'm saying that you did play recently, so it might not be as hard to get back into it as you think. And your fielding has always been solid. No reason you can't still do that!"

"Dad, all these guys who play infield in the majors have great fielding, much better than mine! I know this is all exciting, but let's not kid ourselves. I'm not going to be able to contribute at all against these guys. There's no way."

"Well, I think you're selling yourself short, Jake," his father replied, backing down, "but regardless, this would be such a great thing for you! This is something all kids dream about, and it's been handed to you like a gift. You'll always be able to talk about your days playing professional baseball for the Chicago Cubs! Imagine if you say no and constantly look back on your life with regret because you were afraid to try. I don't think you could live with yourself. I know I couldn't."

"Well, we're two different people, dad! What drives you doesn't necessarily interest me. But there's always the other thing..."

"What do you mean, son?" asked his father.

"Well, professional baseball players make a good salary. I suppose I'd make the league minimum, but that's over half a million dollars."

"Good point!" Justin Riley called out. "You can use that money for graduate school if you'd like."

"Or..." Jake trailed off.

His father knew what he was thinking and quickly rejected the notion.

"No! That money would be for you! We don't need to keep having this discussion. I will not take any money from you! Your mother and I can handle the situation."

"But it's been so hard for you both since everything came up. If this could help..."

"It can help you! That's what's important, Jake!"

"You're important to me, too, dad. It's like I said, we're two different people! In the end, it's up to me what I do with my life and my money!"

"Jake's right, dear," Mrs. Riley finally spoke up. "This is his decision and only he can make it. But I do agree with your father in terms of how great an opportunity it is. It seems like you won the lottery, even better, in fact, and you'd be turning it down only out of apprehension. You have to weigh the decisions for your own life, but I seriously hope you strongly consider this, Jake. We'd help in any way we can."

Justin Riley kept quiet now, his wife speaking enough sense for the whole family. She was right, and both she and her husband knew that Jake still had one last step in his decision making, one they were afraid might sway him despite any rational thinking.

"You're both right," Jake acquiesced. "I have to think about this. I don't know what I'm going to do. Hopefully Angie can help."

With that, Jake walked upstairs to his room, again anxious of the scenario in front of him. His parents peered at each other with a familiar, and rather disappointed, look. It was in Angie's hands now, and only God himself could possibly know what that meant.

CHAPTER 4

Dinner was awkward for the Riley family that night.

Jake was not going to begin the conversation again, especially before consulting with Angie. His parents decided to stay silent, too, wanting to give their son ample time to come up with an answer to such a pulsating question without their influence. The whole family knew Jake would visit his girlfriend that evening and an answer would result from it, hopefully for the better.

Jake hurriedly finished his meal and asked to be excused, retreating to his room to wash up. He texted Angie that he would be over in twenty minutes, to which she replied affirmatively. Jake changed his shirt and said good-bye to his parents before walking out of his home and onto the corner to wait for a bus.

Within five minutes his transportation was there and within fifteen minutes he was exiting the public vehicle, only half a block from Angie's small one bedroom apartment in Ravenswood. She had been waiting for him by the window and when he approached the building, she met him at the front door to let him in. He gave her a small peck on the cheek and they silently walked up the staircase to her apartment.

After walking into the front door, Angie moved towards the couch to get comfortable and let Jake close the door behind them. She looked up at her boyfriend and gave a smile, motioning for him to join her on the sofa. After he sat down next to her, nonchalantly, she took his arm, wrapped it around her shoulder and nestled in next to him.

She looked up at him and realized he was looking right back at her, just as she liked and had trained him to do.

"So," she spoke, now agreeable with their positioning, "how was your day?"

"Oh, I don't know," Jake replied coyly, "same as usual, I guess. You know, ran some experiments, talked with Bryan. Met the owner of the

Cubs during lunch."

"What?" Angie exclaimed, pushing herself from him and looking him in the eye. "You're joking, right?"

"No, I'm not! He was sitting at that restaurant Ruby's with some of his associates or something when I went in to pick up lunch for the bosses."

"So you saw him. You didn't meet him," she answered coldly, as if annoyed by him throwing her off.

"Well, I guess you could say I met him when he called me over to his table, asked me my name and introduced himself."

"No way!" Angie shot back smiling. "Really? What did he want to talk to you for?"

"Why wouldn't he?" Jake answered with an aura of pseudo-confidence. "Big shot lab rat like me, how could he not introduce himself?"

Angie laughed, excited by Jake's extraordinary news.

"So did you really talk to him, or are you just embellishing?"

"Like I said, he talked to *me*. I couldn't understand it myself, but then he completely blew me away with what he asked me."

"What?" Angie asked, backing away farther from Jake to take it all in. "What did he ask?"

"He wants me to play baseball for the Cubs."

Jake had been thinking all day of the right way to tell his girlfriend the news, but he had never got it down just right. While teasing her a little, though, the direct approach seemed to be the right tactic.

The words made Angie mimic Jake's parents when they heard the same information. She looked at him with her eyes wide and her mouth gaped, not believing what she heard, but at the same time knowing it was true.

"He did what?" she asked with exasperation.

"I told you, he wants me to play for his Cubs! I'm not joking, babe. He wants me to play second base for the Chicago Cubs next year."

Angie couldn't respond, so Jake continued.

"I know, I know. You're thinking, 'Why?' Believe me, I was too. He explained it to me as some sort of new fan experience, one that would be a promotional event for baseball. He's hoping it gets Cubs fans more interested in the game and fills the seats next season. Why he picked me, I don't know. I think I was in the right place at the right time."

"And you're thinking of doing it?"

"I am, but I wanted to talk it over with you first. My parents think I should go for it."

"You told them before me?"

"Yeah," Jake responded meekly, "but only because I wanted to tell you in person and I knew I wasn't seeing you until tonight."

"You know it makes me feel bad when you put others before me, Jake. I always put you first in this relationship, but you continue to make me feel like I'm not the most important person in your life. It really sucks."

"You know that's not true, Angie," Jake countered, trying to diffuse the flames. "This was so exciting to me it was too hard to hold it from my folks before I saw you. You know you're the most important person in my life. Please don't be angry."

"Alright, I won't make a big deal about it, but I hope you understand my point, dear."

"I do."

"OK. So let's talk about this. Do you think it's really something that you would want to do?"

"Absolutely I would want to do it, Ange. You know I love sports, especially baseball. The problem is the circumstances. I would have to put the rest of my life on hold to spend a year with the team. I would have to quit my job and not think about school, either. It would be a much different situation than now."

Angie thought about this, especially the way it would affect her. She didn't care about Jake quitting his job. She saw it as a dead-end position anyway. His leaving the lab would probably be beneficial to their relationship. However, the thought of Jake entering into an unknown was a great burden on her. She wondered what kind of time commitment it would be, assuming it would be more than his present occupation. Although she didn't pay attention to sports much and found it silly when Jake would, she assumed he would become quite the celebrity for undertaking such a proposition. The fame he would garner probably meant less focus on her, which she would obviously oppose.

"Would this take up a lot of your time?" she asked.

"I'm guessing it would," Jake answered honestly. "I would have a lot of training before the season to try to get me into good baseball shape, and then would have to travel to Arizona for spring training."

"How long is that?"

"About six weeks."

"That is a long time," Angie replied with some dejection.

"And that's just the beginning, babe. Once the season —which lasts six months — starts, I would be playing games on an average of six times a week."

"Well, the games are only like three hours, right?"

"Yes, but the players get there about three to four hours ahead of time to warm up. Then it takes time after the game to shower and get out of the stadium. It's probably like an eight-hour day altogether."

"Well, that's not too bad," Angie replied hopefully.

"Don't forget that most of the games are at night, 7:05 pm. Those nights I might not even see you."

"That would upset me, I guess."

"And that's for the half of the year we are playing at Wrigley. The rest of the time we will be on the road. The road trips usually last about a week."

"I forgot about that," Angie responded. "Doesn't sound like you and I would be able to see each other much if you decided to do this. Would you be OK with that?"

The trap was set.

Luckily Jake was too smart to jump right into it. He knew if he said yes it would lead to a fight and his chances of playing would be out the window. If he said no, it would seem as if he thought it was a bad idea. He had to come up with an in between answer that would satisfy her if he really wanted to consider joining the team.

He had been working on just such a response.

"Of course not," he started carefully, "if it meant I wouldn't be able to see you at all during those times. However, there is another side to all this."

"What's that?" Angie asked suspiciously. She wasn't too keen on this idea now that she realized the time commitment. She had heard about professional ball player's road trips and the trouble they got into on them, especially with other women. She wasn't about to let her boyfriend go off with a bunch of prehistoric goons while they looked for girls who probably threw themselves at athletes. She could tell Jacob was leaning towards this opportunity and wanted to make sure she thwarted his attempt to convince her.

"The pay," Jake stated calmly. "The minimum salary for a player in the majors is currently $575,000 a year."

Jake noticed Angie's eyes pop open in surprise and he continued on, knowing he had her attention.

"With that kind of money, I thought we could get a nice place by the ballpark. If we lived together, that would automatically increase the amount of time we could spend together. And with so much money coming in, you could take some time off and travel with me on a couple of the road trips, especially the places like Miami and New York. We could have some fun together while I was on the road! Even after the season was through, we'd have enough money to ride out for a few years at least. It could be really good for our relationship."

Angie's demeanor changed and Jake could sense it.

She knew baseball players made a lot of money, but she had had no idea even the lowest paid players would bring in so much. She admitted — to herself — that Jake was right in the sense of them moving in together. It was a point she brought up often and a year in the majors could provide it for them. She also wondered if that kind of money could be used for a wedding. Jake hadn't mentioned it, but Angie was sure she could bring it up at the right time to coerce him into it. Suddenly possibilities were opening up and Angie considered the opportunity more seriously.

"Well," she replied, softer now than she was earlier, "it would be great to be able to live together. And we haven't gone on a real vacation in a while. I would love to go off to New York and Miami with you, maybe even San Francisco?"

"Of course," Jake replied.

"There is still one thing though, Jake."

He knew what it was, and knew there would be some contention between them with it. As soon as he brought up the money, he was sure Angie would see right through him and his intention.

"What's that, babe?"

"I know what you're thinking, Jake," Angie responded firmly. "You think the money could help your father."

"Well," Jake started, seeing Angie give him a stern look during his deliberation, "the thought did cross my mind."

"Did you mention it to him?"

"Indirectly."

"And what did he say?"

"He was upset by the thought of it."

"As he should be," Angie answered without sympathy. "That money would be yours, Jake, and could mean big things for us. That's more important right now."

Jake stayed quiet. He did not agree, and, as always, was upset at how Angie could not see why he would be so intent on helping his father. He wanted to reply, but knew he had her in a good spot and didn't want to ruin the possibility of Angie agreeing with him playing baseball.

Jake had plenty of concern over joining the Cubs, as he had expressed to his parents. The thoughts of his inability to play with the pros, his fear of the fans turning him into a pariah, and the possibility of Mr. Dillinger having sinister reasons for asking him to do so. But he couldn't escape the upsides of the possibility.

Ever since Jake was young, he had always dreamed of playing baseball, especially for the Cubs. He never thought it possible, but it didn't stop him from imagining it. Batting at Wrigley Field with the crowd cheering him on. Having a great at bat that propelled the Cubs into the playoffs. Making a great defensive play to preserve a one run lead deep in the game. All these scenarios had entered his head so many times as a kid he could barely count all the possibilities he dreamt up. Now they could come true.

Sure, it wasn't under the same pretenses he had considered in the past, but the chance was still there. He was too much of a realist to think he would actually do something beneficial to help the team, but the kid inside him couldn't help bringing it to mind time and time again.

His parents were right. If he passed on such an opportunity, his conscience would never forgive him for it. He would always wonder if he had made the biggest mistake in his life.

"So, when do you talk to this guy again?" Angie asked him.

"Tomorrow. I told him I would come up with a decision by then."

"So are you going to tell your work you're quitting?"

"That depends," said Jake with a grin he couldn't conceal, "are you saying you think I should do this?"

"If you want to, I think you should, Jake."

"I only want to if you're comfortable with it."

Angie smiled. That's how she wanted him to respond.

"I am, sweetheart. This could be good for both of us. And you're so excited about it, how can I say no?"

"Thanks, babe," Jake said to her excitedly, hugging her as he responded. "I really think it will be great for us. I'll talk with Mr. Dillinger first thing in the morning, and if it all goes well, I'll tell my work afterwards. Then we'll celebrate tomorrow night. What do you think?"

"Nice dinner and night on the town?" Angie asked expectedly.

"Whatever you want, Ange."

The two kissed and Jake hugged her again, his smile reaching both his ears. He could hardly believe it when Dillinger had asked him to play, but he was even more surprised he was able to get it past Angie. He suddenly felt great about the decision and couldn't wait to inform his parents.

CHAPTER 5

The next day didn't go exactly as Jacob had planned it.

He called Dillinger, and after they agreed to his playing on the team, they set up a meeting for later in the afternoon. Jake went into the lab that morning to say good-bye, at first being reprimanded for not giving proper notice, until the doctors learned his reasoning.

Most of the lab were Cubs fans, so Jake spent over an hour explaining his situation to his astonished coworkers. Everybody congratulated him as he exited. His parents, although secretly thrilled for his decision, remained stoic in order to not overplay their hand. Jake took out Angie for a late breakfast, in celebration, and agreed to look at apartments with her after the meeting with Dillinger.

Jake showed up at Dillinger's office just before three pm and was introduced by the secretary to the men in the room as he entered. It wasn't just Mr. Dillinger in the office. Jake immediately noticed the iconic figure standing to the right of his new boss.

Manager of the Chicago Cubs, Shawn "Bug" Wagner, was looking his new second baseman up and down, much to the discomfort of the one observed. Bug didn't look too pleased.

Bug Wagner was a new manager to the league, just his third year in a four year contract with the Cubs, but he was known for his play as a catcher for the Pittsburg Pirates over the span of eighteen years. He wasn't what you would call overly intelligent, but in the baseball world he was a master.

Standing six foot two with large forearms and a wiry face, Wagner knew baseball like no one else. He had a knack for it, and although a good player in his earlier years, he was now more known for his knowledge of the game and ability to assess every situation methodically and entirely. He set a league record for pickoff throws to first base as he would catch base runners napping and set them up by pretending to not know where the ball was after a pitch in the dirt.

Wagner was a career .278 hitter, just above average, but carried a .349 on base percentage, an excellent stat which told managers how willing he was to get on base for the team and create runs. Bug played hard nose ball, letting inside pitches hit him in order to get on base without ever using any arm gear that would dampen the blow to his body. He believed if you were awarded first base for getting plunked, it only counted if there was a little pain involved. He also ran the bases well, despite his lack of speed, knowing that timing was more important than fleetness of foot.

Bug was given a good contract by Dillinger after just three years of coaching in the minors. His abilities had been noticed throughout the league and Dillinger didn't want to lose him. His results, however, had been poor up to this point. The team hadn't come close to even getting to .500, let alone making the playoffs.

Wagner believed the team needed to be reset. There were too many players on his team not getting on base, not playing the field well, and running into outs on the base paths. Wagner got rid of those players and was grooming the young guys to play the game correctly. There were some improvements, especially individually, but collectively the team had not seen as much benefit as the city would have liked.

"Jacob Riley!" Big Eddy Dillinger called out while standing and offering his hand to greet him. "So good to see you again, and I'm thrilled to hear you accepted my proposal."

"Thank you, sir," Jake replied humbly. "I'm honored to do so."

"I assume you know our skipper, Bug Wagner?"

"Yes, of course I do, Mr. Dillinger," Jake answered, looking over to shake his new manager's hand. "It's such a privilege, Mr. Wagner."

"I wish I could say the same, Mr. Riley," Bug answered gruffly. "I hope you can understand how disappointed I am with this decision."

So it began.

Jake knew there would be resentment from his team, his coaches, and the fans as time went on, but he didn't realize it would surface so quickly. Up until now, everyone had been so excited for Jake's fortune, and all were congratulating him. The honeymoon seemed short lived and reality was now setting in. Jake's stomach seemed to tie in a knot with the rough introduction.

"I am sorry to hear that, coach Wagner," Jake stated shyly. "I promise to do my best to help the team."

"Don't listen to him, Jake!" Dillinger interrupted with a chuckle. "His bark's worse than his bite. I know there will be some disappointed players on the team, but I think you'll experience a good welcome here."

"Are you kidding?" Bug stated, somewhat annoyed. "These guys are going to chew this kid up! Don't you realize what you're doing to him? Kid, I'm sure you have the right intentions, and I'm sure anyone in your shoes would do the same thing if presented such an offer, but you have to think about what you're agreeing to. You're taking the place of a player who has been working his whole life to get to the big leagues. Everyone on the team will be bitter with you getting so much without having to work for it like they have. People are going to despise you for it. And you'll even be taking a starting job from someone, causing disarray on our infield, not to mention how I'm going to fit you into a major league line-up!"

"Starting job?" Jake asked. "I wasn't aware I'd be starting."

"Sure, Jake!" Dillinger answered. "I'm not bringing you onto the team so Bug here can keep you on the bench for the whole year. You're going to really experience the game, just as the others do. Bug and I have been discussing these terms over the last few hours."

"I still don't understand why you're doing this, Eddy," Bug interrupted, as if Dillinger hadn't even said a word to Jake. "The fans are not going to take well to this. This decreases our chances to do any damage in the National League Central. I think you're mistaken!"

"Bug, this is a promotion for the fans, OK? We discussed this already! Attendance has dropped dramatically over the last few years. We need to do something to bring people back into the seats! How are we going to pay all your salaries if we don't get paying customers?"

"But this isn't the way to do it!" Bug defended. "People will be angry. They'll protest this. You'll lose fans, not gain them!"

Big Eddy knew his manager was right and had been thinking that ever since the day of his wager. He wasn't positive how the fans would react, but he was getting pretty confident he made a bad bet and had been suffering for it ever since. It was hard enough to convince himself this was a good idea, let alone anyone who questioned him. He knew the word would be out after today and feared backlash from the media. He hoped it would be something minor and that it would fade with time, but he was beginning to think it wouldn't be that easy.

"We've already talked about this, Bug. Why do it in front of the kid, huh? Let him have some fun with this, will ya?"

"I think it's important he knows what he's getting into, Eddy," Bug replied. "I'm hoping he'll reconsider!"

"If he does, you'll just have to talk to another young man about the same thing, because I'll find someone else to do this. You know that's true."

Bug looked despondently at his boss and shook his head. He wasn't happy, but at least he remained quiet now. Jacob continued to watch and listen with anxiety, wondering if he'd really be able to go through with his decision.

"Jake, let's talk about what we're considering for you this year."

"Yes, Mr. Dillinger."

"So, my thoughts are that you will be starting at second base on opening day. You'll start five games a week, as a normal player does."

"Don't forget about the seventh inning thing we agreed on!" Bug interrupted.

"I'm getting to that, Bug, just stay quiet, will ya? So every game, Bug will have the option of replacing you after seven full innings, but you get to play up until the eighth inning starts in every game you start, unless you get injured."

"I understand," Jake replied, nodding in agreement.

"We're going to pay you the league minimum, which is $575,000 a year, paid every two weeks. That's $22,115 a paycheck. My secretary has your first check and will give it to you on the way out."

Jake couldn't help but show a small smile, irritating Bug. Jake had never seen a check that big before and was beyond excited to receive it.

"Okay, since we're paying you now, we expect you to start working immediately. I want you to report tomorrow to Sid Backman. He's going to be your trainer until spring training starts in four months. You two will be working on getting you into good shape as well as fielding and hitting. He will be reporting to me and Bug on your progress, work ethic, and attitude. If you mess up with him, you answer to me."

"Or worse yet, me," Bug added for affect.

"So make sure you listen to everything Sid has to say, understand?"

"Yes, of course, Mr. Dillinger," Jake answered back. "I have every intention of doing exactly what you tell me to, I promise."

"Well, if you do, you'd be the first," Bug answered sarcastically, finishing with a half-smile.

"Okay, Jake, here's Sid's card. I want you to call him today to set up tomorrow's meeting. Before you leave, meet with my secretary and she'll have you fill out some hiring forms and tax information before she gives you your check. Any questions?"

"No, Mr. Dillinger. Thank you again for this opportunity. It was nice to meet you, too, Mr. Wagner."

Jake left the two as he exited the office to look for the secretary. Big Eddy and Bug watched him intently as he walked out and waited a good five seconds after he closed the door before they began to speak.

"He seems like a good kid," Bug stated. "And he actually carries himself well."

"I noticed that when I first met him," Big Eddy replied. "He has good coordination and an aura about him, don't you think?"

"Yes," Bug answered hesitantly, "but he also lacks confidence. That's obvious. And it might be the one thing he really needs if he wants to survive two weeks in this clubhouse."

"Do you really think it'll be as bad as you say? You know, with the other players?"

"You can't imagine, Ed. These guys are going to eat this kid alive and it'll be an act of God for him to get through it. These are proud men we're talking about, and they protect each other, too. Whoever it is that gets axed in spring training or who gets shafted out of starting second base is going to be the battle cry for the rest of the team. They'll be mostly pissed at you, but you're never there. This kid will be the one they take it out on. I'm worried."

"Well, then you'll have to do your best to protect him through it. It's not the kid's fault!"

"Look, Ed," Bug said gloomily, "I'm upset enough about this arrangement without having to babysit. We'll see how the kid does, and that's it. If he lasts, so be it. If not, don't come crying to me. It'll be better business sense if he leaves, anyway. Believe me."

"Well, we'll see, Bug. Just make sure he gets the training he needs."

"Sid will start that process for us nicely, I'm sure," Bug assured. "What about Klondike? What has he said about all this?"

"Klondike?" Dillinger snorted. "The laziest GM in baseball? That buffoon couldn't care less what I do! He's just waiting for this year to end so he can move on, and I say good riddance!"

"But won't he gripe about you taking someone on without consulting him, first?"

"He doesn't care anymore, Bug. The guy's a millionaire and will retire after this year. Don't worry about him."

"What are your thoughts about Earl?"

"Casey Earl wants two million a year for the next two years and believes he can find a team to give it to him. I say good luck! I'm not giving up that kind of money for his production. He's not your kind of guy, anyway, is he Bug? Doesn't see a lot of pitches and makes a lot of easy outs."

"No, not really," Bug agreed cautiously, "but he does have a great glove, and I'm sure his numbers will be better this year."

"Well, it doesn't matter. You have a second baseman now. Let's see if he can put up better numbers than Earl."

"You say that as if you think it's possible, Ed."

"You don't?"

"Of course not!" Wagner shot back, perturbed by the suggestion. "Eddy, I don't think you have any idea how hard this is going to be for this Jacob Riley. He's in for complete destruction in this league! It's going to be hard enough in the batter's box against big league pitching, not to mention the animosity he will face in the locker room. Add in the boos he'll receive throughout the season from every fan in baseball cursing his role in their beloved game and you'll have a kid with some serious issues come July."

Big Eddy stayed silent as he stared down at his majestic desk. He was pretty sure the world was against him on this decision, but he had been hoping to get a glimmer of hope from his manager. He knew he was grasping at straws, but it was disappointing nevertheless.

He considered dropping the wager and seeing if he could get Maverick to agree to a five million payout, but he knew that was fruitless. Maverick was too confident of his success to take any significantly decreased sum. Besides, the whole group was so excited about the proposition that there was no way Maverick would derail it now.

Dillinger actually liked this kid and thought it fortunate he had seen him in the restaurant. However, maybe Maverick and the others were right. Maybe there wasn't anyone in the world who could do what he had wagered on. Regardless, the wheels were in motion and Dillinger had to get this Riley kid into the best position possible to make an attempt at it.

"OK, Bug, just do the best you can."

"Fine, Eddy. Make sure Sid does his job, though. I need to get this kid into shape in order to get the most out of him."

Big Eddy watched his dejected manager leave the office drearily. There was nothing more to do for either of them at this point. For the next few months, it was all in the hands of Sid Backman and Jacob Riley.

Dillinger decided to get a drink. He had to calm himself down before the press conference he was holding that afternoon about the Chicago Cub's new second baseman.

CHAPTER 6

Waking up the next morning was easier than usual for Jacob Riley.

He was filled with a sense of excitement he had not felt in years. He was starting a new job, one that only entailed working out and playing baseball for the next few months before spring training hit. The thought of not having to perform mundane tasks and experiments in the lab was invigorating. The ability to be able to get into shape while getting paid — very well, in fact — was even more exhilarating. Jake hadn't played organized sports for years, but now it was his duty to. He felt like the luckiest man in the world.

That feeling would change quickly.

Jake took a bus to an old building off of Addison. In it was a private workout facility that was used often by the Cubs players in the off-season. Jake had never heard of the place and was surprised to see it was as prominent as it was in a busy area of town.

He entered without trouble as the door was unlocked and there wasn't any evidence of security or a front desk. A bell rang as he pushed open the door and several of the nine or ten people in the workout room looked up at him.

Jake didn't see anyone who looked like they were expecting him, so he leisurely walked towards the equipment. As he did, he noticed a thin, elderly man watching him and Jake assumed this was his trainer.

The man looked fit, as fit as a man in his seventies could look, but his face sagged with wrinkles. He had a protruding nose and small, piercing eyes that looked Jacob Riley up and down. His hair was a dark gray and plentiful on top of his small head. He had no glasses, which was a shame, for they would have been supported well on his large, cartilaginous ears. His arms, enveloped in a thin sweat jacket were folded across his chest and he balanced himself by leaning back on his heels.

Sid Backman was beckoning his young student, and Jake followed his silent order and approached the old man.

"You Jacob Riley?" Sid asked, already knowing the answer to his introductory inquiry.

"Yes, sir," Jake replied. "You're Mr. Backman, I'm assuming."

"I suppose I am," he answered contrarily, "but most people call me Sid. I'd prefer you do the same."

Jake nodded in agreement.

"So you ready to do this?"

"Yes, sir, I am. How do you want to start?"

"Again, Jake, I'm Sid. Not sir, not Mr., just Sid. Now, I appreciate you being here on time today. That will happen every day. If it doesn't, I promise you it will only take you once to learn. Got it?"

Jake nodded again.

"We start at seven and go until five. We'll take off from eleven till one every day for lunch and relaxation. You should spend at least half an hour of it downstairs in the whirlpool or with the masseuse. It's important you keep your muscles loose and in shape during these next few months. By the time we're through, you'll be able to run through mountains. And hopefully you can hit some fastballs and field some grounders, too. It'll be hard as hell, but you'll thank me when you're in the best shape of your life. I guarantee that."

"That sounds great, Sid," Jake answered excitedly. "I'm really appreciative of all this."

"It's my job, kid. I'm surprised to have to spend so much time on you, with your situation and all, but Dillinger seemed very intent on it. Now let's get upstairs, we'll start with some fielding."

Sid led the two up the stairs of the old gymnasium. Jake was surprised to hear there was a sauna and masseuse downstairs and that he would be able to field in such a place. As Sid opened the door, however, Jake saw a new side of the rundown building.

The beautiful, newly updated second floor was much bigger than Jake imagined it could be. There were six batting cages and two areas with dimensions of about thirty by one hundred and twenty feet, each with a home plate at the entrance, but one surface was coated by what looked like a pseudo-dirt compound which was a light gray. The other was hard wood flooring. The room was well lit and gave a feeling of being outdoors with its high ceilings and crisp air.

The two walked into the cage with the hardwood flooring and a home plate in front. On one side there was a bucket of new baseballs and four wooden bats. The other side held a large black bag which Sid immediately bent down to and unzipped. Jake saw him pull three infielder's gloves that looked new except they were each oiled and broken in. Sid tossed one at Jake who caught it, surprisingly.

"I assume you didn't bring a glove?"

"No," Jake answered defensively, "I didn't realize I'd be fielding today and Mr. Dillinger..."

"It's OK, kid. I didn't expect you to," interrupted Sid. "This one is a great second baseman's glove. Short, pliable, comfortable. Try it out. If you like it, it's yours."

"Thanks, Sid," Jake replied with a smile.

"Don't thank me, Jake. You're in the bigs now. Everything is free, especially if it helps your game. You just tell me what you need, and I'll be sure you get it. Now get out there and let's see how you can field."

Jake was nervous as he ran out about one hundred feet from the plate. He crouched down a little, his glove just able to touch the floor if he let his arms hang limp.

Sid hit him about eighty ground balls, some right at him, some to either side to asses his range. Jake bobbled the ball often and misplayed some of the hops. He felt anxious for the first ten or so, but eased into it after that. He was surprised to see Sid continue to hit balls at him without saying a word. It almost seemed as if he weren't even paying attention to his student, which made Jake feel more comfortable. After the last hit, Sid called Jake back to him.

"Sorry," the student called out as he approached, "I'm a little rusty. I haven't fielded ground balls in..."

"Don't be sorry about anything, kid," Sid responded, looking down at the end of his bat. "I'm here to teach you, and I assume you know nothing. So you'll listen to what I tell you, and you'll get better as you do. Got it?"

"Got it."

"OK, now you did a lot better than I thought you would, but you have a long way to go. I like how you start off, bent over in good position, looking at me. But your weight was on your heels. You have to lean forward more in order to easily slide one way or the other and charge the ball if necessary."

Jake remembered this now. His high school coach taught him and it worked well once Jake was comfortable with it. He had to get back some of his old habits.

"Also, when I initially strike the ball, your first move is to come up. Then you get back down on the ball. You look uneasy and anxious when you do that, so make sure you stay down on the ball the whole time. The only time you come up is if that last hop brings you there. You follow the ball and you'll catch the ball, OK?"

Jake nodded again. He knew he was doing exactly what Sid had noticed, but his nervousness didn't allow him to adjust correctly. Jake was sure he could respond appropriately once he was more relaxed.

"OK, that's the first lesson. Get back out there."

Jake did as he was told and felt a better rhythm fielding. However, after about twenty ground balls he started feeling his calves cramping and his back hurting. It was hard to stay in proper position for so long and still make the plays. Sid would yell at him to get back on his toes and to stay down on the ball.

Jake tried to listen but discomfort made it hard to do so. He missed a lot more grounders than he did the first round and felt worse about his abilities. Sid called him in after about fifty grounders to change the young man's attitude.

"Much better, Jake," he said with a grin.

"I felt so much worse, Sid. I know it's because I'm out of shape."

"Out of baseball shape, at least," Sid replied. "You can actually be overweight and tire out after running the bases, but every big league player out there is in baseball shape. The muscles they need to field a grounder, swing a bat, or pitch a baseball are in perfect condition, and yours will be too. Just give it time. Now let's hit some pitches."

Jake and Sid entered one of the batting cages which, although recently upgraded, held worn baseballs and tattered helmets. Jake picked one out as well as a thirty-three inch bat and headed for home plate.

"Wrong bat, Jake," Sid called out. "Pick up the one next to it."

Jake looked down and saw a large club-like bat leaning against the netting. He picked it up and immediately felt the difference in the weight. This bat was thirty-six inches and much more dense. Jake took a practice swing and realized it would be too heavy for him.

"This bat is too big for me, Sid."

"That's the point, Jake. Use the heavy bat now and build your muscles with the right form so you either get used to it and end up keeping it, or you move to a lighter bat and it becomes easier to catch up to fastballs."

Jake didn't argue and walked to the plate. Sid walked the sixty feet six inches to the pitching machine and set it for sixty-five mph, fast balls, down the middle. Each machine had the options of a velocity between sixty and one hundred and ten mph, straightness ranging from angling right to angling left and from straight to curving downward, and location, from down the middle to varied. Sid wanted to start Jake off easy.

Jake took his stance — the one he remembered from high school — and waited for the machine. The red light turned on and Jake felt beads of sweat on his forehead. This was the first time in a while he was going to swing a bat and he worried about how he would look in front of Sid. The bat was heavy above his shoulders and he knew he would have trouble getting it around quickly enough. Jake also had no idea of how fast the pitches would be coming.

The first few pitches were rough. Jake swung late with the heavy bat and dipped his arms under the pitches. After that he began to hit a few, mostly getting under the pitches and being a bit late. By the end of the first fifty pitches Jake was hitting line drives up the middle and towards left field pretty consistently. He felt better about his abilities, but he knew his swings were becoming more difficult as his muscles tired from the unfamiliar movements.

After the first round, Sid walked up to Jake as he had after the first round of grounders. Again, his demeanor was stoic and unbiased toward the skills of Jacob. He stayed informative and calm, easing Jake's nerves.

"You picked it up in the end there, Jake. Those were sixty-five mph fastballs set for the middle of the plate, a good starting point. Your stance isn't bad, but we will have to work on it a little for when the pitching gets faster. We have to realize you don't have enough time to acclimate to fastballs at ninety-five mph and be able to adjust suddenly for an eighty mph change-up or breaking ball."

Jake understood. He remembered during his sophomore year in high school having to hit a guy who threw faster than most at seventy-five mph. The whole team was putting their arms forward in their stances in order to get to the pitch more quickly. He didn't know how he would catch up to pitches approaching one hundred mph, but trusted Sid to get him there.

"Over the next six weeks or so," Sid started again, "we'll get you up to about eighty-five mph. You might not believe it, but you'll be able to hit those pitches, even with that club you're using. By the time spring training starts, you'll be hitting one hundred mph fastballs like they were nothing. Hard to fathom, I know, but in the bigs that's not the hard thing. When these pitchers frame pitches all over the plate and change speeds on you to throw you off, you'll be praying for straight up fastballs in the middle of the strike-zone. We'll have to train you to hit multiple kinds of pitches in varied locations. Hopefully that trains your muscles and your eyes to know what are good pitches to swing at and allows you to hit at least some of them well. I'm not going to say I can get you hitting major league pitching in four months. That's near impossible. But we'll do the best we can to give you a chance. Understand?"

Jake nodded in affirmation. It was only day one and he was already realizing how crazy all this was. How could he ever get to the abilities of major league ball players in such a short period? He was sure his skills were not nearly as good as theirs and they had been playing their whole lives! He understood that all this training was just to get him to a place where he wouldn't be a complete failure, but he wondered if that would be the case regardless. He didn't have a choice, however, and vowed to work as hard as he could to prepare for the season.

Jake took some more swings in the cage at seventy mph and did well, Sid adjusting his stance slightly and giving him pointers on how to look at the pitch coming towards the plate. The bat became a massive weight as his muscles fatigued and Sid ended the session a little earlier than he had wanted to because of it.

For the rest of the morning Sid and Jake threw the ball back and forth from different distances, Jacob working on his mechanics through Sid's teaching. Jake's right shoulder quickly fatigued, not having thrown a ball in a while. He worked through it, though, in order to push himself as far as he could. Even though he ached, Jake felt he was growing stronger from the activity.

Soon it was eleven and time for lunch. Sid first made Jake drink a protein shake which had specific nutrients in it. He also gave Jake instructions on lunch. Jake could eat anything he wanted, but he had to write it all down when he came back, in order for Sid to analyze his intake. If he was lacking in certain nutritional categories or too high in fats or bad carbs, Sid would make some changes.

Jake found when he wrote down what he ate, he actually wanted to choose more healthy options, even if they were high in calories, because of the drastic workouts he did daily. Sid never mentioned any changes to his diet and Jake wondered if he ever intended to or if he just wanted Jake writing it down so he was self aware of what was going into his body.

The afternoon was more difficult than the morning. The workouts were more generalized and less baseball involved, making them seem more mundane and less interesting. Jake would learn to love the morning routine while loathing the afternoon. He was unhappy to hear he was expected to train on Saturdays, too, giving him only one day off a week, but he was excited to find out the sixth day was only a morning session.

For Jake's first afternoon Sid brought him downstairs to the basement of the facility. The area was darker and more humid, and Jake realized there was a pool. Jake expected a swimming portion of his exercise routine as Sid had told him to bring trunks. The basement also had more free weights than the first floor did, and they were utilized well that afternoon.

Jake started with bench pressing and dumbbell lifts, isolating different regions such as his chest, arms and shoulders. The workout was difficult as his muscles still ached from the morning's activities. Sid fed him energy drinks and protein solutions during specific intervals to both enhance his exercising and build his muscle.

Jake's next regimen consisted of running and cardio routines. There was a track that circled the free weights and totaled one twelfth of a mile. The running was mostly sprints and suicide runs with abdominal exercises sprinkled in.

Jake would find out over the next few months that he had with Sid that he was thankful for the long runs that at times were expected of him. When he was able to stretch his legs and go at a leisurely pace, he felt more at ease. The high intensity runs and calisthenics were very difficult and never seemed to get easier as Sid would push for more and more out of his pupil.

The first run Jake did was a forty meter dash which Sid timed. It was important to know Jake's speed from the beginning to see if he would improve at all over the course of his training.

Sid couldn't believe Jake's first time.

"A 4.5?" Sid called out surprisingly. "That's pretty good! Were you always this fast?"

"Yeah," Jake responded, winded. "I used to be able to run a 4.4. I hope I can get back to that."

"I'm sure you will. You might even dip below that after I'm done with you. Now, in baseball it is important to be fast, but even more important to be quick. Do you know what I'm saying?"

Jake knew. A fast player could get from point A to point B in good time, but to be quick meant a lot more. Quickness was the ability to start from one spot and be able to rapidly move one way or the other, like you would on the field once you picked up where a ball was hit. You could also stop and start again instantaneously if you were quick, but not necessarily so if you were only fast. Quickness involved more than just moving the feet swiftly and was tougher to become good at. Jake was quick once, but felt he needed to train more in order to get back to that state.

"Good," Sid replied when Jake explained the difference. "So you know I'll be trying to make you quick. The fast part you'll pick up on your own with the training, but the quickness I'll have to put some more effort into to get you where you need to be. You're starting on the right foot, though, so I expect big things from you in terms of speed."

The last part of the day was swimming. There was a single lane pool which Jake was to do laps in, mostly for speed. Sid wanted Jake to build up his muscles and endurance in the water. Sid knew the exercise was unparalleled in terms of keeping fit and strong and had the extra benefit of keeping the muscles loose while the exercise was being performed.

Jake hated the end of each day as he was always extremely fatigued and then had to give all he had to swim laps, something he was never very good at. He would cramp if he wasn't hydrated and would swallow water if he didn't keep his form.

The exercise was so difficult Jake knew it must be doing an extreme amount of good for him.

After the first day ended — promptly at five o'clock — Sid told Jake to expect this kind of workout every day he came in. Jake was exhausted and felt he couldn't even understand what his trainer was telling him because of his complete lack of energy.

He left his suit at the facility to be washed and ready for him the next day. He drank two liters of water and ate another protein bar that was left for him. Then he asked the masseuse if she could work some of the knots out of his demolished body.

Jake climbed up on the table and relaxed as she did her work. He woke up two hours later with nobody in sight and the lights to the facility dimmed. Jake looked at his cell phone to see he was now late going home and had three missed calls from Angie.

Jake stood up, slowly, and felt a deep ache in his calves. He grabbed his bag and walked up the stairs to the main floor, each upward step intimidating and excruciating to his glutes. Jake left the building with a smile from the doorman and walked out to the street to wait for his bus. It had been just one day, but Jake wondered if he would be able to make it for many more.

CHAPTER 7

Sid was right.

After four weeks, Jake was hitting eighty-five mph fastballs without difficulty. His club did not feel as heavy as it did the first time he swung it. Jake's fielding had become smooth. He could easily shift to the right or left for ground balls and no matter how hard the ball was hit, Jake was making the play effortlessly.

Jake's body was chiseled now, despite him taking in over five thousand calories a day. He could run like never before and felt his quickness improve to the point where he could stop and start instantly without fear of injury. Jake was swimming much farther and faster then he ever could, and the exercise wasn't even that troublesome at the end of the day.

It might have taken four treacherous weeks to get there, but Jake was in shape — baseball shape — and was feeling great. He felt ready to move on to more difficult tasks, but Sid wasn't as confident.

The old trainer was impressed with his pupil's work. Jake was punctual and diligent and it translated onto the field. He had made some real jumps in his batting and his stance was greatly improved. He hadn't thought Jake would be able to pick up his fielding so quickly, but he admired his student's ability to field balls to both sides of his body without any hindrance.

The most improved aspect was Jake's confidence. Sid saw the young man begin to hit balls with authority, no longer just trying to make good contact. He also saw Jake trying to overcome his best times at the forty yard dash, the half-mile and the mile. Jake was speaking with Sid like they were partners now and not just in a teacher-student relationship.

All these things helped Sid's faith grow in his pupil, but the thought of moving on was still a worrisome one.

Sid knew Jake had to start hitting off-speed pitches and breaking balls, a much tougher obstacle than straight fastballs. This was always a daunting task for any player, let alone one who had only been playing for a month. The pitches the machine could manufacture would fool Jake and he would not be able to hit as solidly as he currently was. That kind of change in his results were always difficult on a player and Sid was afraid it would break Jake's confidence to the point his student would fall back into his old habits.

There was also the topic of fielding. Catching ground balls hit on a smooth surface was easy. There was virtually no chance for a bad hop. Now Jake had to move onto a dirt surface where tricky hops were part of every ground ball. Once the first ball got by someone because of misdirection, it was easy to second guess every ball hit. That kind of mind teasing could pull a lot of confidence from a player in two ways. One, it worried someone that they wouldn't be able to make a good play, and two, it scared someone that a hard hit ball might strike and injure them.

Sid knew both those thoughts had to be overcome in order to be a good fielder and some players were never able to do it.

Regardless of the apprehension Sid had, he knew he had to advance his young student and the next four weeks were dedicated solely to that. As Sid expected, Jake did not transition very well.

His hitting was not improving quickly anymore. The change-ups were usually around seventy mph, a change from the ninety mph he was used to. Jake would often swing way in front of the ball and not come close to hitting it, even if it was right in the middle of the plate. The breaking balls were worse. Jake's mind was taught to only swing where the ball was going in terms of a straight line. When the ball weaved in and out of its original trajectory, Jake would swing above it, to the side of it, and often late.

The change in his hitting was so great that his confidence took a tumble. Jake was frustrated by his downturn and showed it in the batter's box. Sid tried to calm him down and encourage him, but Jacob now was doubting his abilities and his temperament had been pretty glum for a few weeks.

Fielding was more difficult, too, but, as Sid expected, Jake transitioned this part of his game more fluidly.

The different hops and skips the ball took while Jake was fielding made it more tricky to make the play, but the conversion wasn't as dramatic as with hitting and Jake was able to improve. He found he could usually tell when the balls would take a bad hop and could adjust accordingly. He might not have always been able to make the play, especially if it was to his left or right, but he could usually knock the ball down and retrieve it quickly.

This part of his game was improving and Jake tried to take confidence in it to make up for his embarrassment during batting practice.

Jake found out early that his Saturday morning workouts were by himself. Sid preferred to take the weekend off. Jake spent them hitting a lot of balls in the cage and working on his fitness through running, stretching and yoga. He was torn between keeping the day as a restful one and getting all he could out of the four hours he was there. He decided to approach it by assessing how he felt on the mornings he came in. If he was very sore and tired, he would take it easy. If he felt better, he would work hard knowing he would have almost two days to recover before he came back Monday morning.

On the first Saturday, even though he felt run down, Jake worked hard. The second Saturday he decided to take it easy. The third Saturday he was starting to feel better, not having the muscle soreness he was accustomed to the first couple weeks. He started looking for ways to improve his workouts and stumbled across something that would change his approach to hitting for good.

There was a batting cage on the second floor that was more open than the rest. It was the last one against the wall and when it was built, there must have been more room than the architect originally planned. The right side of the batter's box — the one that opened up as if going towards first base — had a lot more room than the others. Jake could imagine himself hitting the ball and then running to first base, just like in a real game. He preferred this cage to the rest when he was alone because of its openness and he would sometimes work on his stance and swing without any pitches thrown.

On that third Saturday, Jake was feeling pretty good. He had been getting in good shape, eating well, sleeping hard every night, and he was no longer constantly sore. He had a spring in his step and felt comfortable in his stance and with his swing.

Standing in the wide cage he started to daydream.

Jake knew this season was going to be rough for him. He was not naive. There would be no way he could come out of spring training in good enough condition to hit big league pitchers well. He hoped his fielding would be good enough to not cost the team too many games, but he knew it would be sub-par nevertheless.

However, all those odds stacked against him didn't stop him from thinking there could be moments of greatness. He dreamt of a time he would make a diving catch at second base or start a nifty double play. He mused about stretching a double into a triple or even scoring from first on a double to win the game in the ninth inning.

At this point, while standing in the batter's box of his familiar training facility, Jake was dreaming of hitting the ball hard down the left field line for a double or triple. It was a common one for him. Jake got into his stance and looked at the pitching machine. He imagined a mammoth right handed pitcher who was ahead of Jake 0-2.

The pitch came, a fastball at one hundred miles an hour on the inside portion of the plate. Jake swung the bat hard, dreaming he ripped the ball on a line shot past third base, chalk flying high as the ball struck the line in left field. Jake dropped the bat and darted out of the box as if he were running to first, but he stopped suddenly.

In his dream, he was going to try to stretch out the hit into a triple, but as he physically tried to get out of the box, he felt he was slow. He needed to be quick out of the box if he was going to fulfill his fantasy, so he picked up the bat and got into his stance again. He took another swing and dropped his bat to run to first. He stopped after three steps. Still too slow.

Jake knew that a quick first step was important not only for stretching doubles into triples, but for getting on base in general. Any weakly batted balls on the infield could turn into hits if the batter got to first quickly. Jake tried multiple times before realizing he didn't have the quickness he desired.

Jake practiced getting into his stance, swinging the bat, and darting out of the box about fifty times that day. Then he decided to try to do it after he hit the ball, so he slowed the pitching machine down to allow enough time in between hits for him to take ten steps towards first every time he made contact.

This became routine for Jake every Saturday and he felt, like he had with everything else, that he was getting better at it with all the work he put into it. By the time Jake had finished his training with Sid, he was as fast as he had wanted to be coming out of the box and he knew it would only benefit him when he was to take live pitching in camp.

The first eight weeks had its ups and downs in terms of baseball and those weeks followed a similar path in terms of his home life. Jake's parents were thrilled he was putting so much effort into baseball. They were excited to hear his stories about training and eager to know he was progressing. They weren't excited to hear he was moving in with Angie, but they helped him pack and move the day it happened without uttering a disparaging word.

Angie hadn't been as happy about the situation as the Rileys were. She was getting irritated at Jake's long days away and then his sluggish demeanor in the evenings. He never wanted to do anything but lounge and eat, blaming his workouts for his indolence. She also didn't like that Jake would go to bed early on Friday nights in order to be ready for his half day workout sessions on Saturday mornings. She felt he shouldn't have to train on the weekends. Furthermore, when she found out he wasn't being supervised, she suggested he truncate his hours or not show up altogether.

Jake was too honest to do such a thing so Angie was left feeling abandoned and ignored.

Not that it was all bad for her. She cut down her hours waiting tables with Jake's new paycheck. Jake agreed to pay for their new apartment off the lake and all their expenses in order for Angie to use her money on herself. She was able to shop, exercise, lounge around her new place, and take walks on the beach, all with more money in her pocket.

She enjoyed this very much but didn't want to let Jake know it in case he would feel empowered because of it. She kept her new found joys to herself but expressed her misfortunes often and vividly. She even had a plan.

It was now eight weeks into Jake's training and he was resting on the couch with Angie on a Friday night watching a movie. He was feeling good enough to go out, but knew he had to get up early for training the next morning. Angie, for the first time in a while, did not act agitated by

Jake's demeanor. She had ordered them a pizza from Gino's and picked out a movie for them to watch. After it ended, she broached the topic she had been molding Jake for during the whole evening.

"I've been thinking," she said while playing with Jake's hair as he nestled in her lap.

"About what?" he replied inquisitively.

"Your job," Angie answered plainly. "You've been doing this for almost eight weeks now, and it's been pretty tough on you. Well, on both of us. I'm not sure it's the best thing for us."

"Are you saying you want me to quit?"

"No!" Angie answered quickly, realizing she was leading him too much. "I mean, not right away. You have about six more weeks left until spring training, right?"

"That's right."

"Well, what if you quit after these six weeks? We would have made about $150,000 dollars, which will last well into next year. It would avoid you having to go out there and embarrass yourself in front of all those brutes on the team. It would also allow you to stay here instead of having to be in Arizona for over a month. We could get the best of both worlds."

"But I promised Mr. Dillinger I would play baseball for him. The media has been talking this up for the last two months. If I quit now he'll look like a fool and I'd be taking advantage of our agreement!"

"He's a business man, Jake," Angie retorted, rolling her eyes. "You wouldn't be the first person to back out of a deal. He knew the risks when he started this whole project! Plus, don't we finally deserve a break? We've both been stuck in these dead end jobs without any hopes of breaking free and then this suddenly falls into our laps! I say it's about time, no reason for us to feel bad for taking advantage of a situation for once!"

"Angie, we can take advantage of this without backing out of the deal. Look at this beautiful place we have! And now you've been able to cut down on your hours. It's all been such a blessing!"

"But what about your having to leave for over a month? Do you really want to be away from me for that long? It's ridiculous for an employer to ask so much out of someone! They are being unfair and it would serve them right for us to collect the money we already have and leave them.

They deserve it!"

"It's not unfair, Ange. All the players have to report for spring training. I agreed to it in my contract. I don't think it would be right to betray Mr. Dillinger like that. Besides, you're taking ten days off to visit me in Arizona during camp. It'll be a great time for us, especially you."

"I can't believe you're siding with them over your own girlfriend, Jake! Can't you at least consider this?"

Angie knew Jake wouldn't. The one thing she found difficult to control was his morality. He would never betray his boss, no matter how badly he was treated. Jake had a sense of ethics that kept him from crossing another person no matter how egregious that person could be. His moral compass was solid, which Angie actually admired and had used multiple times to her advantage, but she knew it would not serve her well now. Her last ditch effort was futile and she realized she would just have to stay upset with him for awhile so he suffered for his decision not to go along with her plan.

"I won't consider it, Angie. I don't want to take anybody's side except yours, but I have to do what is right. If I can't do that, how can I feel I'm good enough to deserve you?"

Angie smiled, although it was small as she tried to suppress it. She appreciated his devotion to her and knew it was genuine. She just didn't want it to become misdirected.

"Well, I'm still mad at you about it, but I guess I'll have to be the better person and accept your decision. But know I still think my way is the best for us. I hope I don't have to say 'I told you so.'"

"OK, Ange, I understand. But know I need your support through this. It's been tough already and I don't see it getting any easier. I really appreciate all you've done for me already."

"And?"

"And I love you, of course," Jake added with a small kiss. Angie smiled back.

"OK, Jake, I guess we have to get to bed if you're getting up early for training tomorrow."

"You're right, Angie. Thank you for understanding."

"I don't understand, Jake, but I'll go along with it. For you."

The two went to bed that night as they usually did. Angie was frustrated, but knew her pitch to Jake had been a long shot. Jake fell asleep thinking not about her, but about baseball and all it would entail over the next eight months.

He was the most excited he'd been in years.

CHAPTER 8

The following Monday Sid informed Jake that they only had six weeks left before spring training.

The last two weeks would consist of live pitching. There were a couple minor league pitchers in the area who would come for two hours a day to assist with Jake's progression. In the meantime, Jake needed to become an expert at the batting cages in order to be able to feel comfortable with an actual human being throwing him pitches.

It had not been going well up to this point.

Jake was struggling with hitting pitches that changed speeds and curved in and out of the strike zone. He was doing a good job of interpreting balls and strikes and rarely swung at bad pitches, but detecting early enough the type of pitch coming to him was the challenging part. Jake was starting to figure out the pitch as it was approaching him. The problem was swinging the bat in time to catch up with it.

After another week of struggling, Sid caved and told Jake they were going to change things up.

"I have to admit that you picked up the fastball better than I expected," Sid told his pupil, trying to give him some confidence before breaking down his faults, "but you've struggled mightily with the breaking balls and off speed pitches. Don't get discouraged. I expected this. You've tried to pick up a whole lot in a very small amount of time and have done as well as you can. But the feat ahead of you is so great we can't expect you to be hitting everything you see. You might never be able to do this, Jake. Most people can't. But my job is to train you to do it the best you can and your job is to work as hard as possible to completely fulfill your potential. Unfortunately, we don't know what that is yet, and we're running out of time. I didn't want to do this, but I have to change course. I want you to switch bats to a thirty-three inch, one with a normal weight.

It's going to feel light to you, given what you're used to, and you'll have more time to figure out the pitches because your bat speed will be greater. However, it's not all positive. You'll have an even harder time with the off speed pitches because you'll be swinging earlier than before, so you really have to look out for those. Got it?"

Jake nodded. He had been hoping he could use a lighter bat soon because he felt it would be beneficial to his timing, but he had never dared ask Sid for it.

Jake had completely followed Sid's plan from the beginning and had him to thank for how far he had come. There was no way Jake thought he could be as good a baseball player as he presently was, despite how hard it was for him to hit breaking balls. He fully trusted his teacher and was eager to move on to the next step. Jake picked up the bat and smiled.

"Now get in the cage and see what you can do."

Jake stepped up with more confidence. The bat felt light in his hands, but as he made solid contact with the pitched balls, he noticed he was hitting them with more authority than before. He still had trouble with the breaking balls, but he noticed when he got fooled by a pitch, he could more quickly try to make up for it and he was able to at least foul off a lot of pitches that he had been missing before.

However, the detriment Sid anticipated was accurate. Jake was way ahead of the change ups and was frustrated he couldn't pick up the pitch sooner.

Over the next three weeks Jake showed some real improvement at the plate. He was hitting a lot more of the breaking balls and he could at least foul off most of them. He recognized fastballs quickly, but was usually late in his swing because he was worried about a change up throwing off his timing. He would still hit the fastball well, but the ball would go towards the right side as was common with a tardy swing. Because of his waiting back on the ball, he was doing a better job hitting the off speed pitches, but he would hit most of them foul off to the left side of the field as, was common with an early swing.

Sid was happy with Jake's progress but wasn't expecting the young hitter to be ready for live pitching when the time came. Now that the moment was upon them, however, Sid could see the possibility of Jake making the transition better than he had expected.

The training had been going on for eleven weeks and there were only two more to go. On the Monday of the twelfth week, a tall, slender Hispanic boy about eighteen years old met with Sid and Jake for batting practice. The kid looked much younger than Jake and although tall, did not have much bulk to him. His arms looked scrawny and Jake wondered how hard a boy like this could actually throw.

"Jake, this is Juan Villanueva. Juan is from South America. Chile, is it?" Sid asked the boy.

"Si," replied Villanueva without expression.

"Juan was signed last year by the Cubs and will be moving up to AA ball this year. He's a top prospect and is going to be providing you with the live pitching we were talking about."

"Nice to meet you, Juan," Jake stated, putting out his hand for a formal greeting. "I appreciate you being here."

Juan loosely grabbed Jake's had and nodded to him without a word. Jake awkwardly released his grip and looked at Sid for support.

"Juan doesn't know a whole lot of English, but he is familiar with baseball, aren't you, Villaneuva?"

"Si."

"OK, Juan, why don't you go to the mound. Jake, pick up the bat. I'll watch from behind Juan."

The batting cage had been altered. The pitching machine was on the outside of the cage and there was netting in front of the pitching mound protecting everything but the upper right quadrant where Juan would be throwing the ball.

Jake stood in the batter's box and looked down at the pitcher, seeing Sid with his arms folded behind Juan. Jake took a deep breath and stepped up to the plate. This was the first time in years he would face live pitching and his heart was beating rapidly because of it.

"Do you need to warm up?" Jake called out to Villanueva.

"He warmed up earlier," Sid called out, Juan not saying a word. "Let's start off with some fastballs."

Jake was happy to hear he would know what was being thrown, especially fastballs, his favorite pitch. He had some extra confidence because he felt this Villanueva kid seemed too young and gawky to be able to get anything on his pitches. Jake took a few practice swings and looked down at Villanueva. He was ready to go.

Villanueva wound up and delivered a pitch down the middle of the plate. The ball was thrown hard and made a sizzling sound, getting louder as it approached. Jake couldn't believe how quickly the ball seemed to be coming at him and he realized he was already too late. He tried to take a quick swing but was tardy and he looked awkward because of it. The ball hit the backstop netting with a thud and Jake was disappointed and embarrassed.

He would no longer judge a pitcher's abilities by how they looked on the mound.

The next pitch was a little low, but Jake was ready for it. He put a good swing on it and connected solidly, sending a line drive just to the right of Villanueva. The next pitch was on the outside edge and Jake hit a shot towards first base. Villanueva then threw a high pitch which Jake held off on. The fifth pitch was on the inner edge of the plate and Jake lined it towards left field, his most solid hit yet.

Jake continued to hit the fastballs well, laying off the balls and tearing into the strikes. The pitches were coming in at almost ninety mph, and Jake was feeling confident in his abilities.

"OK, good work, Jake. Now let's hit some breaking balls."

Villanueva set up and delivered his first pitch. His wind up was the same and his delivery looked exactly like when he threw a fastball, but the trajectory of the ball was much different. The ball appeared to be coming in at the upper edge of the strike zone and looked fat and hittable, but when Jake began his swing the ball dipped and disappeared from Jake, leaving him swinging above it.

Jake had seen this pitch multiple times with the pitching machine, but it was much more intimidating coming from a live pitcher. He heard Sid chuckle as the ball hit the back netting.

"A little different, isn't it, Jake?" Sid called out with a smile. Jake also saw Villanueva giving a smirk which he was clearly trying to hide. Jake stepped back up to the plate.

The next pitch was similar, and Jake was ready for it. Jake watched it come down from its original location and dip out of view. Jake swung late because he was attempting to see the ball the whole way. The bat hit the ball and sent it into the back netting, but Jake was happy to simply get a piece of the biting curve.

The next pitch started waist high, but when Jake swung, the ball was already hitting the ground in front of him. Jake shook his head in disbelief as Juan and Sid smiled.

During the next twenty pitches, Jake began to figure out the pitch and he had a few solid hits. He also was able to lay off a few of the pitches that started low and ended up even lower, clearly not strikes. He wondered how he would fare trying to hit or lay off these pitches if he didn't know a curve ball was coming. He would know his answer soon enough.

"OK, Jake, I'm going to have Juan mix it up now. Let's see how well you can identify the pitches and then hit them. You ready?"

"Ready," Jake yelled back, knowing his honesty had never seen a worse moment.

Juan started off with a fastball towards the middle of the plate. Jake recognized it early, but was afraid it could be a breaking ball and therefore ended up swinging late and fouling it off to the right. The next pitch was another fastball that was high and inside. Jake saw it coming and tried to get out of the way for fear of being hit and was surprised that his instincts caused him to take a swing at it anyway, missing badly.

"Lay off the bad ones!" Sid called out.

The next pitch was an off-speed pitch on the upper portion of the strike zone. Jake swung early and missed badly. That was strike three. In a real at bat situation, he'd be shaking his head in disgust as he walked back to the dugout. He knew he had to get better.

The next sequence didn't provide him much solace.

The first pitch came in as a fastball on the inside corner. Jake thought it was a ball, but when Sid called out "Strike one!" he knew he was down in the count. The next pitch came in on his hands, but then broke in to the middle of the plate. Jake realized he was fooled and tried to swing but missed badly. Jake was sure the third pitch was going to be a breaking ball or an off-speed pitch. He decided he would wait back on it and if it was curving out of the zone, he would let it go and if it was an off-speed pitch and in the strike zone, he would have time to get his bat on it.

Instead, a ninety mph fastball down the middle of the plate sizzled by him and struck the back netting before Jake had time to realize he had been struck out again. He was frozen in the batter's box and now realized how tough it was to hit a good pitcher.

Jake felt wonderment and despondency at the same time.

As the practice went on, Jake started to pick up on some of Juan's pitches and occasionally he had a decent swing on the ball, but most of the time it was because he guessed fastball and was right. It was rare he had any good contact on the breaking balls and he realized he had not once hit a change up into fair territory.

It was depressing, but Jake tried to remain calm and positive, telling himself this was all a learning process and he would get better. However, he was more worried about when he experienced major league pitching in front of thousands of people with millions watching on television. He was sure he would look like a fool. He was right.

"Don't worry about it," Sid said in an upbeat tone after the session was over. "Juan's a good pitcher, and you have to learn some time. Besides, I thought you did pretty well out there. Right, Juan?"

"Si," Juan said expressionless.

"You'll get better at it, Jake. You'll see."

"And if I don't?" Jake asked, his doubt surfacing for the first time.

"Well, there's no way that can happen. You have to get better if you keep working at it. Maybe it won't be as good as you'd like, but what can you expect? You're doing the best you can, and that's all anyone can expect from you."

"I guess," Jake answered dejectedly.

"Juan, go home. We'll see you tomorrow. Jake, let's go work on your fielding."

Jake wasn't worried about his fielding, at least not right now. He felt pretty good with it and sensed he was as good as he could get on an artificial surface. He needed to see how he could do off a live bat on a real diamond before he could assess how well he would do defensively.

Even during the next fielding session, though, Jake couldn't get his mind off how difficult it was to hit Juan. This was a kid in AA ball! In two weeks he'd be facing pitchers who have been throwing in the big leagues for years. How could he expect to do anything then? He became anxious that he would look completely ridiculous and everyone would hate him for it. Jake began to wonder if he made the right decision to be Dillinger's guinea pig in this twisted experiment. Maybe Angie was right when she told him to quit before things got worse.

Jake did improve his hitting over the next couple weeks. Sid saw it as a big improvement while Jake only saw it as small steps. Admittedly, he could recognize the pitches better out of the hand of Villanueva, but he was still late in making a decision on whether or not to swing. He had difficulty getting any balls in play.

He was better at fouling pitches off and was greatly cutting down on his strikeouts while seeing more pitches in his at bats, but Jake knew that wasn't enough to get hits in the big leagues. Even if he could hang around for a couple more pitches, a strike out was a strike out, or so he thought. His only solace was the possibility of laying off enough pitches that he could get a good hitter's count and make the pitchers throw fastballs, the only pitch he was really able to hit with authority.

He knew it was a long shot, but at this point it was the only hope he had. Jake's confidence was low, not something he wanted going into his first week of spring training, but he didn't know how else to feel.

Angie didn't make it easier. She complained on multiple occasions of Jake leaving for Arizona for so long and not knowing when she would see him again. Jake was irked by these maudlin dramatizations, but tried to hold it in for her sake. He felt bad for her because she was hurt by his future absence and he knew it was his own doing. Jake suppressed his fears and anxiety in order to keep from upsetting Angie any further because he felt it was the right thing to do.

The one positive Jake had going for him was his fitness. After extreme training for fourteen weeks and eating right most of the time, he was in the best shape of his life. He was quick and energetic and his endurance lasted hours longer than it ever had in the past. He felt powerful, too. His arm was strong and he could throw the ball harder than he ever had.

His swing also benefited from his increased strength. When Jake was given straight fastballs, he felt he hit the balls hard and directly. Although he couldn't be certain, because the cages only allowed for the ball to go so far, Jake felt some of the balls he had hit were on pace to go well over three hundred feet, probable home runs in most ballparks.

Jake tried to see his fitness as one of the positives, as well as his monetary development. Between the two, Jake knew he was in much better shape than he had ever been in and that this whole ordeal would be worth it in the end, no matter how frustrating the next few months would be.

He tried hard to focus on that as he made his way out to Arizona, but his anxieties seemed to overcome his overall state and Jake was feeling as nervous as ever. He prayed it would be better than he anticipated.

CHAPTER 9

Jake had feelings of excitement and nervousness as he headed for Sloan Park in Mesa, Arizona.

The ballpark was the Cub's spring training facility as it provided a climate better suited for baseball during the winter months than frigid Wrigley Field. This year the position players were to report on February 22nd, approximately ten days before they were to start their exhibition games.

That meant Jake had a little over a week to meet his teammates and try to hit their pitching before playing in an actual game against people who were going to be trying to strike him out every opportunity they had. It was frightening to ponder, but it was all he could think about on the plane ride from Chicago.

With Jake's mind preoccupied with big league pitching, he didn't have time to think of another problem that had begun to surface a few months earlier, his unwanted popularity among Cubs fans and the media. It wasn't all good popularity. Most of the press was sinister and Jake had to try to ignore it as he worked out with Sid. He was sure it would follow him to Mesa where the media would be asking him questions about his preparedness for the season and what he thought of Eddy Dillinger for putting him in this position. He had heard it all before hundreds of times and it seemed to forever encapsulate him except for when concentrating on his training. He was hoping the media in Mesa would allow him to focus on baseball, but he doubted that would be the case.

The news of Jake playing for the Cubs had come out shortly after he accepted the position from Dillinger. Big Eddy had called for a press conference later that day to let the public know of his decision. Dillinger felt the sooner it got out, the less it would look like something hidden and suspicious and the sooner it would blow over and take the pressure off himself and Jacob Riley.

It didn't quite work out as planned.

In the beginning, some fans were fine with the idea and even thought it a good one. Having a common person on the team would make it fun to watch. The fans knew it would be a difficult transition and make for exciting news, almost like a reality show, but as the media continued to press the situation and more people became aware of the implications of an untalented second baseman playing for their team, bitterness developed.

At first it was only directed at Dillinger. Fans blamed him for instantly making their beloved Cubbies even worse than they already were. The media called him ignorant of baseball and even demanded he step down from his position. Players began to back the media, calling the move a selfish one, one that was only intended to put fans in the seats and to make more money for the owners. The players' union wanted to back the players, but were in a tough spot as they now also represented Jacob Riley and didn't want to disenfranchise him just for being fortunate enough to get his position.

After it was clear Dillinger was sticking to his guns and would not stop Jake from entering the majors or step down from his position, people started turning their cynicism to Jake. They blamed him for accepting the offer and stated he wasn't a true Cubs fan if he was okay with making the team worse. There were people who recognized him on the street and made rude comments to his face for hurting the Cub's chances in the upcoming season. Jake was starting to feel ostracized and the pressure thickened as more people became aware of the situation.

The positive for Jake was that many people didn't blame him. They heard him tell the media that Mr. Dillinger was going to select somebody for the spot, so he felt it might as well be him. Jake also said he considered himself better suited than most for the opportunity and hoped he could be somewhat productive in order to not bring the team down as much as another person might. Jake reiterated the sentiment many of the fans shared: if it was offered to you, you would do the same. It was a hard point to argue, as everyone was jealous of the good fortune Jake stumbled upon and, truthfully, most fans would have taken his place at the drop of a hat if offered it.

Young people — especially children — even looked up to Jake for it. They considered him some sort of hero who was just like them and now was able to play for the Cubs. It gave them hope as they dreamed of one day being able to do the same. These people were rooting for Jake. If he could somehow make this work, no matter how bad the chances were, it gave them hope for their own aspirations. This was a powerful motivator and even those who opposed Jake's promotion couldn't deny it. As irritable as some might have appeared on the outside, almost everyone would have loved to see Jake succeed and were secretly fantasizing about it.

None of this, however, did any good, or bad, for Jake's progress on the field.

As much pressure as there was outside of the facility, Jake was able to completely focus on baseball while he was in training. The task seemed so difficult and insurmountable that no amount of criticism was going to surpass it. Jake stayed determined to get better in every way possible and worked harder than he ever had in order to accomplish that. Jake might have been far from the level of a major league player as he took that plane to Mesa, but there were very few people in his spot that could have been in a better position for a chance at succeeding.

Bug Wagner, the manager of the Chicago Cubs, had been getting updates from Sid Backman on the progress of Jacob Riley. Bug was pleased with the reports, but not because they made him think Jake would succeed. In fact, the manager had no expectations whatsoever of his new second baseman and when he heard that his defense wasn't awful and that he was actually making good contact on fastballs, it was all a bonus.

Bug was hoping he would have something to work with come opening day that wouldn't make his team lose every other game they played. He knew this kid would never be able to contribute, but the less Jacob Riley took away from his team in errors and consistent strike outs, the better.

Although the reports of Jake being able to field ground balls appeased Eddy Dillinger in the sense that he wouldn't be a complete laughingstock, it didn't help at all with his bet. Dillinger was upset to hear of the struggles Jake had with hitting live pitching and cursed the boy's name because of it. He was still sure that with the proper training, a decent athlete could hit major league pitching so he deduced that Jacob Riley must have been a poor choice.

Dillinger had put a lot of pressure on Sid to get Jake shaped into a major league hitter even though Backman told him that probably would not happen. Eddy even sent his best minor league arm in the Chicago area, Juan Villaneuva, to help in the development of his new player. Supposedly, that didn't go very well either. Dillinger didn't know what else to do as it was out of his hands. He just hoped Jake could find that spark necessary to bat over .200.

When Jake arrived at the airport, there was a car waiting to bring him to the facility. He would barely have enough time to get acclimated and get some dinner before he met with one of the coaches. One of Bug's staff had already stopped by Jake's room to leave him his schedule and drop off some uniforms.

When Jake arrived at the team hotel, he headed for his room, but as he approached it, he saw Bug Wagner in the hallway talking to another man wearing a baseball cap.

"Jake!" Bug greeted him politely yet firmly. "It's good to see you made it here okay."

"Thanks, Bug. Good to see you again."

"I want you to meet Stan Oliver, our bench coach. He'll be helping you acclimate here in Mesa and with the stadium. He's also going to keep a close eye on your progress for me so we do right by you and the team. Be good to him. He can really help you out."

"Mr. Oliver, good to meet you," Jake stated happily. "I've heard good things and appreciate your dedication to the Cubs over the years."

Jake wasn't lying. Although he didn't recognize the man at first, he was quickly aware of who he was when Bug introduced them. Stan Oliver had been with the Cubs for five years now and was beloved by his players. He was said to be helpful to all the needs of the team and he would work as hard as he needed to fulfill the expectations the players had for themselves.

Jake knew he could be a good ally if he got on Stan's good side.

"Well thank you, Jake," Stan said. "But please, call me Stan. We'll be working together for the next few weeks and I'm going to really keep close to assess your needs. I'm assuming they will be plenty, no offense, but Dillinger has put you in a bad spot. I'm going to do my best to take as much pressure off you as I can."

"Thanks, Stan," Jake stated. "It will be nice to have someone who's looking out for me. I assume I'll be in a somewhat hostile environment come tomorrow."

"Well, I'd be lying if I said otherwise," Stan replied. "You have to understand that we baseball folk don't like changes that much, especially when it means someone attaining a position that everyone else has worked hard for their whole lives, not just a few months."

The words stung Jake. He realized what he was up against, the feelings his teammates would have and how they would express them. He now realized even nice guys like Stan Oliver were inwardly against him, even if they were forced by Dillinger not to express their opinions.

In thirty seconds Jake went from feeling accepted to feeling like an outsider. He didn't know what to do next. The only thing he could think appropriate was to ask for an autograph.

"I'm not trying to spook you, Jake," Stan started again, breaking the awkward silence, "but realize this is going to be a tough road. I can't fault you for it, even though I've tried, because I can't think of a single rational person who wouldn't have done the same thing. But I still don't approve of the situation, and neither does the rest of the team. You're going to have to have some thick skin these next few days. Your teammates will be the roughest, I'm sure. I'm going to try to get you through it because it's my job and it's the right thing to do, but I'm not saying I'm going to like it."

"I understand," Jake said despondently.

"Now, don't get all gloomy, Jake," Stan said with a faint smile. "I'm one of the nice ones! Besides, you seem like a good enough kid. If you keep that demeanor and keep quiet while working hard, you'll win over some of us. It's human nature."

"Right, I've thought that too," Jake replied. "I promise you there will be no one out there working harder than me. I figure I have to do that just so I don't strike out every time I bat this year."

"You might be right, Jake. Don't worry, we'll help you with that, won't we, Bug?"

"That's the plan, Stan."

"OK, then I'll leave you gentlemen alone. It's nice to meet you, Jake, and I wish you the best of luck come tomorrow."

"Thanks, Stan."

Stan Oliver walked down the hall and through the exit door to the stairwell without looking back. His disposition had been pleasant, but his words were harsh. Jake understood that they were at the same time truthful and he respected Stan for saying them cordially.

Bug broke the silence.

"Jake, here's your schedule. Breakfast at the stadium at seven am. You know how to get there, right?"

"It's right down the block. I was told there's a player's entrance."

"Exactly. You have a badge in the packet I gave you allowing you access through that door. From there it's pretty evident where you go. After breakfast I'll have someone show you the locker room. Bring some of those uniforms in your hotel room with you to put and keep in your locker. There's a laundry service in the locker room that will keep your equipment clean. Tomorrow's a big day for you."

"Sure is. I've been working hard to get to tomorrow. I hope I'm ready."

"For tomorrow? No, you're wrong saying that. Tomorrow helps get you ready for opening day, as do all our exhibition games and all the training you've done over the last few months. Don't think tomorrow means anything more than another opportunity to get better. Unlike most of the others, you have a starting spot already guaranteed, so you don't need to feel the pressure to impress, just to improve. And we are all here to help with that. People might not like it, but your part of our team now, and an important one. You're our second baseman. We need to realize that our team gets better with every improvement you make. I know Stan just freaked you out a little, but I'm going to do my best to make everyone on the team realize what I've just told you."

"Thanks, Bug, that means a lot. I don't want to let you down."

"With what I heard from Sid, you won't, kid. All I expect from you is one hundred percent, and I'm told you give that in everything you do. So keep that up and I'll be happy."

Bug walked away and exited the same door Stan Oliver had a few minutes earlier. Jake watched him go, happy he had Bug as a manager. He knew things could be a lot worse.

Jake entered his room and did some stretching while attempting to reflect on the positives. He was still happy about his opportunity, no matter how difficult it would be over the next few months. He was also happy to have a good paycheck and a healthy body. He was thankful for his parents and their support throughout it all.

He was even appreciative of Angie. After all, she had let him participate in this new dream of his, despite her being against it most of the way. He was aware that Angie didn't always approach things in the right manner and she might not always act as ethically as she could, but Jake saw those as flaws all people had. He didn't want to judge her too harshly and wanted to be grateful for the good moments he did have with her.

He admittedly didn't know much different in the way of girlfriends, but Angie had made him feel that all she was to him, good and bad, was the norm. For that reason Jake continued to believe that he was in a good relationship and that he had someone who was there for him. He also thought it was possible he could get all his teammates to accept him and not give him a hard time.

It was a toss up which thought was more delusional.

CHAPTER 10

Jake made sure to get to breakfast early the next morning.

He was trying to do his best to avoid any awkward moments between him and the other players. Despite showing up fifteen minutes early, there were a few others already congregated at a table eating their buffet eggs and pancakes.

When Jake walked in, the three at the table looked up at him and mumbled to each other as he went through the line to get his breakfast.

Jake sensed the others watching him and he knew they had spotted him as the player who won the golden ticket. Jake carefully picked out some bacon, hard boiled eggs, sausage, and high fiber cereal with a small glass of juice and water. Once he had gathered his food, he wasn't sure what to do next. Should he sit by the other players or take a seat at an empty table? He didn't want to seem conceited and sit by himself, but he also didn't want to be intrusive and break up a conversation among friends, something that might get the veterans mad at the new guy. As he walked towards the table, still undecided, someone made the choice for him.

"Hey, Riley!" called out Cam Burton, the starting right fielder over the last two years. "It's Riley, isn't it?"

"Yeah, that's me," Jake answered sheepishly.

"I knew it! I recognized you from the news. Come sit with us."

Jake put his tray down across from Burton and sat next to Shawn Hammel, the shortstop. Next to Burton was a shorter Hispanic player with a large grin and a mouthful of teeth, smiling widely as Jake sat down.

Jake knew the two starters and was instantly intimidated by having to eat with them. He would have been excited to see them on the street and have a story to tell friends, but now he felt he was at a party that no one invited him to and he didn't know what to say.

"So Riley," Burton began cordially, "I heard you've been training with

Sid. How'd that go?"

"Oh, Sid's been great," Jake answered, happy to be offered an ice breaker. "He's really helped me try to get back into baseball."

"What do you mean by that?" Burton quipped. "I thought you've never played before."

"Well, with what you guys consider baseball, that's probably true. But I did play a little in high school."

"High school ball isn't going to get you very far here," Burton replied, the others chuckling. "Hopefully he taught you more than that."

"Sure," Jake stated, again feeling out of place, "but I'm sure it's nowhere near what I'm going to see today."

"Or for the next five weeks," replied the unknown member of the table.

"Give him a break, Cools," defended Hammel, turning to Jake after the comment. "Look, I'm Shawn Hammel and this over here is Cam Burton."

"I know," Jake said, "I love watching you guys play. I'm Jacob Riley. Most people call me Jake."

"Okay, Jake," replied Hammel. "You might not know Cools Perez. He played triple A ball last year and is up to make the team this year on the infield."

"Right!" Jake answered, forgetting his shyness. "I saw a special on how you're the next big middle infielder. Wow, it's great to meet you."

"Well," Cools answered softly, "I'd like to say the same, but you being here is going to make it difficult for me to make the roster. No offense, of course."

"Oh, right," Jake stammered, embarrassed. "None taken. Sorry to put you in that spot."

"Nah, don't worry about it," Cools replied uneasily. "I'm sure I would have done the same thing if I was you."

"Listen to Cools change his tune now!" Cam blurted out, laughing. "This guy was the biggest Riley hater out of all of us!"

"Why you gotta be a punk?" Cools replied, red-faced and looking down.

Jake wasn't liking where the conversation was going and he suddenly felt stupid. It was obvious they didn't like him and their banter was delivered as if he weren't even there.

Jake only had one person there who wasn't so eager to push against him.

"Alright guys, let's show a little more class to the new guy, huh?" Hammel said, quieting Burton at least for the moment. "Some people forget how hard it is to be the new guy, Jake. Hopefully we'll be able to help you out a little."

"Come on," Cam shouted back. "No one helped me out when I came up, and I did it the right way! Everyone has to suffer a little."

Bug started to make an announcement from the front of the eating area, and Jake realized that the room was now filled with players. Jake couldn't think of a better time for the manager to interrupt their conversation. He had been so engrossed in conversation with the three at the table that he didn't realize the rest of the team had been filtering in and it was past seven o'clock.

"OK, guys!" Bug called out, getting the attention of the room. "Day one for the position players. Pitchers and catchers have already been here for two days, but now the team is complete. I want everyone on the field by eight and we'll divide up from there. Those who haven't been here before, get someone to show you where the lockers are. It's not too difficult. Get ready to have a day. This is day one of a great season. I feel better things for us this year, Cubbies! And it starts right now. I'll see you out there."

"Optimistic Coach Bug," Cam said to his dining partners. "What would spring training be without him?"

"Well, hopefully he's right," Hammel rebutted. "We should have some improvement in our rotation and most the rookies who were in the pen will be a year older. I see them being a strong point of the team. Our outfield should be better in terms of power and on base percentage. That is, if you can learn to start taking a walk, Cam."

"Oh!" Cools called out. "He got you!"

"Yeah, you're right," Cam said back with a chuckle. "But we can't ignore our new friend here and the hole he's going to put in the lineup, not to mention the infield."

The other two were quiet as Jake looked down at his food, not knowing what to say. The verbal abuse he had been taking was getting to be too much and it was even making Hammel and Cools uncomfortable.

"I'm not trying to be disrespectful, Riley, but..."

"For not trying you're doing an awful good job of it," Jake interrupted, now fed up with the conversation.

"Ooh, the rookie's got some bite!" Cools blurted out with a smile.

"Thanks for inviting me to your table," Jake continued. "It was nice meeting you all. I'll see you on the field."

Jake got up and took his tray with him, following some of the others who were headed for the locker room. Cam and Cools giggled under their breath as he left while Shawn Hammel looked back over his shoulder at Jake, embarrassed by the other two.

"You guys can be real dicks," Hammel said to them, looking down while getting another forkful of food.

Jake found the locker room to be no more exciting than any other he had been in. He found his locker quickly as they were all in alphabetical order by the player's last names. Jake put his equipment bag down and unzipped it while sitting down on a wooden bench. He emptied out some of his uniforms and his cleats and placed them in his oversized locker. He then pulled out his two gloves.

Sid had given Jake both of the infielder's gloves and Jake had used his favorite one about ninety percent of the time. He felt one with his glove just as he remembered feeling as a kid in little league. The glove fit him well and Jake knew all the good and the bad of it. His back-up mitt was good, too, but his go-to glove was like his best friend now and he hoped he would not have to part with it. Jake felt ease from the tension he had experienced at breakfast as the oneness between him and his glove gave him comfort.

After dressing, Jake walked out to the field. He didn't bring a specific bat because Sid told him there would be a lot of bats around to hit with during spring training and after that he would have his own bats ordered for him during the exhibition games. Jake hadn't grown fond of any one bat he had used with Sid so it wasn't disappointing to him one way or another. He also knew that bats crack all the time in the big leagues and it was foolish to get sentimental with any specific one like he had when he was in high school.

Jake followed the group to the front of the home team's dugout and a few of the players introduced themselves. Most of the introductions seemed to be forced. Either the player was standing right next to Jake or he would be with another person who was also introducing himself. The feeling Jake got was that no one was too excited to meet him, but at least most of them didn't seem as eager as Cam Burton to tear him down. Jake preferred to proceed quietly after his initial encounter with his team during breakfast. That encounter hadn't given him much confidence going into practice.

Jake was sent off with four other infielders as the team was divided up for drills. He would be fielding first and he went off to his position at second base with Cools Perez. At shortstop were Shawn Hammel and two minor leaguers who were trying to make the team. They were both long shots because Hammel was the starting shortstop and Cools was versatile enough to play shortstop, third base, and second base.

Jake was of course going to be the starting second baseman. The back-up second baseman had not yet been seen by Jake, but he started running out toward the infield right before the drill began. It was Casey Earl.

Earl had tried to get a new contract and had asked Dillinger for two years at two million a year, but Dillinger balked. Earl then tested free agency when Dillinger would only give him a one year deal at just over a million. However, no other team was willing to take a chance on the gold glover who barely hit over .200. The fear was that he was in a decline with his hitting and therefore would be a detriment to any line-up.

Surprisingly, Earl then came back and agreed to the original contract that Dillinger had offered, despite his knowledge of Jacob Riley's position. Earl had figured the amateur wouldn't be able to take the pressure and quit or be so bad that Dillinger would have to pull the plug on his experiment, giving Earl the starting job back as long as he could keep Cools Perez from stealing it. Besides, even if Riley kept at it for an extended period, Earl was informed the last two innings of the game would be his and he would start every seventh game. Either way, Earl was going to fight for his spot by any means possible and he had no problem hating Jacob Riley before he even met him.

"Sorry I'm late, boys," Earl called out confidently. "Good to see you, Cools."

"You too, Case."

Earl ignored Jake and instead went up to the front of the line of the three second baseman to field ground balls. Cools was positioned to take the second hit and Jake the third. Jake felt a little nervous, but he was happy to be starting off with fielding rather than batting.

The first ground ball went to shortstop and Hammel fielded it easily and threw it to first. Jake was in awe seeing him up close and amazed by how fluid Hammel was with his motions. The next ball went to Earl at second and Jake was even more impressed. Earl looked so natural with the way he shifted to his right, scooped up the ball and side-armed it over to first. Jake was sure he didn't look that good.

The three rookies received their first chances next, and all of them looked good, especially Cools. His defense had been touted as some of the best talent in the minors, and he was a power hitter on top of it. He could hit the long ball well, but struck out too much for the likes of the coaches the previous year and they had him working on his contact in the minors because of it. Cools was only twenty-two years old.

Jake stepped up next for his ground ball, and he knew all eyes were on him. The field seemed extraordinarily quiet and the moment felt like it was going in slow motion. Jacob saw the coach hit the ball and it came almost right at him. Jake had to make a small shift to the left, but was able to easily see the ball into his glove. He then flipped the ball over to first with a natural motion, taking a breath of relief when he saw the ball get to the first baseman accurately.

He'd completed his first play in the presence of other major league players and Jake had felt himself shaking a little, but he calmed down as he felt the relief to get the first one out of the way.

Nobody said a word to him as he shifted to the back of the line. It seemed as if everyone was disappointed he had not yet made a mistake.

After about twenty ground balls to each of the infielders, Jake had held his own. He had bobbled one ball that probably would have been an error on a tough play to his left, but that he was doing as well as he was surprised the others. Jake was feeling confident in his fielding and happy he didn't look too much worse than his counterparts. He was no longer nervous.

"Alright," the coach who had been batting balls yelled out to the players, "Now I want you to turn two. Each pair of you will do it twice before you rotate so everyone has a chance to field it and pivot for the throw to first."

Double plays. This worried Jake. He had worked on some pivot work at second base, but there had never really been any emphasis on it because he was only throwing into a net that represented first. Jake was getting the hang of it with Sid, but didn't feel completely comfortable because it hadn't been the real thing. He started getting nervous again.

The first group, Hammel and Earl, performed the task superbly. Their motions were so fluid, it seemed they were teaching a class on the perfect double play. The next group did well, too, as Cools flashed some fancy footwork getting the scoop from shortstop and turning to fire the ball perfectly to first base. Jake stepped up for his first attempt and knew the ball would first be hit to shortstop and he'd be covering the bag at second.

When the crack of the bat was heard, the ball was heading up the middle of the infield just to the right side of second base. Jake ran to the bag to get the throw from the shortstop, who cleanly fielded the ball and flipped it perfectly to second. Jake realized he was getting off easy on the first play, as the ball was hit so close to second that it was a simple flip to him which would be easy to grab and then throw to first.

The ball came right to him, and Jake caught it in his glove, quickly reaching in his mitt with his throwing hand to make the throw to first. Unfortunately, Jake felt the ball slip a little in his glove while he was trying to retrieve it, and he didn't get a good grip on it. Instead of being able to throw it right away, he had to take an extra step with his feet toward first and then pump his throwing hand while he developed a good handle on the ball. From there Jake made a solid throw to first, but the play already looked slow and Jake was sure the double play would not have been turned if there were actual base runners.

"You can't pump on this play, Riley!" the coach hitting balls yelled out. "You have to throw right on the turn!"

Jake knew what he did wrong and the coach, who he didn't even know yet, just made matters worse by calling it out to the rest of the players. Jake wasn't sure, but he thought he heard Earl say something behind him and Cools chuckle.

The next ball hit was right to Jake and he fielded it cleanly and then looked over at second to make the flip. As he went to release the ball, he was thrown off by the way the shortstop was approaching the bag, causing him to second guess the location of his throw. Because of that, the toss to the bag was low and late, making the shortstop wait for the ball and lose his momentum and then have to reach down for the ball as well, leading to an awkward throw to first. The shortstop did a good job of it, but Jake knew he had just made a simple play difficult.

"Gotta get that ball up higher, Riley. And more quickly!" yelled the coach again.

Jake turned red as he returned to the end of the line.

The next few times were a little better, but Jake knew he wasn't fully comfortable with the double play turn from either spot and he knew he would have to work on it more. A weakness was exposed, and the other players started to feel better concerning their initial thoughts about Jacob Riley.

Jake knew what was materializing and his confidence was waning. He started to worry even more about batting practice.

Luckily for Jake, the first day was only hitting balls out of the cages, and it was meant to be easy to get the players back into the swing of things. Jake saw almost all fastballs during his turns in the cage and he hit them fairly well, as did almost everybody else. At least this was not something that caused him even more anxiety on his first day. He knew that time might come, but he figured as the days rolled on he would get more comfortable and hopefully not be as bad as he was imagining.

The end of practice was filled with running and stretching, low stress activities for the new second baseman. He got through them without any problems and without too much flak from the rest of the team. Most everyone ignored him while joking around with their peers, but Jake had expected that. He knew it would take a lot to get people to like him and he wasn't going to push it. He figured he would continue to work hard and try to gain people's respect that way.

He saw no other option.

Jake finished practice and then showered and picked up some takeout to eat in his room. He didn't want to run into anyone in a restaurant and have to face another situation like he had at breakfast. He called his parents and Angie, watched a few shows on television, and went to bed early. His first day hadn't been as bad as he thought it would be, but he knew he had a lot of work to do. He was able to sleep easily that night and hoped he would have more nights like that, feeling good about the day's accomplishments.

Unfortunately, his future evenings in Mesa wouldn't be as pleasant as his first night had been.

CHAPTER 11

The next morning of practice was set up identically to the first day.

Jake joined Hammel, Earl and the others in fielding practice, which went well. He then hit out of the batting cages, and that also went well. Going to lunch, he was feeling good about how the day had gone up to that point, but he was fearful of what would happen in the afternoon.

Everyone was going to hit live pitching in a pseudo-game format. There would be four players on a team that would either play the field with another four players or take a turn batting. Each team was given three innings, each consisting of three outs. After that, the teams would rotate and one team would come in to bat. There were different pitchers who were each assigned three innings for a team. The pitchers were told to throw mostly fastballs and change ups with a rare breaking ball, all at eighty to ninety percent.

Jake's team consisted of shortstop Shawn Hammel, outfielder Cam Burton, and first baseman Bob Oates. Jake already knew Hammel and Burton from breakfast the prior day. Oates, surprisingly, came up to introduce himself to Jake when they divided into their teams.

"Jacob Riley, right?" Oates asked and noted Jake's nod. "Bob Oates. I'm the first baseman. Nice to meet you."

"Sure, Bob, I've watched you play over the last few years," Jake responded. "I remember when the media really hyped you as one of the big up and coming first baseman, but bemoaned your fielding. I was really surprised to see how much you improved on your defense over the years. It's great to watch you play."

"Thanks, Jake," Bob answered without much enthusiasm. "People want to tell you who you are and what you can do just by watching you play a little. Media does it all the time, but it's amazing anyone listens to them after how many times they're wrong. When they told me I'd be a defensive liability, the first thing I did was try to prove them wrong. I guess you'd probably like to do the same."

"Well, yeah," Jake replied delicately, "but I realize it's different with me. They probably have a right to criticize me. They also have a much higher chance about being right about my abilities."

"Not necessarily, Jake. Let me tell you, I think everyone has been surprised at how well you've fielded your position so far. We all, me included, thought you'd flub half the balls hit to you. I can tell you've been working hard and even have some raw talent. It was a nice surprise, at least to me. Most of the guys would love to see you fail, but I want to win. If you're on my team, I want you to do well. I know it'll be tough in your case. You were put in a bad position, but keep playing hard and we'll see how you can do. It's really the only choice you have."

"Yeah, you're right, Bob. Thanks for the compliments. So far they've been few and far between."

"I bet. Well, don't let it get you down. You're here to play baseball, not to listen to haters. Just concentrate on what you need to. There'll be enough people around to help you out."

Jake was appreciative of the words and felt he might even have a friend in Bob Oates, but he didn't want to push it. Just having someone who wasn't out to see him crash and burn was a good start. Jake sensed some encouragement from Bob as he entered into the hitting session and felt empowered because of it. He hoped he'd see enough fastballs to put together some good swings.

Jake's team batted first, and he was set to hit fourth. Hammel started off with a sharp single to center and Burton then quickly doubled down the line to put runners on second and third. Oates then took an easy swing at the first pitch he saw and hit a line drive over the shortstop's head to score both runners.

It wasn't unusual for all three players to get hits in the scrimmage. With the pitchers throwing mostly fastballs and only going at around eighty percent, the hitters were supposed to win most of the battles. The pitchers were not discouraged by it. They were simply trying to get work in against live hitters to prepare them for the exhibition games.

Jake walked up to the plate and felt his heart race. He had felt more calm before his three teammates had all performed so well. He had hoped one of them would make an out or at least look bad on a pitch in order to take the pressure off him. Now he felt he had to get a hit or he would be considered a failure.

Jake stepped into the batter's box and thought about the pitches his teammates had hit, all fastballs. He figured he would see a couple fastballs as well and wanted to jump on the first one in the strike zone. He looked up at the mound and saw Steve Furst, one of the relief pitchers the Cubs had picked up the previous year. He knew Furst was accurate, but not overpowering. He threw mostly fastballs and relied on good placement in order to get players out.

Furst wound up and Jake studied his motion. As the pitch came out of his hand and started to travel towards the plate, Jake was pretty sure it was a fastball and it looked like it would be in the zone. Jake decided he was swinging. He took a good cut at the pitch, but it had come in a little high. Jake tried to adjust his swing and his bat got underneath the pitch. The baseball shot up high in the sky off Jake's bat, a routine pop-up to the shortstop. The play was made easily, and Jake's team had its first out.

Hammel again lined a shot into center, putting runners on first and second. After four pitches, Burton hit a long fly ball to left that was tracked down for the second out of the inning. Both Oates and Hammel were able to tag up on the play and were now at second and third. Oates had to come off the bag to bat. It was assumed there was still a runner at third.

Oates hit a ground ball that pushed itself through the infield just out of the third baseman's reach. The phantom runner at third scored by assumption and Hammel stopped at third, leaving runners at the corners with two outs. Jake stepped up to the plate for his second at bat.

Jake looked up at Furst and still assumed he'd see a fastball. Every first pitch had been one up to this point. Unfortunately, the pitch was outside and Jake laid off it. It was called a ball. The second pitch looked like it was coming right down the center of the plate and Jake took a big swing. He realized quickly when he came up empty that Furst had thrown him a change up. Jake continued to struggle with that pitch and he was getting frustrated by it.

The next pitch thrown was a fastball that was coming in around the knees, but had some sinking motion to it. Jake recognized the pitch and took a hack at it, but he was a little late because he was worried another change up was coming. Because of the downward direction, Jake hit on top of the ball and sent a routine ground ball to second base.

Jake, as he had practiced, got out of the box in a hurry, hustling down to first base. Cools Perez was playing second base and waited on the ball, considering it routine and guessing he had plenty of time. When Cools felt the ball hit his glove, he was surprised to see Jake coming down the line in a hurry. Cools quickly transferred the ball to his throwing hand and made a hard throw to first. The first baseman stretched out for the ball and caught it, just after Jake touched first base.

"Safe!" called out Stan Oliver, the Cub's bench coach. He had been monitoring the drill while playing the role of first base coach/umpire.

"Great hustle out of the box, Riley!" Stan said with a smile on his face while he patted Jake on the butt.

Cools could be heard calling out "Damn!" as he kicked some dirt at the spot where he had picked up the ball. Although the ball was hit softly, everyone on the field thought it would be a routine play. Now Jake was on first with his first hit, even though he didn't stay for long because Hammel lined out on the next pitch, giving the team three outs and a restart of the inning.

They kept the same order and Hammel led off with a hit to left field and Burton followed with the same, putting runners on first and second. Oates hit a long fly ball to center which was tracked down by the outfielder on the run, allowing both runners to tag up, Hammel ending up at third and Burton at second.

Jake stepped up to the plate and wanted to make some good contact. He was happy with his last hit, but he knew it was his legs, not his bat, that provided it. He wanted to lace a ball into the outfield and believed a first pitch fastball was the way to do it.

Furst was still the pitcher, and he had remembered Jake's reaction when he threw him a change-up. Although the pitchers were supposed to be taking it easy, Furst did not want to be the one to give up a solid hit to Jacob Riley.

Jake dug into the batter's box and waited for the pitch. When Furst released it, it appeared to be a fastball that was coming in at the knees, a good pitch to hit, but at the beginning of the swing Jake realized the ball wasn't getting to him as quickly as it was supposed to. Another change-up!

Jake tried to elongate his swing by extending his arms, hoping to slow the bat down and allow the ball to catch up. It worked, at least to a small degree, and Jake made some contact. The ball was a hopper to the left of the infield and the shortstop had to move to his right to get there. Jake was again out of the box in a hurry, trying to leg out another hit.

Hammel started running home from third while Burton held up at second, knowing he would be an easy out at third base for a play that was moving towards the bag. The shortstop was already thinking about Jake's quick departure from the box on his last hit that left Cools looking foolish.

The young shortstop quickly ran to the ball and tried to make a fast throw to first to get Jake out. The play would have been close, but because it was rushed, the throw was wide of the bag and took a short hop before getting to the first baseman, causing him to miss it completely. The ball went off towards foul territory in right field and Jake and Burton both moved up on the play, Burton to third and Jake to second.

"Did you all see that?" Oliver called out from the first base coach's box. "Because Riley hustled on both of those ground balls, he forced the defense to hurry up, resulting in an error and our guys winding up at second and third. That's why we hustle! Great work, Riley! Keep putting pressure on the defense and you'll be at first base more than you think!"

The ball wasn't a clean hit out of the infield — it wasn't even a base hit — but it made the coaches take notice of Jacob Riley in a positive way.

Jake realized all the hard work of running hard in the off-season and using his Saturday mornings to practice getting out of the batter's box quickly was paying off. He knew he had huge gaps in his game, but maybe the little things he was doing well would help make up for some of that. He started to feel some confidence again.

Jake did have a solid single in another at bat, but he also struck out, the only player to do that in the drills that afternoon.

After his team played out their three innings, Jake took over at second base as the second team came to the plate. Hammel took over at short, Oates at first, and Burton in right. Jake was feeling so good about his at bats that he was hoping to have a ball come his way and was excited about playing the field and hopefully making a good play. It didn't take long for him to get that chance.

After the first two batters singled, leaving runners at first and second, Cools Perez came up. Cools was a switch hitter and because the pitcher was a righty, he batted left handed, giving himself a slight advantage over a right handed batter in the same situation. The first pitch to him was a fastball on the outside edge and Cools swung hard. His contact was good and he sent the ball screaming to the right of Jake on one hop.

The ball looked ticketed for right field, but Jake had a good jump on it and while diving to his right he felt the ball catch in the webbing of his glove. From one knee he quickly tossed the ball to Hammel covering second and got the force out, robbing Perez of a single. The play wasn't a superb one — Jake wasn't fully extended when he got down for the ball — but it was a difficult play and he made it. He even heard Hammel call out "nice play" after it was over.

Jake was turning heads not because he looked good, but because he didn't look as bad as people were expecting. That was good enough for him at this point. However, every player has his down moments, and Jake would be sure to have more than his fair share. One of them occurred just moments after his nice catch.

The new team was in their second inning and Perez had just led off with a hit. The next hitter took a couple pitches low before swinging at the third and hitting a high pop fly into shallow right field, causing Jake's pupils to dilate and his palms to get clammy. The play was clearly Jake's, but he wasn't sure how far the ball would drift.

He realized he wasn't prepared for a pop up. In all the sessions he had fielding with Sid, they never had any pop flies because the ceilings in the facility weren't high enough to do so.

The ball was now drifting on Jake as he backed up to make the play and he felt uneasy about where it was going to land. He remembered in high school that it was always easier to come up if needed than to go farther back, so he tried to quickly take a couple extra steps into the outfield. Unfortunately, that cost him some concentration and he lost the ball in the air.

As he continued to move to the spot where he thought it was going to come down, he tracked it once again, but too late. The ball dropped in front of him as he tried to throw his glove under it at the last instant. Perez got to third on the play and the batter to second.

Jake had looked completely lost trying to field a routine pop up that should have been an easy out. Jake was embarrassed and could see other players shaking their heads in disbelief.

It didn't help that he was barely able to grab another pop up hit to him just twenty minutes later. This ball was more routine, but Jake ended up amateurishly stabbing his glove at the end of the play and he barely caught it.

It was clear that a flaw had been exposed and Jake was upset it was one he hadn't even been aware of. After practice, Jake went over to Stan Oliver to talk to him about his misplays.

"Coach, I know practice is over," Jake said politely, "but I was wondering if I could stay late and you could hit me some pop flies. I'm afraid I didn't work on that this winter and I felt pretty lost out there."

"You looked it, too, Jake," Stan replied. "Of course I'll stay late to hit you some if it'll get you more adept at it. I'll tell you, I was a bit surprised you had trouble with such an easy play only because you impressed me so much with how well you did fielding your position before that."

The last part made Jake feel better. Although it was humiliating to look bad on such an easy play, it was nice to hear he was doing a decent job otherwise. He knew the others would be looking at the bad plays and focusing on them, but it was reassuring to see that at least one of the coaches had noticed some bright spots.

Jake got ready to go home about an hour later than the others because of the extra practice. It was actually calming to Jake to be in the locker room by himself, not worrying about what everybody else was thinking of him.

Although his second day wasn't as good as the first, he still felt better than he had expected at this point. He was eager to keep learning and hopefully to keep getting better. Before going to bed that night he called his parents and Angie and told them his sentiments so far. Otherwise, he kept his evening quiet and relaxing.

Anticipating a new day and new challenges in his new, exciting life, Jake felt relaxed and he slept well again.

CHAPTER 12

The next eight days of spring training had some ups and some downs for Jake.

His fielding was doing well although, as expected, he was still the worst of all the infielders. His practices were always extended by at least an hour to work with one of the coaches on one of the multiple weaknesses of his game. One day was pop ups, another was pick off plays, yet another was cut-off throws from the outfield.

Every day seemed to hold a new challenge for Jake, but he didn't let the fielding aspect get him down. He was improving and he felt the more practice he got, the better he was becoming.

His hitting was another story. As the days went on, the pitchers were progressively given more freedom to throw what they wanted and at any capacity. Jake was starting to see a lot of off speed pitches and breaking balls and the pitchers worked hard to make him look stupid at the plate. They were succeeding. Jake realized the pitchers were putting forth an extra effort against him because of his position, but he tried not to let it get him down.

Actually, he realized it was helping him because he began to get used to the pitches he had been less comfortable with and he noticed that now he was recognizing them much earlier in the sequence. Jake started to hit a few of the off speed pitches more consistently, although usually for foul balls. Either way it was an improvement, and Jake tried to look positively upon his progress.

The coaches, though, were worried. They saw Jake struggle with any pitch that wasn't a fastball. They even noticed Jake swinging late on a lot of fastballs now that he was continuously looking for the off speed pitches. They knew it equated to a young, inexperienced man getting overpowered by professional pitching and there was little they could do about it.

They tried adjusting the way he looked at the ball coming in, but without much success. They didn't want to change his swing as they were trying to keep things as simple as possible. Besides, they felt Sid had done a good job, but Jake just wasn't producing hits at this point because he couldn't recognize what he was swinging at. Therefore they let most of it go, hoping with more practice Jake would continue to improve.

Jake's trouble with the bat extended into his first few exhibition games. He was now hitting against pitchers whose main goal was to get him out, and the pitchers were winning. Jake batted nine times in his first three games, getting only one weak infield single, but striking out seven times. He wasn't seeing that many pitches and he often swung at the first offering, hoping they would be fastballs.

It was obvious Jake was guessing at the plate instead of trying to determine what pitch was being thrown after the pitcher threw it and then reacting accordingly. The more Jake struggled, the worse his approach became.

Bug tried to get the hitting coach, Jim Bilker, to work with Jake before and after the exhibition games. Jim would always appear satisfied with their sessions and he believed the young hitter was improving, but as soon as Jake stepped into the batter's box, his mind became occupied with what the pitcher was going to throw at him and his training seemed to be forgotten.

Ten games into spring training, Jake was three for twenty-nine with only one walk and nineteen strike outs. The frustration that filled his mind every evening before bed festered after he laid his head on his pillow, and his only comfort came when he finally fell asleep.

There was one positive, though. The few times Jake was on base, he was asked to steal because of his speed and quickness. He was four for four in that department, and only one time was it even close. The pitchers knew of Jake's inexperience and usually didn't pay much attention to him when he was on first base. This allowed him to get a good jump towards second when he attempted to steal, resulting in his successful percentage.

However, Jake realized he wasn't great with pick-off attempts. It was difficult for him to tell when the pitcher was going to throw over to the bag and try to catch him leaning the wrong way. Because of his anxiety over getting thrown out, he wouldn't take too big a lead. The coaching staff wasn't picking up on his timidity to take bigger leads because they saw he was doing well with stealing bases.

Jake knew once the pitchers did uncover this flaw, they would capitalize on it any way they could and decrease his chances to steal.

There was one person who had already noticed all this and was thinking similarly to Jake. After one of the exhibition games where Jake went one for four and had a stolen base, Shawn Hammel pulled him off to the side. Jacob was surprised by this as he was usually ignored by his teammates. He feared he was going to get castigated by Hammel and he had hoped at least Hammel would have the decency to do it in private.

"Jake, how you feeling when you get on base? I noticed you've been able to swipe a few bags with your speed."

"Yeah," Jake answered shyly. "I guess it's been going pretty well in that department…when I finally do get on base."

"I'm not sure I agree with that," Hammel countered.

"What do you mean?"

"Well, you look scared out there. Playing shortstop, I get a close look at you when you get a ball hit to you at second base. I've been impressed by how calm you are when you make the play. I can tell you're at ease with your fielding, which is unbelievable considering how little time you've been able to spend on it. But when you're at bat, we all know you're worried by what's coming. It's been obvious to everyone. I'm sure you're aware of that."

Jake listened. He knew Shawn was right but was uncomfortable with what point he might be trying to get at.

"So when you get to first and take a lead-off, I realized you look more like when you're batting than when you're fielding. And you also take a short lead. Most guys as fast as you are trying to get big leads in order to steal bases and make the pitcher worried about them. They have confidence they can get back in time if the pitcher throws over there because they know they're quick enough. But you don't, even though you should. I know what the problem is."

"What's that?" Jake asked, not wanting to admit he was afraid of being picked-off.

"You don't know exactly when the pitcher is committed to throwing home. If you recognized when he entered the part of his motion that forces him, by the rules, that is, to go to the plate, you would feel more comfortable. Am I right?"

"Actually, yes," Jake admitted, letting down his guard in hopes of Hammel genuinely wanting to help him. "I always feel the pitcher is going to throw to first, and it seems like I'm not comfortable drifting farther off the bag until I see him throwing the ball home. I must be losing some time when I try to steal because of it."

"Exactly!" Hammel said conclusively. "Now you know the rule of when the pitcher has to throw home, right?"

"Sure, I even looked it up online to be certain. Once a right handed pitcher is set, any movement with his right foot on the rubber commits him to the plate, so I run on movement. For a lefty, I need to watch the right foot. Once it crosses in front of his left knee, he's committed to the pitch, so I can run then."

"Well, you know the rule perfectly, so why aren't you taking advantage of it? You know that any other move the pitcher makes after he's set will probably be towards you. If you watch for that, you should be fine."

"I know, Shawn, but I think I still am unsure of myself. Sometimes I feel it's hard to recognize the pitcher's intent."

"Yeah, they'll try to use different windups to throw you off, but I think it's more you just getting the feel. It's like when you first learn to drive and come to a four way stop. It's confusing and you're worried about when you're supposed to go and when you're supposed to wait. But after a couple weeks it becomes so natural you can't believe you had trouble with it. That's the point you have to get to, and because you're not getting on base much, you're having a hard time. When you do get on base, you have to push it, because even if you do make a mistake, it's now when you want to do it, not on opening day. You understand?"

"Sure. I probably need to take on some more risk. I'm just so worried about doing the wrong thing. I guess I'm being too conservative."

"Easy to do, especially in your situation. But you can't win big by holding out. We only have three weeks before the games count, and I need you to be ready. Promise me you'll chance looking bad now in order to play better later."

"Alright, Shawn, it's a promise. Thanks for the advice."

"And you know what else, Jake? If you're not holding back and being confident on the field works, and works similarly on the base paths, you might want to think about trying it in the batter's box, too. Get it?"

"A good overall philosophy is what you're saying."

"Right. OK, I'm going to go get Dunston."

"The relief pitcher? Why?"

"So we can work on your leadoff. I'll play first base?"

"Right now?"

"What, you too good to work after practice?"

"Well, no, I've been doing that most of my time here, but..."

"Oh, I get it," Hammel stated knowingly. "You think I am. Or you think I think I am."

"Well, I was just surprised you would stay late to help me. And are you sure Dunston will?"

"If I ask him, he will. Look, Jake, I don't like what Dillinger did to get you here, but I don't want us to suck, either. I have to make you as good as I can. I'm not going to go all 'rah rah' on Jacob Riley, but you seem alright, despite taking over for Earl. I'll look out for you, just kind of under wraps. If you're okay with that, of course."

"Sure," Jake said, surprised. "I mean, that's great! Thanks."

"Right. OK, wait here. I'll get Dunston."

Jake felt better about his lead offs after working with Dunston and Hammel, but not as good as he felt about having someone who seemed interested in his development. Oates had expressed the same sentiment earlier, but the two hadn't connected at all since then. Jake was getting lonely as the Cub's outsider, knowing most of his teammates didn't care for him and were rooting for his failure. It was nice to know a couple of teammates who would at least look out for him and join him in his path to become better.

Jake's confidence did rise after his discussion with Hammel and their practice session. He found himself trying to learn as he failed, instead of just trying not to fail.

At first he was picked off once, but after that he had stolen five more bases and was getting much better leads than he had in the past. He also had badly missed a few change ups while refusing to guess which pitch was coming and simply reacting once he saw the ball leaving the pitcher's hand. Now he was starting to recognize the pitches better and he found himself able to foul off a lot of the off speed pitches. He even drove one breaking ball to right field for a hit.

Jake's percentage of success was rising. In his next ten exhibition games Jake went five for thirty and had twelve strikeouts. He even hit a fastball down the left field line for a double, surprising everyone on both benches. He was scoring runs more frequently and starting to feel like he was contributing.

His teammates would even slap his hand after he scored a run, something he didn't expect. Jake felt a shift in the attitude of his team towards him and for about a week he thought he was more comfortable with everyone around him.

His opinion changed after one game with the Orioles, though, sending Jake back to his original feeling of isolationism and despondency.

The game was the Cub's twentieth of the pre-season. They were eight and twelve, a respectable record for exhibition play. Jake's first at bat was a good one, off of one of the best pitchers in baseball, Todd Cummings. Cummings threw nine pitches in that at-bat, Jake fouling off four good breaking balls to force a full count. The ninth pitch was a fastball and Jake smacked it into right field for a hit.

He went on to steal second and third base and score on a sacrifice fly, his best all around at bat and base running feat of his time with the Cubs.

This did not make Cummings happy. It was one thing for Jake to have gotten a bloop hit. Cummings could have seen past that. But to work the count like a regular hitter and then line a solid hit into right was too much for the big, veteran right hander.

On Jake's next at bat, Cummings's first pitch was a fastball at ninety-seven mph which struck right between Jake's fourth and fifth ribs. Jake tried to spin out of the way, but the ball was coming too fast and it ended up knocking the rookie to the ground in pain.

The pitch had intentionally been aimed right at Jake. There was no doubt about that. In a situation like that, usually his team would rally around him, yelling at Cummings, maybe even threatening him. The coaches and manager would've been barking at the umpire to throw Cummings out of the game, as they would have if it had been any other player.

Unfortunately, Cummings was a respected player in the league. Nobody dared to side with Jake because it would be like they were siding against their profession. Some of Jake's teammates were even glad he got hit. He deserved it after all, they thought. They didn't blame Cummings for doing what they wanted to do all along.

The others who might have felt sorry for Jake didn't want to look bad in front of everyone else so they collectively just watched as Jake was lying on the ground grabbing his left side.

When the pain started to subside and Jake was able get up with the help of the Cubs trainer, he felt more alone than ever before. Nobody was saying a word. As Jake looked into his dugout while hobbling to first, some of his teammates even seemed disinterested.

When he reached first base, Stan Oliver, the first base coach at the time, only asked, "You okay, kid?"

Jake realized all he had worked for and all that he thought he had gained as a member of the Cubs was a mirage. They would only be decent to him if it was convenient for them. It was him against them, no matter how he looked at it.

In his anger, he decided he was fine with that. He wasn't quitting and he was going to do everything he could to prove them wrong.

Jake, still wincing from the plunk, took his lead off first. Without any signal from his coaches, Jake took off for second on the first pitch and stole it easily. Jake took a bigger lead at second, staring down Cummings as if he dared him to try a pick-off. When Cummings instead went into his wind up, Jake darted for third base with everything he had, sliding in well before the ball even got to the base from the catcher.

Jake took his lead off third, fire in his eyes. The pain had been dulled by a feeling of revenge. When Cummings looked over at Jake's lead, Jake stared deeply into the pitcher's eyes. Cummings gave a scowl back and threw to third, Jake safely sliding back. Jake took an even bigger lead and shot Cummings another scornful look. Cummings again threw over to third, but this time directly into the right side of Jake as he was sliding head first into the bag. The ball made a loud thud on his ribs, everyone in the park feeling the pain of the intended shot. As Jake stood up and looked at Cummings, he saw him chuckle, pleased with hitting the rookie again.

Jake wasn't finished.

This time his lead was a ridiculous one. Jake was twenty-five feet off the bag. When Cummings looked up to see it, his eyes grew wide. He couldn't believe this Jacob Riley was daring him more. Cummings had been certain he had taken the life out of him. Instead he seemed to have invigorated Riley.

Cummings stepped off the rubber, expecting Jake to scuffle back to the bag. But Jake just stood there, hands on knees, his eyes sending daggers through Cummings's torso. The large pitcher felt threatened and was surprised when he felt a shiver of fear go down his spine. He quickly regained his senses, not wanting to get shown up by the six foot, one hundred eighty pound traitor. Instead of throwing to third, Cummings took two steps towards the base runner and Jake took off for home.

The pitcher threw to the plate, knowing he had Jake by a large margin. Jake, however, also knew this would be the case and stopped well short of the plate and turned back for third base, causing the catcher to run at him with the ball, exactly what Jake knew would happen.

When Jake got to within twenty feet of third, he turned around again, knowing the catcher had to throw to third and that only one person could be covering home. Cummings. Jake ran as hard and as fast as he could for home plate, knowing the third baseman would throw to Cummings and that he had no chance of scoring. However, what he saw while running full speed to home was exactly what he had hoped for.

Cummings was awkwardly running back to the plate to cover for the catcher and looking for the ball from third base. Jake had no intention of continuing this run-down. He saw the ball float over his right shoulder as he was twenty feet from the plate and he saw Cummings put up his glove to catch it. The large pitcher was still moving back towards the plate while he was going for the ball and Jake was closing in.

The pitcher saw Jake coming hard down the line and started to worry about the ball getting to him accurately. It was there in plenty of time and Cummings brought his glove in front of him to tag Jake before he got to home plate.

Jake had no intention of scoring. He continued in a straight path for Cummings just as the pitcher stopped his backpedal and was attempting a tag. Jake put up both his forearms and rammed the unsuspecting pitcher in the chest and below the chin.

The pitcher's head jolted back quickly as his body was headed for the ground. Jake's momentum kept him right on top of Cummings and he landed right across the front of the pitcher's body, his forearms still in contact with Cummings's chest and chin.

Cummings lay on the ground in shock as much as in pain while the other members of the Orioles team were grabbing Jake off their prized player and trying to wrestle him to the ground.

No matter what the Cubs players thought about Jake, their natural instincts to clear the bench kicked in. Both teams were out on the field in a large scrum, punches being thrown by some while some players wrestled others to the ground.

Jake was at the bottom of the pile, but felt on top of the world.

After the riot was broken up, the umpire tossed Jake out of the game. As Jake walked to the bench, he looked over to see Cummings walking off the other side of the field rubbing his jaw with blood running down his chin. He had two trainers with him and was being taken out of the game as a precaution.

Jake was told to head for the showers.

Jake was also told he'd have to sit out the next few games, but he continued to practice on those days with the other coaches. He didn't care about the suspension and he didn't care about what the other players thought about him. He was invested in his decision to join the Cubs and he was going to do the best job he could regardless of what any of the others on the team thought.

Jake was convinced he was right. He accepted the position from Dillinger just as anyone else would. He worked as hard during the off-season as anyone could have expected. He came to camp in great shape and proved that although he might not have been anywhere close to the others in terms of ability, he was doing much better than anyone thought he could.

He was right with what he had done to Todd Cummings and he would do it again, if necessary.

When Jake rejoined the team after his suspension, nobody said anything to him about it. The truth was the whole team had a new respect for Jacob Riley regardless of whether they liked him or whether they were going to support him. What Jake did to Cummings was gutsy and the players couldn't help but be impressed.

What they had seen on the field impressed them, too, they were finally beginning to admit.

Jake was playing with more confidence now and he gave the impression of being on a mission. He worked hard and appeared focused. He was still doing things poorly in terms of major league standards, but he was improving and he seemed intent on continuing to do so.

His knowledge of the strike zone continued to improve and his ability to foul off more pitches got him deeper into counts, resulting in the chances for more walks or more fastballs he could drive for hits. In his remaining ten games, Jake went seven for twenty-nine, a .241 average, and he had five walks and eight runs scored. He had made a couple of errors, boosting his total to seven on the preseason, worst in the league. He was making some more difficult plays, but was still having trouble with turning double plays and getting the ball into the infield appropriately on cut-offs.

Jake was struggling, but it was a controlled struggle. The team had seen Jake improve and some were happy while others were not. The coaches did feel better about Jake not costing them too many games after they'd witnessed the upswing in his play, but they still hoped they could convince Dillinger to put an end to the situation.

Dillinger refused, however, every time he was asked. He was also keeping an eye on Jake and was impressed with his spunk and his improvements. He noted that Jake actually batted .191 in spring training and was on the rise. Big Eddy was feeling like he could still win this bet.

No matter the case, spring training was over and the Cubs were traveling back to Chicago for opening day against the Pittsburgh Pirates. Jacob Riley was slated as their opening day starter at second base with Casey Earl as the back-up. Cools Perez was sent down to the minors during the last of their cuts and many on the team rekindled their hatred for Jake when they saw their friend get demoted because of him. Jake perceived this but didn't care.

He knew what he had to do, and it all would start on opening day at Wrigley Field.

CHAPTER 13

Chicago was bitterly cold when Jake returned from Arizona on April 3rd, 2025.

Game time temperature was supposed to be fifty-one degrees, about thirty degrees cooler than what Jake had been used to. Even so, it was nice for him to be back in his city and with his family.

Angie had picked him up from the airport and they went back to their apartment together. She had prepared a welcome home dinner for Jake and had even invited his parents over to their place for it. The whole family knew the game was starting at 1:20 the next day and that Jake would need to be at the park by nine so the evening ended early, everyone happy that Jake was home and excited about opening day.

Even Angie seemed excited to go to the game and to be able see her Jake on the field.

Getting to the park the next morning was easy as Jake lived just fifteen minutes away by foot. He had to bundle up as the morning temperature was only thirty-nine degrees. He could be seen by the other players as he walked to the park at 8:30 am while the rest of them drove by him and parked in the players' parking lot.

Jake was dressed in a thermal undershirt and a hooded sweatshirt as he did his stretches on the field. The grass was dewy and crisp and although uncomfortable, Jake loved every minute of it. He looked around the friendly confines and was happy being on the inside. He could never have imagined he'd be performing at such a level.

Jake did feel butterflies in his stomach, though, every time he thought forward to his first at bat. He wanted to make a good impression, especially knowing that there would be many in the crowd against him. That wasn't such a big deal to him anymore as he had been getting used to it at training camp in Arizona.

Jake took his batting practice a couple hours before the game and hit some strong line drives around Wrigley. He felt good. His swing was crisp and his muscles loose. He even hit a ball deep into left which hit off the wall and he initially thought it was a homer. His fielding also went well in practice, although the dirt was cold and clumpy and he feared some bad hops during game time.

The temperature actually warmed more than expected and with the sun shining brightly, Jake was comfortable in his thermal undershirt and uniform jersey over it. He wondered what all the fans were thinking when they saw him run out to the field with a big number seventeen on his back and "Riley" just above it. He was sure his parents were reveling while Angie barely understood all the excitement.

The first couple innings went by without much excitement, just one hit from each team and no runs. Jake even made a routine play at second, a simple two-hopper right at him. He had made that play hundreds of times in the last five months, but he admitted later that he was nervous when the ball was coming towards him and he felt relieved when he had made the play cleanly.

The bottom of the third inning had the pitcher leading off in the eighth spot and Jake batting ninth. When the pitcher grounded out weakly to the shortstop, Jake stepped up from the on deck circle into the batter's box. The crowd clapped softly when they announced his name, but some people were booing. Jake heard them, but remained unfazed.

It was time to bat, and Jake had to concentrate.

The Pirates were opening up their season with Thom Bradman, a hard throwing right hander who had been in the league for six years. He had a strong fastball, a great change up, a knee-buckling curve ball, and a nasty slider. The fastball was where most hitters were able to take advantage of Bradman, and Jake was no exception. Jacob had been studying film on the pitcher to see what pitches he used in different circumstances and what kind of movement he had on his curve and slider. Jake was running all this through his mind as he stepped to the plate.

Bradman looked down at Jake with disgust. He, like most of the people around the league, hated Jacob Riley and the whole situation attached to him. Every pitcher vowed to make things as difficult as they could for him and Bradman was the first to get that opportunity. He already knew what he wanted to do to make Jake look stupid at his first at bat and had already talked with his catcher about it.

The first pitch was a fastball. The ball came in at ninety-five mph and was painted on the outside corner. Jake was looking for a fastball and when he saw it, he took a good cut at it. The location of the pitch was too good, though, and Jake was only able to foul it back and to the right. Although still a strike, Bradman was mad that Jake even touched it.

The next pitch was the Bradman change-up. It came towards Jake looking like a fastball and Jake immediately tried to get his bat on it, swinging early and missing badly. Bradman laughed as he received the ball back from his catcher. He had Jake set up on a 0-2 count and he was ready to make him look ridiculous.

The catcher signaled for the curve ball, the same pitch Bradman used on multiple occasions over the years to make great hitters look like chumps. Bradman nodded in agreement to his catcher and wound up for the delivery.

Jake was watching it come, knowing he would probably see a breaking ball from the big right hander as that's what he usually threw in these circumstances. Jake wanted to be ready for anything and he concentrated hard on the pitcher's release.

When the ball came out of Bradman's hand, Jake saw it coming for the heart of the plate. Jake's instinct was telling him to swing, but his mind was trying to wait. Sure enough, just before Jake committed to the swing, he saw the laces of the ball spinning hard, and he knew the ball was about to drop out of sight.

He froze his bat about a third of the way into the strike zone as the ball fell to the dirt. It was a ball, and Bradman couldn't believe he didn't strike out the amateurish Riley on three pitches.

Bradman caught the returning ball in disgust while Jake took a deep breath, relieved his first at bat didn't result in a three pitch strike-out. He realized his chances of success were low, but he was now proud of winning that one battle and living to see another pitch.

Jake wasn't sure what he was going to see next. Another curve? Maybe a fastball or possibly Bradman's rarely used slider? Jake knew he could be badly fooled if he tried to guess and decided to wait and see the pitch. Bradman wound up for the delivery and Jake breathed deeply again, trying to control the rate of his palpating heart.

When the ball came out of Bradman's hand, Jake thought it was a fastball and saw it was headed for the outer part of the plate. It looked like a strike, but Jake knew this could be a slider that dipped way out of the zone at the last second. He tried to hold his swing and decided if it was a fastball he would try to foul it off to stay alive.

When the ball continued on it's trajectory to the outside corner as it had on the first pitch, Jake realized he needed to swing. He quickly flipped his bat out to the other side of the plate and was relieved to feel contact.

At first he thought he had successfully wasted a good pitch, but he was even more surprised than Bradman to see the result.

The ball ricocheted hard off of the end of Jake's bat and the speed of the pitch had enough power to send it well over the head of the first baseman.

As soon as Jake saw the ball headed into the field of play, his training pushed him hard out of the batter's box and towards first base. Jake was already half way to the bag when he saw the first baseman coming down from his jump without the catch and Jake could tell his squarely hit ball was curving toward the line. It hit cleanly with chalk spraying into the air.

The umpire pointed his arm toward the field of play, indicating a fair ball, and Jake's heart raced with excitement as the play unfolded right in front of him.

Jake rounded first base and headed for second, his back to the play now. The ball was running up against the wall in right field where there was little room between the fans and the line. The Pirate's right fielder tried to retrieve the ball while running hard towards foul territory, but as he tried to bend over to pick it up, he slowed his body down while the ball kicked up awkwardly against the wall and he couldn't grab it cleanly.

Jake touched second base and looked up at the third base coach. He saw his arm waving him to third. Jake moved even faster with even more adrenaline flowing through him.

The ball was finally picked up and thrown to the cut-off man, who then wheeled around and fired to third. Jake was already sliding in head first tagging the bag well ahead of the throw.

He'd started off his major league season with a triple.

When Jake looked up, he saw thousands of Cubs fans out of their seats jumping up and down cheering. The whole stadium was now alive with excitement and Jake felt it pulsating through him.

He hopped to his feet and remained on the bag while his third base coach gave him a pat on his butt. The crowd was only twenty feet from him, and he could see them having the time of their lives, all because of him.

He was so filled with energy he was sure he could run right through a brick wall.

He led off from third as the pitcher prepared to throw to Hammel, the lead-off hitter. Jake picked up his first base coach, who was giving him a sign to run on contact. Jake knew this meant he'd be running as soon as he saw a ground ball in order to increase the Cub's chances of scoring.

The first pitch was a strike and Hammel hit a bouncer to short. As soon as Jake saw the ball headed for the ground, he bolted from his stance and headed for home. The fielder picked up the ball and thought he had a play so he fired it home, but Jake was already sliding into the plate when the catcher got the ball.

He was safe. The Cubs had their first run of the ballgame and of the year. The crowd roared again and Burton, who was on deck and had instructed Jake to slide, had a large grin on his face as he gave Jake a high five.

The moment was one Jake would remember his whole life. Giving the fans so much to cheer for, just with a swing of the bat, was exhilarating.

All was good in Jake's life for that moment. His teammate's contempt didn't matter, his frustrations with hitting off speed pitches didn't matter, Angie's scorn didn't matter. Even the dire situation Jake had been facing with his father over the last few years didn't matter. Everything seemed right.

Baseball had given that to Jake and he would always remember it.

The Cubs couldn't produce much more offense that day and they lost the opener six to two. Jake struck out his next two at bats and played a clean second base until he was pulled after the seventh inning for Casey Earl, who singled in his only at bat.

The season was under way, and Jake couldn't have been more thrilled with the results.

CHAPTER 14

The first few weeks of the season were cold ones.

The Cubs played their first six games at home, the next six in St. Louis and New York, and then another seven in Chicago. The Cubs had a hard time stringing wins together and found themselves a struggling seven and twelve to start the season, as most people had expected.

Bug Wagner wasn't deterred, however, and he saw his young team doing many things they hadn't been able to in the previous seasons. His players were looking at more pitches, drawing more walks, and playing better defense.

The pitching staff was not as good as he had hoped, and the plan had been that they would turn things around and get the Cubs moving in the right direction. However, even an optimist like Bug Wagner couldn't help but be worried this struggling start was a precursor to another losing season in the friendly confines.

As the Cubs struggled, so did Jacob Riley. In the young season he had already committed five errors, the most in baseball. He was still having trouble turning the double play quickly despite the coaching staff working on it with him tirelessly before games.

Jake's defense might have cost them a game or two, and his hitting hadn't been much better. Jake was seven for fifty-four, a .129 batting average with only five walks. He had struck out twenty-one times, although his manager actually saw that as an improvement.

Most of his actual hits were weak ones on the infield.

The other problem was that teams were beginning to understand Jake's play more. Pitchers saw him waiting on fastballs and therefore gave him fewer to hit. Defenses saw him waiting back on pitches and hitting to the right side so they shifted, causing a couple balls that looked like they should have been hits to end up as routine plays.

The one thing that hadn't wavered, unbelievably, was Jake's

temperament. He was still concentrating on baseball and, more specifically, on getting better at it. He knew he could get help from the coaches and a couple of the players, but he was mostly doing it by himself. Few cared if he succeeded or not, so he relied on his family for support and himself for character.

Jake was getting better, but against professionals he was still too heavily disadvantaged.

In the last game of the Cub's home series, there had been an injury. Brent Gruber, the Cub's power hitting third baseman, had been hit by a pitch in the fifth inning. He was struck on the hands and ended up coming out of the game when he couldn't swing the bat because of the pain. The Cubs had their back-up shortstop, a veteran named Pierce Harley, who had just beat out Cools Perez for the final roster spot, as well as Casey Earl available to play the position. Bug, seeing he needed someone to get in at third, asked Earl to fill in.

"Casey, why don't you go out and play third for Gruber," the Cub's manager called out to the veteran infielder.

"Why don't you have Harley do it? I'm coming into the game in the seventh at second. Besides, I don't play much third base."

"Earl, you understand that Gruber might be out for some time if he has a sprain or fracture. I might need someone who can start at third for the next six weeks. Why don't you get out there and you might start playing every day. This is your chance to get some more time in."

"Then put Riley at third and I'll play second. It doesn't matter where that kid plays. He's a disaster. Might as well put me at a comfortable spot."

"Riley can't play third base," Bug reciprocated, irritated at Earl's defiance. "He's never done it. I need you to do it. I make the decisions, not you. Now are you going to third or not?"

"Well, I guess if you're making me do it..."

"Forget it!" Bug shot back, fed up with Earl's arrogance. "I'm done looking for playing time for you if you're not going to appreciate it! Harley, you're in at third!"

Jake couldn't believe what he had heard. Not the part about Earl calling him a disaster—he expected things like that and it rolled right off him—but he had never heard of a player trying to tell a manager what to do, especially when it was to keep that player out of the game!

It was lazy and insensitive, and the tension was thick in the Cub's dugout, everybody else sensing it too, but nobody said a word.

After the game, Cools Perez was called up from AAA ball and made the road trip with the Cubs out west to face the San Diego Padres and San Francisco Giants. He was named the new starting third baseman until Gruber got back. Perez was finally going to play in the big leagues, and the Cubs fans were excited to see what the young prospect could do.

Jake felt good about the move because he was still holding some guilt about being the reason Cools got cut in the first place.

The road trip started off with a close game. Jake had actually singled in a run, his first RBI of the year, and the Cubs had a four-three lead over the Padres in the seventh inning. Their opponent's relief pitcher, Suds Milkin, had walked the first two batters before getting a force out at second to put runners on the corners with one out.

The next batter hit a bouncer to Perez at third, and Cools ran up to grab the ball and throw it to Jake at second. Jake grabbed it, made the pivot, and threw weakly to first. The runner was called safe on a close play.

The Padres tied it up that inning and went on to win the game by a run in the ninth. After the game, Cools approached Jake in private.

"Hey, Riley, you got a second?"

"Sure Cools, what's up?"

Jake knew what was up. He knew he should've had more on the throw to first and the Cubs could have come out with a victory. Cools was ready to lay into him, and Jake was ready to take it.

"That double play was bang bang, you know?"

"Yeah, close one. If I had more on my throw, we might've got him."

"Maybe," Cools said compassionately, "but maybe not. Hard to know and you shouldn't worry about it. But you should work on that throw to first off the pivot. You have a better arm than that and should be able to get it there quicker."

"Coaches and I have been working on it. It's coming along, but I know I probably have my limitations. I am trying, though."

"I know. I've seen the coaches helping you, and I know you're working with them. Man, I can't say I like you being here, but you're doing it the way you're supposed to. You're not letting any of us get to you and you're trying to get better for the team. I have to give you credit for that. And I like you for that. But if we're going to win games, you need to get better, and I know how. At least with your pivot."

"Well, did you talk to the coaches about it? I'm doing everything they're telling me to."

"I know what they're telling you to do, but they don't get you. Man, they only get the game as they see it. But I know you, at least I think I do, and I'm telling you they're punking you."

"What do you mean?"

"They think you're only capable of so much, so they're trying to get you to play it safe. The bad part is if you do that, you'll never get good at throwing it over to second. Never. If I threw it like they've taught you, I'd have nothing on it either. You want me to show you?"

"Yeah," said Jake, intrigued.

Cools was taking a real interest in him, but Jake had to suspect there might be a sinister reason behind it. However, it didn't hurt to listen, especially considering Jake felt like he owed Cools for taking his spot on the roster. The two went into the media room and Cools pulled up video of their last couple games.

"Watch this, Jake. Here's you turning a double play. Watch your lead foot as you pivot and throw."

Jake watched, but he knew what he was looking at. The coaches had gone over it multiple times with him before. It looked to him like he was doing exactly what they told him.

"Got it? Now look at the Cardinals turn a double play in the same game and watch the second baseman's lead foot as he pivots."

Jake watched the play in slow motion. He saw the difference immediately.

"What'd you see, Jake?"

"I have a shorter pivot step, kind of like I'm throwing too quickly, instead of taking a wider step and getting more on the throw."

"Right! You have to give yourself a chance and swing that left leg around with authority, giving you more on your throw. Your left foot is barely moving on your pivot and your foot plants without a chance of extending and getting off a good throw."

"Why would the coaches have me do it this way?"

"Because they know it's safe and quick. You turn on your pivot straight up and you can see first clearly and throw to the base quickly. The problem is you get nothing behind it. If you do what I tell you, there's a better chance of you throwing blind and the ball soaring for an error. I'm telling you, though, if you don't go for it, you'll never be good on that turn. I can show you if you want me to."

"Now?"

"No time like the present!" Cools replied, smiling to Jake.

Hammel helped out, playing first base while Cools picked up balls at third, threw to Jake at second, and Jake made the pivot throw to first. Hammel shouted out his opinions as well, not always congruent with what Cools was saying and causing the two to playfully argue. Each one of them thought they had the perfect way for Jake to change his form. They agreed, though, that it would depend on how Jake responded to the changes. Either way they knew it would be for the better.

Jake listened intently to the two infielders. He respected both of their opinions because he admired their fielding abilities and he decided they were both out for his good, or at least the good of the team.

Jake tried to pivot the way they told him – it was difficult at first — and compare it with the way the coaches had taught him. He realized Cools was right. When Jake allowed his foot to come out farther, he was able to get more on his throw.

He noticed it was harder to control his precision Cool's way, but most of the time he was pretty accurate. After practicing for about an hour, Jake was getting it almost every time and feeling much better about his ability.

"Now, it will be different in the game, with someone running at you and all the endurance," Cools warned. "That's why it's so important to get it down now."

"Cools is right," Hammel interjected, "but I'm sure you've figured all that out by now. How hard was it the first time you caught a ground ball in a game?"

"Really difficult," Jake answered. "I was surprised I made the play."

"Exactly," Hammel responded. "So you know what to expect. This is just like the base running we talked about, Jake. You have to get comfortable with it and take some chances. Stop worrying about making mistakes. They're going to happen. Just make sure at the end of each day you can say you did as good as you could have. If, instead, you are happy because you didn't make a mistake, you're not playing the game like you're supposed to."

This was not how Jake liked to do things, but he was finding it to be the only way to approach baseball. He knew his whole life had been forged by his making the safe decisions. It had always seemed like the smart thing to do.

He had been afraid of committing to too much and then being disappointed later, but this situation was different. He had made the decision to play baseball because he was afraid of regretting it if he didn't. Now he had to do things the way others were telling him to. If he didn't, he'd be ignoring the best minds in the world on the game, and he theorized that wasn't a logical way to go about it. Therefore, Jake was forced to go out on a limb.

So far he was enjoying it, even if it was a bit scary.

Over the next week, Jake did his best to practice his pivot as well as attempt it as fearlessly as possible during games. It was working. He felt he was getting more behind his throw and more easily turning the double play.

He did have one play that was much more difficult. It caused him to swivel quickly and attempt to throw out a faster runner going down the line at first, but when he turned, he saw the runner from first barreling down on him. Jake had second thoughts about getting more behind his throw. At the last second he decided he needed to go for it and swung forward his leg exactly how he had in practice.

The release of his throw was mistimed and he ended up throwing the ball to the right of the bag, allowing the runner to be safe at first and advance to second. Jake was disappointed by the outcome, but he knew this was to be expected and he commended himself for attempting the throw the way he did.

He realized it was only unsuccessful because he had thought about it instead of just doing it. He would have to work on that. He knew at times his biggest enemy was his mind. It was hard for him to accept that because it had done him so much good throughout his life, but he could see he had to start trusting his instincts as well. That would take more time.

In terms of a baseball season, time was not on his side. In the terms of life, however, there was always time to make himself better. Jake was starting to see the correlation.

CHAPTER 15

The next few weeks were better for Jake.

He started hitting the ball more solidly and he had a few line drives into the outfield, one going for a double in the right-center field gap. He had ten hits in his last fifty-seven at bats, a .175 average in that span, and that raised his average to .153. He realized this still wasn't acceptable and was hurting his team, but he saw it as an improvement and hoped he could continue getting better.

Jake was seeing more pitches and fouling off good breaking balls, recognizing them earlier in the count. He also walked another eight times, lifting his on base percentage to .241, which was poor, but improved.

His fielding was also getting better and he found he was making more plays to his right and left, increasing his range considerably as he progressed. He was still making too many errors, ten in just over six weeks. He beat himself up over this more than he did over his hitting because he felt he should be better at concentrating on the routine plays.

Jake's coaches, however, were in awe that he was doing as well as he was. They had figured he would have had twice the amount of errors in that time frame.

The Cubs continued to struggle, though, and were now fifteen wins to twenty-three losses, last place in the NL Central and seven games out of first place. That's not to say there weren't a few bright spots. Hammel was batting .311 with a .392 on base percentage from the leadoff position, and Bob Oates, the first baseman, had already hit nine home runs and registered thirty-three RBIs, fourth best in the league.

The pitching staff had done well, too, at least for being so young. The starting pitcher's ERA was 4.01, not great but respectable, and the bullpen was doing their job holding leads late. Overall, Bug Wagner was happy with the progression of his young team and felt they were ready to take the next step.

Cools Perez, however, was struggling mightily. He was at a new position and his fielding wasn't as crisp as expected. His hitting showed flashes of power, but his strike out rate was unacceptable. He was leaving too many runners in scoring position and not taking enough pitches to draw walks. He was batting seventh, just in front of the pitcher and Jake.

Cools felt his window to impress was closing as Gruber — the Cub's regular third baseman — was recovering from his wrist fracture and would be back in four to five weeks. Cools's spirits were down and Jake, as well as the rest of the team, had noticed it affecting his game.

During the time of Cools's darkness, Jake and the Chicago Cubs saw a light. For about ten games, Jake had started seeing the ball better than he ever had before. Pitches were looking fat and hittable, screaming for Jake to hit them hard, and Jacob Riley complied. He went through a five game hitting streak, going seven for nineteen. He had two more doubles — one off the wall in left-center field — and he scored seven times in that ten game span.

He also had stolen five bases during that time, increasing his season total to ten, and he was only caught twice.

His fielding had gone the way of his hitting and he was errorless during the streak. He even made a beautiful diving stop of a ball ticketed for right field, doubling off a wandering runner at first. The play made *Sportscenter's* top plays and Jake watched it over and over until they weren't playing it anymore.

The Cubs went seven and three during that period, taking two of three from Milwaukee, splitting a four game set against the Cardinals, and sweeping a three game series from the Astros. At twenty-two and twenty-six, they had moved up to fourth place ahead of the Brewers and started to feel some momentum as a team.

Casey Earl had done well in his limited time at second base and Shawn Hammel and Cam Burton had led the way for the offense, totaling fifty-two runs in the ten game spurt. Bug Wagner was beaming and he pushed his team even further.

Jacob Riley was feeling more confident and thought he might even start contributing to the team on a consistent basis, erasing his blemish as an embarrassment to baseball and the Chicago Cubs.

Sometimes things always seem good right before the rug is pulled out from underneath and Jake experienced this the hard way.

As quickly as the baseball had become a beach ball for Jake, it turned into a golf ball. Pitches seemed to vanish on their way to the plate, and Jake was lucky to make weak contact, if any at all. He began to strike out at an alarmingly high rate and his hits were few and far between. Jake went on a two for twenty spurt, dropping his average ten points and his confidence even further. In those twenty at bats, Jake only walked once and struck out twelve times.

His hitting affected his fielding, too, and Jake made two more errors, one costly one in the sixth inning of a close game leading to a Cubs defeat.

Jake couldn't understand what was happening. Recently he had felt so good about his improvements, but now he felt his hitting was worse than when he had started spring training. Pitchers were dominating him, pounding the strike zone and mixing up pitches so well Jake found himself again guessing what was coming instead of evaluating each pitch individually.

His mind was aching with baseball and it was too much on him. He welcomed his one day off and tried to relax his mind, but the next day was no different. He struck out all four at bats and began a streak he would remember for the rest of his life.

The next two games were as frustrating as the last few. Jake found himself continuously thinking about his poor hitting and that led to even poorer at bats. He was over-thinking every situation and coming up empty time and time again. He struck out three times on ten pitches in the first game and another three times on twelve pitches in the next.

His mind was concentrating so much on his hitting that he also made two errors in one game, causing the winning runs to score. Jake had fallen into his first real slump and had no idea how to handle it. Despite his coaches attempting to talk him through it, this was something Jake had never experienced and he realized how mentally difficult it was to handle such a situation.

Since the time Eddie Dillinger announced Jake's signing, many talked about how there would be a multitude of broken records because of Riley's inexperience. The thought was he would have the lowest batting average, lowest on base percentage, lowest fielding percentage, most strike outs, etc. One of the most talked about items was consecutive strikeouts. The record was twelve straight plate appearances with a strike out.

This was the first record Jake was about to break and the media was attacking it. He was now with ten straight.

Jake was trying not to think about breaking the nefarious record, but he found it impossible to escape dwelling on it. He had already been doing better than most had thought, though he was still under-whelming overall, but now he was getting to the point where he probably would break most of the records everyone had talked about.

This was the first time he could sense the actuality of it, and it was unnerving. He found himself thinking about it every time he reached two strikes in the count and he couldn't keep a level head after that. He didn't know what to do.

The day after Jake had reached ten consecutive strikeouts was unbearable for him. He stayed awake most the night before, thinking about each at bat over the last few days and how he had failed every time. He tried to imagine how he could be more successful in his next attempt, and thousands of scenarios flashed through his head. Jake knew how much attention would be on him and the egregious record he was approaching.

Now the day was here and Jake was at the field warming up, no longer being able to hide from the inevitable.

The Cubs performed well in their first inning, scoring three times and going through seven batters before Perez whiffed with a man on third to end the inning. In the bottom of the second, the pitcher led off with a soft ground out to the second baseman — something Jake was longing for — and up came the ninth spot in the order.

The overhead announcer called out, "Batting ninth, Jacob Riley." There were a few claps from the audience, but a good amount of boos with it, something Jake was used to.

Perspiration was flowing off Jake's forehead.

The first pitch was a perfect strike on the outside corner, and Jake knew it. The second pitch was a good curve that he missed badly. Jake was already down 0-2 and he started to panic. He tried to guess which pitch was coming, sure it would be a change up. He waited back on it, but the pitch came in hard at the letters, and by the time Jake realized it was a fastball and started to swing, the ball was already in the mitt of the catcher.

His streak went to eleven, and the crowd booed even more loudly.

The Cubs wouldn't go as quietly, however, and put up four runs in the third, leaving runners on second and third with only one out when Jake came to the plate. He heard the crowd boo harder when his name was called, and he admitted to himself it was starting to bother him significantly.

The first pitch was again a good fastball on the outer part of the plate and Jake fouled it back, but he felt good about just getting a piece of the ball. The next pitch was high and Jake laid off, running the count even.

A little confidence came back in. Jake wasn't down 0-2 for the first time in what seemed like forever. However, the next pitch was a beauty, a knee-buckling curve right over the heart of the plate, and Jake was down 1-2.

After he swung ahead of a change-up for strike three the crowd really let him have it. Boos erupted over the whole stadium and chants of "Riley sucks!" could be heard.

Jake sat down on the bench, dejected, now co-owner of the longest strike out streak in baseball and only one away from it being all his.

The Cubs went down quietly the next two innings, which led to Jake leading off the bottom of the sixth with the home team leading seven to one. Jake thought leading off would be less rattling on his nerves, but the crowd had other ideas.

Fans began booing loudly the second his name was announced and someone threw a cup of beer at him from the stands as he walked to the plate, hitting his arm and slightly dampening his right sleeve while dampening his spirits even more.

The first pitch was a curve ball taken for a strike, and boos emerged again. The second pitch was a fastball that Jake missed entirely and the whole stadium was on its feet, screaming for the blood of Jacob Riley. Jake saw the pitcher chuckle, enjoying the moment of a fallen insignificant, and it became too much to bear.

Jake called for time and stepped out of the batter's box.

"I can't do this," he thought. "I can't strike out again! I can't face myself anymore if I do!"

Sweat was falling heavily down his temples and anxiety was building up quickly. He noticed all the members of the opposing team were at the rail of the dugout, enjoying the scene. He wondered what his team was doing and turned to look. He saw all of them up and watching, too, but not as cheerfully as the visitor's dugout. The thought that his teammates weren't enjoying it was refreshing until he saw one of them smiling.

It was Cam Burton. He was grinning from ear to ear, reveling in the moment of Jake failing. He didn't even flinch when Jake caught his eye. He didn't even realize he was being a jerk about it. That's the way it always was with Burton, and it angered Jake even more now. He thought Cam would have given him some encouragement at such a troubling time.

Jake realized he would need to search somewhere else for strength, and he found it inside of himself.

He wasn't going to strike out again. He wouldn't have been able to take it.

Jake used his mind to come up with a way out of it, just as he had done with everything else in his life. He knew what he was bad at. Guessing pitches. There was no place for that now. He also knew what he was good at. Judging balls and strikes and fouling pitches off.

Jake stepped back up to the plate. He knew what he had to do.

His stance this time was different. His feet were in the same place, but his torso was not as twisted. He crouched a little with his hands in front of him, not allowing for much to come from his swing. He was also choking up on the bat and he waggled it in front of the plate as the pitch came to it.

The pitch was a change up, but Jake hardly noticed. As soon as it got close to the plate and looked like a strike, Jake poked the bat at the ball and saw it weekly foul off to the right. The next pitch was a curve ball in the middle of the zone, and Jake did the same thing. The fifth pitch in the sequence was a high fast ball that Jake let go for the first ball. He fouled off three more pitches until the ninth pitch dropped in the dirt for ball two. After fouling off two good fastballs on the inside and outside corners, ball three was called inside.

Twelve pitches had been thrown already, and Jake had looked the same for the last ten.

The crowd was no longer booing and the opposing team was no longer smiling. Everyone was watching the epic battle between Jacob Riley and the world record of consecutive strike outs. Jake was not going down without a fight and it was a great show for all.

Pitch thirteen was probably outside, but Jake took no chances, now confident in his ability to at least foul the ball off, and he poked it to the opposing dugout. Pitch fourteen was a high strike and Jake fouled it straight back. Pitch fifteen was in the center of the plate and it got fouled back as well. Pitch sixteen was on the inside corner and Jake spoiled it by chopping it foul down the third base line.

The opposing pitcher was no longer chuckling. He was not amused by this sorry excuse for a player spoiling his best pitches and now running his pitch count up by sixteen in one at bat. He wanted to throw something more off the plate, but was too fearful of walking Riley and not allowing him to break the strikeout record. On the other hand, he didn't know what else to throw. Riley seemed to be able to get a piece of every pitch.

He decided to keep pounding him with fastballs and hopefully come out of the prolonged battle victorious. It didn't work.

Pitch seventeen and eighteen were both fouled straight back. Pitch nineteen was fouled down the right field line. Pitch twenty was grounded slowly to the left side, past the third base coach.

After the twentieth pitch, Jake heard something he hadn't heard for a while. Clapping.

Jake stepped out of the box for a breather and looked up into the stands. Everyone was on their feet, most with wide eyes, not believing what they were seeing or who it was that was giving them the show. Others were clapping with smiles on their faces, truly entertained by one of the greatest at-bats in the history of the game.

Jake looked and saw the opposing dugout was no longer laughing, but smiling in awe of the achievement placed before them. Jake looked back around for a second and saw his own teammates were having the time of their lives, cheering him on and laughing amongst themselves at the show they were being given.

Jake stepped back into the batter's box with confidence now.

The next pitch was a low fastball, but not low enough to let by, and Jake foul tipped it behind the plate. The pitcher, clearly frustrated now, finally shifted out of his fastball groove and threw a curve ball that started belt high.

Jake watched it closely as it approached the plate and he saw it start to dip. He knew it was a curve ball, and a good one. He held back as long as he could, not wanting to swing at a bad pitch, as it continued its downward course. Jake started to move his hands forward, thinking he might need to poke at the ball at the last second, but he finally held back as he saw it fall out of his view and into the dirt.

Jake had walked.

There was no strike out recorded and Jake trotted to first among great cheers from the crowd and his teammates.

He did break a record though. Twenty-two pitches seen in one at bat was the most in major league history. The previous record was twenty pitches to Ricky Gutierrez in 1998.

Jake had avoided the strikeout record and had won over some fans, at least for the time being. He felt great and couldn't hold back a smile as his first base coach laughed and slapped him in the helmet.

He felt even better after stealing second base and scoring on Hammel's RBI single.

The Cubs won big that day, 12-2, but cashed out even higher from the confidence boost in their second baseman Jacob Riley.

Jake realized now what he could do and how he could help this team offensively, or at least not strike out so much. Jake went to bed that night with a smile on his face, the first time he had done that in a while, and it felt refreshing to the young Cub.

CHAPTER 16

The next day the excitement continued.

Jake's first at bat lasted thirteen pitches and ended in a walk. The second lasted fourteen before the pitcher grew tired of the inexperienced Riley showing him up and ended in a fastball between Jake's ribs. Jake smiled, despite the pain, as he ran to first base and the umpire ejected the starting pitcher for a purposeful hit batsman.

The third at bat was the most memorable, if you didn't count the nasty bruise that the second one had left.

The Cubs were tied 4-4 in the seventh and there were two on with two out. Jake had already seen eleven pitches and it was a 2-2 count. The pitcher was growing tired, and Jake could sense it. The velocity of the tenth pitch seemed significantly reduced from the first fastball he had thrown Jake.

When Jake saw another dull fastball come down the inner half of the plate, he flexed his arms and swung hard at the ball, lifting it over the third baseman's head and into the corner.

Jake was out of the box as soon as he struck the ball and he was already at second by the time the left fielder had a good grip on it. Jake headed for third and made it standing up, a two out, two run triple, that ended up being the game winner.

Jake was on a roll and the baseball seemed like a beach ball once again.

The Cubs were playing well, too, and were now two games below .500 and six games out of first place. The team was rolling and they continued to improve as they took three out of four games in Colorado and two out of three in Los Angeles. They just missed a sweep of three games in Arizona and settled for a seven out of ten road trip before going back to Wrigley.

Jake, for once, was not a detriment.

He played in eight out of the ten games and went five for twenty with nine walks, seeing an average of nine pitches per plate appearance. His patience and ability to spoil good pitches wrecked the opposing pitchers both physically and mentally. Throwing thirty pitches a game to the number nine hitter was significantly increasing their pitch count, knocking them out of the game early, and frustrating them to the point of sometimes giving up and throwing pitches out of the zone, hoping Jake would swing at a bad one. He rarely did, striking out just three times in his twenty-nine plate appearances on the road trip.

His teammates and coaches started thinking the kid wasn't so bad after all.

By the All-Star break, the Cubs were 46-42, one game in back of the Cincinnati Reds and three games in back of the St. Louis Cardinals. The Cubs had been one of the hottest teams in baseball over the past thirty games and most of the credit was given to the maturing of the starting rotation and the emergence of the young hitters. The whole team was getting on base more and hitting the ball for power. Their quick turn around surprised all the opposing coaches.

A few people even threw some credit at the improvement of Jacob Riley, who was now hitting .183 and, more importantly, getting on base at .293. Most people, however, still just felt the Cubs were doing well despite their anchor at second base.

Not everyone was happy with the club's performance. Casey Earl, for one, was inwardly miffed. He was sure they couldn't go anywhere without him being in the line-up, but instead this off the street substitute was reaping praise for the upshift. Casey had been sure Riley would be gone by now and the job at second his, but that was based on Riley doing so poorly that the team was well out of contention.

Instead, the Cubs were now in a better position than they had been in half a decade. The city was actually excited about the lovable losers and didn't have time to complain about Casey being on the bench. Earl had even seen people wearing Riley jerseys. He couldn't believe anyone would be rooting for such an atrocity. He was searching for any leverage he could find to squeeze out Jake, but his window was closing fast.

Another who had not been as happy as most was Cools Perez. Since he had taken over for the injured Gruber, he had hit a mere .239 with an on base percentage of only .284. He had swatted ten homers, but only had nineteen RBIs to show for them. Worse yet, he had struck out over eighty times, nearly half his plate appearances. Cools's major league debut was not going as well as some had thought and the rookie third baseman couldn't seem to stop striking out.

Gruber's recovery had been slow — over eight weeks total — but he had already finished a three game minor league rehab stint and was scheduled to be back with the team after the All-Star break. Cools knew he was likely to be sent down to the minors for more work on his swing.

The one person who should have felt the best about the Cub's position, the owner, didn't seem to notice his team's ascension. Big Eddie Dillinger was more wrapped up in the batting average of Jacob Riley and until that average was safely above .200, he wasn't too pleased with his rookie second baseman. He expressed this daily to his General Manager, Tex Klondike, the only man who knew about the wager outside of Dillinger's lunch table at Ruby's the day the bet was made.

Sampson Klondike — called "Tex" because of his college ball in Texas — was a large white man in his early seventies who wore button down, checkered shirts with boots and a white cowboy hat. He often had on large, dark sunglasses which hid his eyes during his wide-mouthed grins. He looked every part the man from Texas who was misplaced in Chicago but didn't seem to think anyone noticed. He was often loud and obnoxious in the finer restaurants in the city and he had made himself look ridiculous during charity events by treating them like a party that was held in his honor.

Tex was ready to get out of Chicago and out of baseball for good. His contract was up at the end of the year, and it couldn't come quickly enough. He was done trying to finesse players into coming to teams for no good reasons he could think of except that they would be paid a small fortune for it. It seemed like every other big name he lured to a team ended up being a bust and the fans, coaches and owners would always blame him. The whole process seemed more like a gamble than anything else.

Like many other GMs, Tex would shrug, "You win some and you lose some."

His latest gig with the Cubs was his worst one yet. It was difficult to get anyone to play for a losing team with an unlikable owner and a no-name manager. There were no franchise players to start with, which made it difficult to get any player with credentials to consider playing for them. Players also were not fond of the poor weather conditions of Chicago, and Tex could hardly blame them. He wanted out of the frigid climate as well.

The whole situation had left Tex with a sour taste in his mouth and a desire to get out for good. He felt he only had a few more months to put up with Dillinger and then he could say good-bye as a class act, fully living up to the contract he signed, but Big Eddy hadn't been making it easy.

Every day Eddy would talk about Riley's at-bats, how many hits he had, how many strikeouts he had, what his daily average was, where he was trending. It was frustrating for Tex to see somebody show so much concern for one player when he should have been worrying about the whole team. Now especially, when the Cubs were actually showing signs of promise and possibly being in a playoff hunt, Eddy continued to be upset by Riley's performance because of a bet he had made.

The bet itself was problematic to Tex. He wasn't exactly a man of ethics, but when it came to baseball, he was a purist at heart. He was perturbed by the whole process and felt constrained because he couldn't tell anyone about it. Eddy had confided in him and it was Tex's last duty as a General Manager to keep that dirty secret quiet, no matter how much it tore him up inside to do so.

"Kid's only at .183 now. That means he has to hit over

.220 the rest of the way to end up above .200! No way he's going to do that, don't you think, Tex?"

"I don't know, Eddy," replied Tex, uninterested as he sat on a couch in the owner's office and thumbed through *Golf Digest*. "Seems to me he's done a pretty good job just being where he's at."

"Nonsense!" blurted Eddy. "Anyone could do what that kid is doing. I was a damn fool to pick him! He's going to make me a complete laughing stock!"

"Don't blame the kid on that," Tex replied coolly.

"Do you think it gives me credibility that he's close? I was thinking about that. From the very beginning the guys thought I was crazy that any average Joe off the street could hit .200, but this kid is only seventeen points away! Doesn't that give me something?"

"Not in terms of the ten million," said Tex dryly. "If Riley bats .199 you still owe the full amount. But aside from the money, yeah, it makes you look credible."

Dillinger flashed a slight look of satisfaction. He was grasping for any respectability he could find at this point.

"You know, Eddy, this kid has actually saved you since you made that ridiculous wager."

"How so?"

"Well, as bad as he might be, he's much better than anybody thought he would be. You heard Bug rave about him earlier today. He actually makes most the plays at second and has some decent range. He also gets on base pretty well and can steal bases. The fact that Riley isn't a complete disaster is very positive from what the writers were predicting at the beginning of the year. You've shut a lot of them up, and this kid could keep getting better. Maybe even win you this bet."

"You think so?" asked Eddy, hopefully.

"Well, no," Tex exclaimed, causing Dillinger to sulk, "but it's a possibility, and that's more than anyone thought you'd have at this point. Be happy about that. I would be, if I were you."

"If you were me. That's really soothing, thanks," Dillinger replied sarcastically. "Don't you realize I can't stop thinking about this stupid bet? It's all that's been on my mind the whole season! I'm sure I've blown multiple business deals on account of not concentrating on anything but the batting average of Jacob Riley! I was a fool to accept this wager, I admit, but I don't deserve to be in this state, do I?"

Tex sat motionless, refusing to answer such a loaded question.

"What else am I to do? Even now, during the All-Star break, all I can think about is what Riley is doing right now to get better for the second half and how it's going to turn out. I'm completely obsessed by all this and I don't know how to get out of it!"

"Just quit thinking about it!" Tex interjected. "You think I care to hear about this every single day? I'm actually trying to enjoy my last season in the bigs and you bring me down every afternoon with this nonsense!"

"Tex, you have to understand, you're the only one I can talk to about all this. You're the only one who knows."

"Well, lucky me!" Tex shot back, rolling his eyes. "I didn't ask for you to divulge all this to me, you know. I was happy just getting through the season and enjoying myself. Now I find myself half rooting for this kid to succeed for the team's sake and half wanting him to fail just to see you lose!"

"You're just saying that, Tex. You don't mean it."

"The hell I don't! You embarrassed every player in the game and cheapened the sentiments of everyone who cares about baseball with a selfish wager, and nobody even realizes it except me! Now I'm supposed to go on grasping every positive shred of evidence that comes out of camp Riley so that you can win some stupid bet. Well I'm sick of it! The Cubs are actually playing well, despite their anchor at second base which you, by the way, tied to their feet. The Cubs have a chance of making the playoffs, and your team is one of the most talked about in baseball and all you care about is Riley. Snap out of it! As the owner, you're supposed to care about this team and try to get them into the playoffs. Do your job and maybe you'll get your mind off a single player's batting average!"

"Well, Tex, maybe you're right," admitted Eddy. "Maybe I should get into this Cubbie fever. I should be proud of the team we put together and maybe they can make the postseason after all. The team is playing so well it has taken a huge burden off of me, and I haven't been appreciative of it. You put things in a fair perspective, Tex, and I'm grateful for it. I'm sorry it's been so hard on you. That was not my intent."

Eddy did have a way of apologizing that left the one being apologized to feeling guilty about ever attacking, no matter how warranted. It was one of Dillinger's business techniques that had given him so much success over the years. It's not that Eddy did it just to get an edge over his opponent. He did often feel bad abut his actions and the way he portrayed himself. The tactic had worked so well it became reinforced many times over his life and he became better and better at invoking it. He knew it was successful this time when Tex sighed deeply and turned away.

"I'm not trying to berate you, Ed," he started.

"It's OK, Tex."

"It's just that I can't go on like this anymore. Let's enjoy the season and work on making the Cubs better, huh? Maybe we can do something nobody's done here in a while."

"I read you, old friend," Dillinger smiled back, knowing the two were good once again. "I'll get Bug in here tomorrow and we can talk about what he needs to stay in this playoff hunt."

"Now you're talking!" Tex smiled back at Eddy, feeling a need to now act on his rant. He hadn't felt inspired in a while to really help a team compete, but his speech to Dillinger invigorated himself more that he thought it would. He was now ready to make one last push at a champion before he retired, and maybe, as silly as it seemed, he had Jacob Riley to thank for it.

"So," Dillinger started up again, "you think Riley can really make a second half push and still get to .200?"

Tex sunk lower in his chair and pushed his white cowboy hat over his eyes so that Eddy wouldn't see them rolling.

"What?" asked Eddy. "What did I say?"

CHAPTER 17

The All-Star break was a time for most players to sit back and rest.

Only a few were chosen to play in the star-studded event and Jake was looking forward to the five days off. A baseball player's schedule was gruesome. Every week promised at least six games, and half of the time they played in different cities. There was so much traveling and so little time off that the grind could really get to a player's psyche.

The All-Star break was a chance to regroup and try to recharge both the body and the mind. Jake was excited to do both, all in the comfort of his home city, Chicago.

He spent the first day and a half at the apartment with Angie and noticed little had changed. Angie was still dismissive towards him because of the lack of time he was able to spend with her throughout the season. She had mentioned it multiple times, but Jake still wasn't sure he knew exactly what she wanted him to do. His schedule was rigorous, even when he was in town for a week, and he didn't think he could spend a lot of time relaxing while he was hitting below two-hundred as well as remain on pace to commit the most errors of any baseball player in the history of the game.

Angie wasn't mad all the time, but her demeanor to him was one of dissatisfaction. Jake constantly felt he was not giving his girlfriend the attention she needed and was letting her down on an emotional level. Not that Jake had done anything wrong outside of signing a contract, but when the person who means the most continuously acts like the other is just a bad person, it's hard not to think it's the truth.

Jake was hurting emotionally because of his relationship with Angie while mentally he was slowly being reduced to nothing. He wasn't sure which part of him would completely collapse first, his heart or his mind.

Jacob loved Angie, at least he believed he did, and wanted her to be happy, but it was hard for him to understand the need for he himself to be happy, too. Angie found ways to make everything he did seem like a selfish act, which she supposedly took the brunt of.

Angie was only happy when she wasn't, and she made sure to drag everybody else down with her. Secretly she admired Jake's perseverance and the amount of attention he did provide her, but she was afraid if she acknowledged this it would lead to his feeling content with his effort and therefore stop working as hard as he was. Jake's love was taken for granted and rarely does that ever lead to something positive for either member of the relationship.

The end was near for both of them, but neither of them yet realized it.

Jake decided to spend his second night off over at his parents, much to Angie's further disappointment. She claimed, as she often would, to have other things going on, and Jake went alone.

Jake's mother and father were delighted to see him. Jake walked right in through the front door as he always did, finding no need to knock in his own home. His father was on the couch and his mother in the kitchen when he announced he had arrived, and both immediately got up to welcome him. His mother gave him a big kiss and his father hugged him joyfully. Jake could feel that they had been waiting for this moment all day.

"So good to see you, dear!" said Loretta Riley, grinning like she couldn't hide her excitement. "No Angie tonight?"

"No. She was busy."

"Well, we sure are glad to see you," Justin Riley exclaimed, as if it hadn't already been obvious. "I can't wait to talk to you about how great you've been doing! Your eye has been so good lately and you really are getting on base. I can't stop talking about it with the guys at the club!"

Justin Riley had golfed once a week for the last twenty years at a golf club close by and Jake was sure he was boring the members to death about his son.

"Well, something has clicked lately and I'm hoping it continues," Jake responded.

"I think it's just going to get better, son. I can tell!"

"Would you like something to drink, Jake?" Loretta offered. "Dinner won't be ready for another half hour. We can talk in the family room in the meantime."

"Sure, mom. How about some juice?"

Loretta went into the kitchen while Justin reclaimed his spot on the couch and Jake sat in the recliner.

"I bet Bug has been thrilled with your improvement, huh, Jake?"

"He has been happy to see me getting on base more, especially by cutting down on the strikeouts."

"And the amount of pitches you're seeing!" the elder Riley interjected. "You're wearing those pitchers out! I read that Bug is probably going to bat you eighth now. He should, too, you've been a better hitter than the pitchers for quite a while. I bet you could even bat up in the order, the on base percentage you've been displaying."

"I wouldn't get ahead of ourselves, pop. I'm happy that I haven't completely sucked lately, but I now understand how cyclical this game is. I can fall into a funk again at any time. It wasn't too long ago I had struck out twelve straight times, you know."

"Ah, that's behind you now, Jake," Justin rebutted, accepting a cool drink from his wife, who took a seat next to him on the couch. "You have to start thinking bigger now. Getting more hits and raising that average to a point where they'll have to consider keeping you on the team next year."

"Dad, listen to yourself!" Jake interrupted, a bit annoyed with his father's incessantly positive attitude. "I'm here for one year, that's it! I'm making the best of it I can, but that's all I can do. You don't understand these guys, they're so good. It's amazing I'm doing as well as I am, and I'm still so far behind them!"

"Yes, but they don't understand Jacob Riley," Justin interposed. "The way you have found a way to get on base and raise pitch counts, that's so you! Your innovation has always been your best quality, and now you've done it on a level that everyone in the sport is talking about it!"

"I don't know about that."

"They are! Even the Jacob Riley doubters and haters are all saying how you've really made the best of all this and found a way to contribute when nobody thought you could. You think anyone could have done that? No way!"

"I'm lucky to have done what I did, and that's that, dad."

"Okay, you two," Loretta broke in, not wanting the tension to get any higher. "Why argue about this when we finally get a chance to be together?"

"I'm sorry," Justin said, decreasing his tone. "I'm just so proud of you, son, that's all. That's what I should have said."

"I know, dad," Jake said with red cheeks. "I shouldn't have been upset by it. It's been really tough these last few months, and I guess I'm on edge. I'm glad to give you something to cheer about right now and I'm hoping it can last."

"Well, let's go and start dinner," Loretta stated. "It's hard to argue with good food in your mouth."

"Well said!" Justin replied as he got up to help with the table.

Loretta Riley was right. The next hour was filled with happiness as Jake and Justin devoured the exquisite meal prepared by the woman of the house. Their laughter became contagious as they reminisced about old times when Jake had roamed the house as a teenager and even as a small child. Stories were recollected and mysteries of the past were solved as the three gleefully welcomed each other's presence.

If one had never met the Rileys, they could easily see just from this one dinner that it was a family of love and good times with deep mutual respect for each other. Justin and Loretta were parents many would die for, and Jake was a son who loved them fully because of it.

The meal and the affirmation of their ties had been a long time coming, and each of them reveled in their fulfillment by it.

After dinner, Justin insisted on cleaning up so that Jake could spend some time alone with his mother. They both went back to the family room and sat on the couch together, Loretta with her cup of coffee in hand and Jake with his arm around her. They were happy to be together, but both knew there was more to talk about, and now was the right time.

"How's dad been?" Jake asked, finally moving to the place they needed to be.

"He's been better, Jake."

"How so? What's been happening?"

"He went to see the doctor again yesterday. The news wasn't good."

"Since when has the news been anything but bad, mom?"

"Yeah, I know, but it's getting worse. The treatments haven't been helping."

"Did you tell dad I gave you the money for the last treatment?"

"No. He thinks we put it on credit. But we really do thank you, Jake. It's at least giving him a chance."

"Anything I can do, mom, I will. That's one of the reasons I did all this with the Cubs. I know it gives us a chance to pay for more opportunities."

"Dad doesn't see it that way, and I bet Angie doesn't, either. Have you told her you gave me the twenty thousand?"

"No," Jake answered sheepishly, "not yet."

Loretta nodded slowly as she took another sip of her coffee. She was fighting back her tears, as she had been the last few months with her husband on a nightly basis. She felt she was getting quite good at it, but it didn't seem to make her feel any better about the situation.

Justin Riley had been diagnosed with cancer over two years earlier. It was colorectal cancer, and pretty advanced by the time it was diagnosed. Justin had been a smoker for years and he knew this was the primary reason for the disease. He had stopped smoking immediately at the time of the diagnosis, but it was already too late.

The cancer was first found in his liver and his lungs, although in small amounts. Initial chemotherapy coupled with a partial colectomy and radiation had given signs of promise in the beginning. The liver and lung lesions had seemed to disappear, but the lymph nodes continued to irradiate on the PET scan a year afterwards.

The oncologists had told him his five year mortality rate was under thirty percent, but hopes were high after the metastatic lesions seemed to improve. Just prior to Jake's meeting with Big Eddy Dillinger, the Rileys had learned that cancer had reappeared in Justin's liver, requiring more chemo that didn't seem affordable at the time.

With Jake's help, the therapy was given, but the doctor begged them all to understand that the disease was so far advanced that new medicine probably wouldn't be curative.

That hadn't stopped the family from hoping.

Loretta explained to her son that the latest scan showed two golf ball sized lesions in Justin's right lung, proof the cancer was now spreading rapidly. The time for hope was over, and now thoughts about palliative care were being pursued. There were services that helped a patient move towards comfort for end of life issues, and it appeared Justin Riley was now at that stage.

The war was over, and the Rileys seemed to have lost. They were now just hoping for fair concessions.

Justin walked in to see his family sitting on the couch, Jake holding his wife's hands. His boy's eyes were red from the strain of holding back tears. Loretta was not crying, but obviously was deflated and defeated.

A frown appeared on Justin's face as they looked up to him.

"I see you told him, Loretta."

"I'm sorry, Justin..."

"Don't be, dear," Justin comforted, sitting down next to her on the couch. "I realize this isn't only hard for me."

"Dad, I'm so sorry."

"You're sorry?" Justin replied lightly. "That's funny. You're sorry. I'm the one who did this to myself, smoking all those years. I knew it was no good for me and yet I did it anyway. Now the whole family is strained because of my stupidity. I'm the one who should be sorry."

"You didn't know, dad."

"I did. I knew what could happen, at least. I admit I didn't think it would happen to me, but I guess all us idiots think that."

"Dad, we all do dumb things. This was just unlucky, that's all. Don't beat yourself up over it now. We don't blame you."

"That's because you love me so much, and for that I am so lucky. My greatest solace in all this is that you never took it up, Jake. If you did, I could never forgive myself."

"That's because you love me so much, dad. I know it and I always will."

"Thanks, son," Justin answered thoughtfully. "Even in these terrible times, I do feel so blessed to have you both. Really, I'm only upset because of what it's doing to you two. I've lived a great life and I'm not afraid of dying. I am upset I'll miss so many things in your life, but I guess that would be the case no matter when I die. There's a time for us all. Mine's just a little sooner than we would like."

"How long are they giving you, dad?"

"Doctor says I'd be fortunate to live another six months. It's coming up quickly now."

"Six months!" Jake exclaimed, obviously hurt. "That's hardly any time at all!"

"Honestly, Jake, I don't think it's going to be that long. I want you to brace yourself for the worst. I can feel it coming on fast. My lungs are really struggling now, and I get short of breath walking up the stairs. I don't know how much longer I can live like this."

"Then I have to quit playing baseball and spend more time with you! I have so little time left with you. I can't waste it on this, this baseball stuff. I'm sorry dad. I had no idea it would be so soon."

"Don't talk foolish, Jake," Justin replied calmly. "This is quite a time for you, and I won't let you cut it short so you can sit around here slobbering over me. You know that's not what I want!"

"What about what I want, dad? I want to be there for you and mom during this time! I can't even fathom you not being here, and it's coming up on us so fast. I won't be able to forgive myself if I miss just a little part of it. I need to be here with you!"

"Now listen, Jake. There is a time coming up where I won't be around, and you're going to have to live with that. I know it's scary and unpleasant, but it's reality. The other reality is you have your life, no matter what happens to me, and you have to protect it and flourish. If you don't, what does it say about the way I raised you? In a few months, the reflection of my whole life will be on how my son succeeds. I'm not going to let you take a hit now and hamper your chances of attaining your full potential. You know that's the way it has to be, son."

Jake had tears in his eyes now, frightened by a world without the man who loved him and who he loved so dearly. He knew his dad was right. The best way for Jake to honor his dad was to live his life to the fullest. It was just hard right now, and he realized it was only getting harder.

"Dad, I don't know if I can do this! I love you, but you're asking so much of me!"

Jake's mother held her son tightly and he melted into her arms like a four year old child. Justin pitied the sight and blamed himself for his undisciplined past. He knew he had only a little time to right things, and it all hedged on his connection with Jake and what he could do to encourage him. He had been a good father, always loving and devoted to his son, but the one place he felt he had failed was in raising Jacob's confidence.

Not that this had been an easy task. For some reason Jake was filled with a feeling of inferiority the minute he came into life, and maybe nothing done by his parents could change that. Although Justin Riley knew this, he also knew it was no reason to give up on something so important.

"Jake, you know how hard it was for me to hear the news that the cancer was not only back, but stronger than ever? It ripped me apart inside. Your mother, too. We came back from that appointment in the worst spirits I can ever remember. When we got home, we turned on the

TV, knowing you were playing a day game. I watched you work fourteen pitches before lining a single up the middle and I was enraptured! One act from you erased all my fear, all my despair. This last month has sucked, and I've felt like shit because of it, but to see my son succeed has been my shining light. You need to keep going out there and playing, Jake. For me. It's meant so much, you can hardly imagine. I love you, son."

Jake looked over to his mom and saw the tears in her eyes flowing along with his as she nodded assertively at her husband's words. Jake stood up, his mother by his side, and hugged both of them tightly.

He loved them dearly and at that moment knew he had to do everything he could to help them, even if it was playing baseball.

"Dad, I'm so glad to hear that you're proud of me. I'm not going to let you down."

"That's my boy," Justin exclaimed, embracing his family warmly. "That's my boy."

CHAPTER 18

Tuesday night arrived, and the All-Star game was on in Jacob and Angie's apartment.

They had ordered a pizza and agreed to watch it together, although Angie wasn't excited about more baseball. Jake, despite wanting to watch the game, felt obligated to do so as both Shawn Hammel and Bob Oates would be representing the Cubs as substitutes, Hammel just losing out for the starting nod at shortstop.

The game had been somewhat boring and Angie was starting to yawn when the sixth inning rolled around. Just before Hammel came to bat, the doorbell rang.

"Who's that?" Angie asked. "Are you expecting someone, Jake?"

"No, I'm as surprised as you are, Ange," Jake replied, pausing the game and heading for the intercom.

"Who is it?" Jake asked while pushing the button.

"Cools Perez. Can I come up, Jake?"

"Sure, Cools," Jake answered with surprise, buzzing up his teammate.

"Cools Perez?" Angie asked. "How do I know that name?"

"Because he plays third base for the Cubs and bats right before me," Jake answered matter-of-factly with a hint of sarcasm.

"What does he want?"

"I don't know, Angie. That's why I buzzed him up."

"Well, try to get rid of him. We're spending alone time right now."

Jake opened the door and saw Cools standing there, wet from the light rain outside. Cools looked dejected, and Jake knew why.

"Hey, Cools," Jake welcomed unassumingly. "What brings you over here?"

"Hey, Jake, sorry for the interruption. Mind if I come in?"

"No, come inside."

Jake opened the door further and moved away to give Cools room to enter. Cools looked around as he took a few steps in.

"Wow, nice place."

"Thanks. Can I get you something to drink?"

"Jake!" Angie called from the other room. "What's going on?"

"Nothing, Ange, it's just Cools stopping by."

"What does he want?" she called out, leaving Jake in an awkward situation as Cools looked at him with a forced grin.

"I don't know yet, honey, I just let him in."

"Sorry to intrude," Cools called out to the unseen figure in the other room.

"It's OK, Cools," Jake answered for her. "She just gets edgy at night."

"I understand, Jake. Don't worry about me."

"So what's up? What brings you by?"

"Well, I'm sure you've heard."

Jake looked down, not able to meet Cools eyes to let him know he had heard. Brent Gruber was being called up from his wrist injury and would be starting at third base after the All-Star break. Cools Perez had been sent back down to AAA Iowa to work on his approach at the plate.

"Look, I understand the situation," Cools continued, "and I don't even want you to think this is because of you. Even though you take up a roster spot, I was given an opportunity, and I didn't exactly run away with it. I blame myself for this, and right now I'm looking for someone to talk to before I go back tomorrow."

"Well, why me? You have so many friends on the team. I thought you barely considered me an acquaintance."

"Well, I do have others I can go to, but I think you can help me more than the rest of them."

Jake looked back at him confused.

"Jake, I respect you, man. You have gone through all this adversity and somehow made it work. You've looked past all of us criticizing you, laughing at you, pretty much wanting you to fail, and you've ended up succeeding because of it."

"Well, I don't know about that…"

"Look, man, you've done what nobody in that locker room thought you could do. You have some sort of gift for the game. Not like I do or like Hammel does, but a way of understanding it, of dissecting it and learning from it. You found a way you could be successful where no one has before, and I can't help but respect that. I want to learn from that. I want you to teach me how not to strike out. After all, you were the king of it before!"

"You don't have to remind me," replied Jake, smiling.

"Come on. Come out with me to watch the last few innings of the game. I could really use it."

Jake thought about it, worried about Angie's response but acknowledging that Cools needed him right now and it would be wrong to send him out empty handed.

"Come with me, Cools," Jake instructed, leading him into the other room.

"Angie, I want you to meet Cools Perez."

Angie looked up from the couch, her head poking out of a sea of blankets.

"Nice to meet you, Cools," Angie greeted him hesitantly.

"It's nice to meet you, Angie," Cools said politely. "Jake talks very nicely of you. And quite a place you have here."

"Thanks," Angie said as she looked towards Jake. "Are you planning on staying?"

"Cools is going through a tough time right now, Angie," Jake interrupted. "I'm going to go out with him for a couple hours to talk it out if you don't mind."

"What about our night in together?" Angie countered, without the scorn Jake initially expected.

"Sorry, babe. We'll make up for it tomorrow."

"Fine," Angie answered coldly, turning her head away from the both of them.

"First, though, we have to watch Shawn bat," Jake said to Cools while grabbing the remote.

"He's up?"

"Just came up when you rang the bell so I paused it."

"Nice!" Cools exclaimed excitedly.

Angie gave a grunt and grabbed the blankets as she retired to her room, barely saying goodnight to their guest.

"Goodnight, Angie, it was great to finally meet you," Cools called out behind her.

Jake started the game up again and they watched Hammel work a full count before lining a single to right. They both cheered, but knew the moment had been tainted because of Angie's abruptness.

Jake pulled out two umbrellas as he knew it was raining and the two of them walked out together to head for one of the local bars.

"Here," he called out as he handed Cools the umbrella.

Cools opened it to see a large, obnoxious Cubs logo on the front.

"I'm not using this," he blurted out. "I like to try to hide the fact that I play for the team."

"Okay," Jake said, somewhat embarrassed. "We can share this one."

Cools looked at him with a surprised expression.

"I don't think I'll be walking down the street sharing an umbrella with you, dude."

"Fine," Jake said, now even more embarrassed, but trying to play it off. "Have fun getting wet!"

They walked three blocks to get to the sports bar off Clark street and sat down at a small two top, both facing the bar to get a good look at the game showing on two large screen televisions. The game was in the seventh with the National League up 2-1.

"So, I leave tomorrow for Iowa," Cools said, breaking the silence.

"You doing okay with it?"

"No. Well, maybe I am. I don't know," Cools was acting distraught while trying to be strong. "I got this great chance with Gruber being out, and I feel I blew it. For that reason, I'm okay with Bug's decision to send me down, but I'm upset with myself for not coming through when I needed to."

"That makes sense," Jake answered sympathetically.

"Does it?" Cools joked. "Because it sounded pretty messed up from this end."

"I know what you're saying, Cools."

Cools nodded, not knowing what to say next. He wasn't good at this kind of thing and he hoped Jake would be able to offer some solace while he struggled. Cools knew Jake was the one who had taken his spot to begin with, but he had gotten over that back in spring training when he realized if it wasn't Jake, it would have been someone else. Now he really didn't blame Jake.

Even with a legitimate shot to show some ability at third base, Cools still failed miserably. He realized he had only himself to blame. Now he looked at Jake as a friend and, surprisingly, a teammate.

Both began wondering where this conversation was going to lead and if it had been a good idea for them to both go out in the first place.

"Is that your real name?" Jake blurted out.

"What?"

"Cools," Jake answered confidently. "I always wondered how you got that name and if it was given to you by your parents."

"Ha!" Cools replied, a smile on his face. "I'm not sure anyone has ever asked me that before."

"Well, I never heard the name before, and assumed it was a nickname, but all your baseball statistics read 'Cools Perez.' So it got me thinking."

"Well, it wasn't my original name, that's for sure! You really want to know how I got it?"

"Yeah," Jake said excitedly. He realized he might be the only person on the team to know the truth. Jake enjoyed things like that.

"Okay. It actually happened when I was fourteen. I lived in Miami. It was a real poor neighborhood, mostly Hispanics there. We had this crappy park we played baseball at, but we were all pretty good. Playing ball was all we ever did and we took it seriously. So one year we won our district league and were asked if we wanted to play teams from around the area for an all star circuit. We were really excited because we only played in our little neighborhood and didn't get to travel much given our financial situations. The city said they would pay for uniforms and our travel, so we accepted.

"The first tournament we participated in was in the middle of Miami, and there were these four unbelievable fields we were able to play on. We had never seen fresh chalk or white bases. They even started the games with new baseballs. We were all so pumped. They told us we had to turn in official lineups, but we had no idea how to do it. We scribbled our names down on the back of a score sheet and gave them to this announcer who then called out what we wrote over the speaker system as we approached the plate. We couldn't believe we were hearing our names echoing across the field and everybody at the game would know who we were.

"Well, I was batting fourth and kept listening out for my name. My family was in the stands and I was looking out at them right before they announced me. I guess when we wrote out the lineup, our penmanship hadn't been the best, and my friend wrote out my real name, Carlos, all jumbled together. So this old white guy who was dressed in a suit couldn't decipher the writing, and instead of 'Carlos' he called out, 'Batting fourth, Cools Perez.' Everybody in our dugout, including me, started busting out laughing! Cools was so perfect, especially considering this white guy probably thought it made sense that some Hispanic kid like me from the poor side of town would be named 'Cools.' He called out 'Cools' every time I came up or made a play at short stop that game. After that, we wrote 'Cools' on the lineup card every time. I ended up being the MVP of the tournament and still have the trophy with the name 'Cools Perez' etched into it. Everyone on my team thought it was great, and I, the cocky kid I was, actually found it fitting, so it stuck. I always introduced myself as 'Cools,' and now that's what everybody knows. Great story, huh?"

It was a great story, at least in Jake's mind. He had been listening attentively, thoroughly entertained the whole time.

"I think I'm going to start calling you Carlos," Jake joked.

"Don't you dare, man!" Cools replied with a laugh. "I don't want anybody else knowing this!"

"Just joking with you, Cools. I really am sad you're going back down. I'm sure you'll be back up soon."

"Not if I keep striking out like I have been," Cools answered dejectedly. "That's one of the reasons I wanted to talk to you."

"Me?" Jake replied surprised. "No one has struck out more than I have!"

"Overall, maybe. But not as of late. You've really been seeing the ball well and getting the most out of at bats. That's where I've had trouble, and I've been doing this forever! You seem to have figured things out in just half a season, and I was hoping you had some advice for me."

"Cools, this might only be a lucky hot streak for me. I don't know baseball like you do, or especially like our coaches do. You should probably ask them for advice, not me. I might even make things worse for you."

Cools frowned. He didn't know Jake all that well, but he had seen this side of him. Cools was a great baseball player, but he also was good at reading people. He felt this was an advantage he used in dealing with pitchers. He could read what they were thinking and what kind of pitches they would throw in certain situations. It had helped him his whole life until he attempted the move up to the majors. Now he was listening to Jacob Riley underestimate himself again. He wasn't sure if it was because of humility or a lack of confidence, but figured it to be the latter. Either way, he was slightly irritated and even concerned about it.

"Riley, I'm not sure what it is with you—if you have some sort of inferiority complex or you can't handle a compliment—but I know you're not an idiot. You're probably the smartest guy on the team. It should be pretty obvious to you that you can do things us other guys can't and that you've figured out more about this game in six months than anyone else could have. You skipped college ball, all minor league levels, and still seem to be figuring it all out. You have talent, no doubt, but not the kind most of us do. You succeed because you have discovered how to make your strengths work with the game while the rest of us try to change ourselves to mold with the stereotypical baseball player. You see the difference there?"

Cools paused and looked Jake in the eyes to see if he was getting what he was saying.

"You could have never come into this league and caught up to the other players by doing things the same way we all have. It's impossible. You tried it, too, but realized it was too much. You had your ways of using speed and quickness to help you beat out close plays and steal some bases and you even used your work ethic to make you a somewhat respectable defender, but you found out it wasn't enough. That's when you started to wear out the pitchers in order to get on base and force good pitches which you could handle, giving you more hits. I've been here for the whole thing and I've noticed it hasn't just impressed me, but all the guys on the team and the coaches as well. You're no superstar, of course, but you are helping the team win games. I'm not sure there's another person on earth who could have done what you are doing."

"Well, others have done things similar..." Jake started.

"See? You're doing it again! Just take the compliment, man! You think it's easy for me to tell the guy who is keeping me in the minors that he's doing a good job? Just say thank you and use it to keep improving. You have a real problem with this!"

Jake acknowledged the criticism. It had always been true and the only people who called him out on it in the past were his family. It was easy for

Jake to ignore his parents when it comes to compliments. It always seemed as if they had a biased opinion and were only trying to push him forward.

When Cools told Jake the same thing, it made him understand the truth of it, and it had hit him squarely. He was in a sort of trance as he tried to process it and looked straight down at the table, seemingly ignoring Cools.

He wondered for a second, too, why he had never heard it from Angie.

"Are you even listening, Jake?"

"Yes! Sorry," Jake said, looking up and breaking out of his stupor. "I've listened to every word of it, and I thank you for it, Cools. You're right about it all, and I've always had a hard time accepting the truth when it comes to my abilities."

"Well, I didn't think anything I told you was news," Cools explained. "Maybe you've been so focused on baseball and improving that you haven't noticed how far you've come. But again, that's not why I invited you out tonight."

"Yeah, it seems like your problem somehow turned into us talking about me."

"Well, maybe that's necessary. See, I need you to help me. I know I can be a better hitter, but I have trouble making contact. You were the same way, but now you can fend off pitches with the best of them. I need to be able to do that. If I can, I'm sure I can cut down on my K's and start to produce better. That's how I'm going to succeed in the bigs."

"What if it cuts down on your power, though?"

"I think it will only make it better," Cools began. "If I can work counts into my favor and coerce pitchers to throw me the pitches I'm looking for, I can hit them with more authority."

"I never thought of it like that, Cools. I've always been trying to not strike out and get on base, but I guess I have gotten better pitches to hit as a result."

"That's why your average has started to climb. I also feel your first homer coming soon, if you can get a good pitch before you go into two-strike mode. So you think you can help me with it? Maybe I can work on it in Iowa and if I improve, hopefully I'll be back up as we make a little playoff push."

"Yeah, of course. I'll do what I can. Maybe tomorrow we can meet at the field and hit some balls."

"Remember what I told you when you wanted to wait until the next day to practice your pivot at second?"

"No time like the present?"

"You do remember! I've noticed that if I wait for things, I often never get around to them. If I feel an urge to improve myself, I do it immediately."

"But how are we going to..."

Jake was interrupted by the feeling someone was staring at them. He looked to his right and saw the bartender standing four feet from them, an embarrassed smile on his face. Cools saw Jake look over and turned to see the same man smiling at him. An awkward silence made things more uncomfortable.

"Can we help you?" Cools asked in an annoyed manner.

"I'm sorry to interrupt," the bartender answered uneasily. "Aren't you guys on the Cubs? You're Cools Perez, right? And Jake Riley?"

"Yeah, that's us," Cools replied frigidly.

"I knew it!" exclaimed the bartender excitedly, starting to attract some attention from the others at the establishment. "Joey! I told you it was Riley!"

Joey, the other bartender, walked over with a smile.

"Jacob Riley! I'm a big fan of yours. I've been rooting for you from the beginning!"

"Well, thank you," Jake answered politely.

"You, too, Mr. Perez," Joey added, turning to Cools. "I can't wait to see you start hitting for more power. I know you're in a transition period, but all us fans know you're going to be great for us!"

"Thanks," Cools said, warming up a little to the complimentary fans.

"Hey, Mr. Riley," Joey said, turning back to Jake, "can you show us all your two-strike stance? Everyone is talking about how great it is! How do you do it? How did you come up with it?"

"Uh, well, I just kind of let it happen, you know? I was tired of striking out every time at bat!"

Laughter burst out all around the two, forcing them to look around.

The whole bar was now surrounding them, eager to get into the conversation with the two local celebrities. Everyone seemed happy to be there and they hung on their every word.

"So, can you show us that stance?" Joey asked Jake again, proving it wasn't an empty request.

"Well, it's kind of hard to do without a bat," Jake said, trying to get out of it.

"Oh, no problem!" Joey responded happily. "I've got one in the back! And a wooden one, too. Not those cheap aluminum bats. Howard! Get me my bat! And bring two shots out for Mr. Riley and Mr. Perez. On the house!"

"See, Jake?" Cools stated, slyly looking at his friend. "No time like the present."

Jake smiled back. He had to admit this was kind of fun, regardless of how uncomfortable he was with all the attention. Jake hadn't ever received this much admiration and he handled it somewhat awkwardly at first, although Cools took it in like a pro.

The bat was brought out and the next two hours was filled with Jake and Cools demonstrating swings, stances, and anything else the crowd desired of them. Jake and Cools could say or do no wrong, the bar enjoying every minute of the entertainment as the bartenders continued to fill the two ballplayers with complimentary liquor. Nobody knew the outcome of the game as they stumbled home long after closing time. Jake and Cools had had a great time together and that allowed Perez to forget about his demotion, at least for the time being.

Everything seemed to be well until Jake awoke the next morning with a headache, much exacerbated by the scorn of an agitated Angie.

CHAPTER 19

The second half of the season started off as well for Jake as the first half had ended.

It was hard without his new ally, Cools, but his other teammates had started to accept him more than he was used to and much more than he had even thought possible. As Jake's ability elevated, so did his adoption into the sacred camaraderie of baseball. Even the opposing teams didn't show the hatred they once had.

Some of the treacherous media who had given Jake hell for months began to warm to his style and technique, too, and one source called him a "breath of fresh air to the rotting aura of Major League Baseball."

Jake continued his hot streak, bashing out twenty-six hits over the next twenty-five games and walking over twenty times. His average moved up to .196, and his on base percentage was at .298. Opposing starters loathed pitching to him, as he averaged over eight pitches per plate appearance, the most in baseball, and that number continued to climb.

Jake's confidence was soaring with his statistics and everyone in Chicago seemed to notice. Jake moved up in the order to the eighth spot and had his first intentional walk in the second week of the second half. It was a sign of respect, and Jake loved it. Everybody seemed to be excited about his ascension except, of course, Casey Earl.

The Cubs were enjoying Jake's contributions and they continued their rise in the standings. They were now eight games over .500, four months into the season, putting them in third place in their division and sixth in the league. It was the best ball they had played in years and most of the credit was going to Bug Wagner. People talked about his ability to mold the young players and his patience with them over the last few years.

Now that they were blossoming, the manager responsible was finally getting the respect he deserved. His team hung on his every word, believing their wise manager could lead them to greatness. With most of the team on board, the players had common goals and helped each other in their success, and the Cubs kept winning.

The only real outsider in the system was Casey Earl. He wasn't particularly excited about Jacob Riley getting into a groove. Earl's plan had been to have Riley out of the game before the start of the second half. Now it looked like Jake was there for the remainder of the year. Earl was still only playing after the seventh inning of each game or in the one of six games Jake had off.

His bitterness affected his play as much as his inconsistent appearances did. Casey was only batting .229, not much higher than Jake's average, and his on base percentage was even lower than Riley's. Earl knew his defense was still much better, but the gap had closed since the beginning of the season.

Not only that, but the other players seemed to warm to Jake in a way that infuriated Earl. In the beginning, everybody seemed to be on board with Casey's criticism of the rookie second baseman. Now they had grown tired of it. A couple of the players even told Casey to take it easy on Riley, criticism that burned a scar in the center of Earl's soul. He was losing the battle and he only blamed Riley all the more for that.

The game played on July 27th finally threw Earl off the cliff he had been dangling over for months.

Jake was still playing better. His approach at the plate had been beautiful, wreaking havoc with the psyche of the opposing pitchers. Jake had been to bat three times against the Cincinnati Reds at the Great American Ballpark. He had walked, singled and doubled with two runs scored and three RBIs. He stole two bases, committed no errors, and even made a great play at second base.

The Cubs were up a comfortable 9-2 in the eighth inning when Jake's spot in the lineup came up.

There had never been a question about when Earl replaced Riley in a game. Ever since the beginning of the season Jake had been pulled in the eighth inning for the veteran.

Today Jake sat on the bench as the seventh batter was in the box. Earl was up and he was moving into the on-deck circle when Bug called him back in.

"Earl, sit down," Wagner called out. "I'm going to let Riley finish this one out."

Jake heard this and his eyes grew wide. He was excited by the opportunity, of course, but also worried about the repercussions. He didn't want to disobey his manager and he quickly got up from the bench and headed towards the on-deck circle, passing Earl while doing so.

As Jake was trying to get around his teammate, careful not to make eye contact with Casey, he felt a hand on his chest resist his forward movement.

"Hold on there, Rook," Casey said to Jake before he turned to his manager. "What's the deal, Bug? It's my turn to go in."

"Jake's played a great game, Casey, and we already have this one won. Let the kid finish a game for once. He deserves it."

Jake didn't move, nor could he in the close quarters of the dugout with Earl's hand firmly on his sternum. The others on the bench couldn't look away. They didn't want to side with either party, but they were more than interested in where the confrontation was going.

"Now look here, Bug," Earl responded coldly. "I'm the second baseman on this team. The only reason I get such little playing time is this gimmick Dillinger threw at us. Now I know he's been playing better, but he's still a joke to this team and to our game. Maybe it's not his fault, but it ain't mine, either! I have to sit here and suffer as he gets all my playing time. I'm not giving up an ounce of it to him, no matter how good it makes you or him feel, got it?"

It wasn't uncommon for a player to disagree with his manager or even call him out during a game, especially a veteran like Earl, but it was still disrespectful. The other players knew this but stayed silent and let their manager answer Earl's scorn.

"Well, Casey, it's just two innings," Bug answered calmly, not wanting an escalation of Earl's attitude and insolence. "I have to make the decisions around here."

"Then decide to put me up to bat, Bug," Earl said condescendingly through clenched teeth.

"Just sit down, Casey," Bug said, the other players remaining silent. "I need you to respect my calls."

"I can't respect this one, Bug!" Earl attacked, his arm now more forceful upon Jake's chest. "Now I've sat back calmly and waited this whole ridiculous thing out, but it's not getting any better. Now I'm supposed to give up my at bats because he's playing a little better? Let me bat!"

The tone was showing Casey Earl on top of this argument, but Bug was not backing down. The Cub's manager didn't expect such hostility from a player, but now he felt he couldn't change his decision without losing respect from his players.

Bug was ready for an all out war with his veteran second baseman when someone rushed to his side. Shawn Hammel, fire in his eyes, stepped up to Casey Earl and shoved him forcefully onto the bench.

"Sit your ass down, Earl, and get your hands off Riley!" Hammel shouted at the oppositional veteran. "Jake, do as Bug said and get up to bat!"

Jake hurried past Hammel to the on-deck circle while Earl looked away, ashamed he let Shawn Hammel get the better of him.

"Now you're taking Riley's side?" Casey whined.

"No, I'm taking my manager's side," Hammel replied. "Just like everyone else should be doing! This is the guy that's righted the ship here, and my allegiance is to him. Yours would be, too, if you thought of the team instead of yourself."

"Come on, Hammel," Casey pleaded, trying to recover some dignity in front of the rest of the team, "you know this team would be better off if I was playing instead of Riley!"

"It would be a hell of a lot more convincing if you could bat over .230," Hammel retorted to the chuckles and snorts from the rest of the bench.

Earl had been put in his place, and now it was by the team's best player, not Jacob Riley or even Bug Wagner. Casey realized he was losing his position and his status with the Cubs and now the respect of his teammates as well.

What happened next solidified his sentiments.

Jake was happy to get away from Casey and the confrontation in the dugout. Conflict was never his thing. He had been uncomfortable and afraid Earl would escalate to the point of violence. Jake took his practice swings, but could only think of what had just happened on the bench. When he came up to the plate, he wasn't thinking of his regular swings or his need to work the count in his favor. He was only feeling his heart beating out of his chest while his cheeks were hot and red from the conflict he had avoided.

He didn't even realize what he was swinging at when a 2-1 fastball came in belt high.

Jake was filled with rage and fear, and his swing accentuated it. He was not even concentrating on the pitch, but his instincts kicked in perfectly. Jake swung long and hard at the fastball, sending it high into the air towards left-center. He didn't realize what he had done until he saw the ball soaring towards the seats and then all his concern, anger and trepidation vanished.

His cheeks grew cool and his lips turned upward as the center fielder looked up hopelessly at the wall to see the ball sail into the stands. Jake's first major league home run was almost effortless and it came at the most unexpected time, sending a rush of adrenaline through his body.

He clenched his fist as he rounded first base and noticed he couldn't stop smiling. He touched all the bases and was welcomed in the dugout by a team full of excited players slapping his hand and congratulating him on his first dinger.

Jake had almost completely forgotten about the incident that preceded his at bat until he saw a warm, proud smile on his manager's face, but a dejected Casey Earl sitting on the bench, looking straight down at the pavement.

That was the last time Jake would let Casey Earl get to him.

CHAPTER 20

Casey Earl was no dummy.

He had always been well versed in the game, but his intelligence outside the game was well known, too. He had great business sense and did well managing his money. Earl appeared in multiple fundraising stints to build his reputation with the fans of the city and he always said great things about not only the city he played in, but every city he visited, knowing one day he could be at the mercy of its fan base.

Casey had rarely burned bridges, but this season he found himself doing so often with the Chicago Cubs.

Earl's temper was the only thing greater than his intelligence, and it was getting the best of him. Casey couldn't hide his frustration with his decreased playing time and rusty skill set. He knew it was getting harder and harder to justify a good contract after the season if he continued to rot on the bench while Jacob Riley continued to garner support from the city and from baseball fans. He had already made an enemy in Bug Wagner and he had started to do the same with some prominent teammates.

He felt his time in Chicago might be close to over and he began contemplating his next move.

Casey knew he wanted to be traded and was hoping to a contender. He believed the Cubs could get a team to give them something valuable for the veteran. If he were able to play more, he knew he could get his name out there and his average up in order to make a good salary for at least next year, if not longer. He had always hoped it would be with the Cubs, but now he sensed that time had passed and he had to move on.

Where to move on to was a serious question, but now it was the ultimate one.

The best fit would probably be the New York Mets, as he was raised in the area and the fans knew him well, but their second baseman had been excelling and it was doubtful he would get any more playing time there than he did with the Cubs. That left the Cardinals, who were currently in first place, but had a switch hitting second baseman who was hitting lefties poorly and not doing a great job defensively. If Casey could get to St. Louis, he knew he could at least play against lefty pitchers, and maybe more, because he was an upgrade in defense over their current player.

How to get this trade was tricky, but Casey was a smart man. Ever since he had come over to the Cubs, he had become good friends with the General Manager who had brought him there, Tex Klondike. The two could be seen regularly having drinks after games or dinners while on the road. Casey liked the big Texan because of his demeanor and his respect towards the game, but the best thing about Tex was that he knew things.

Tex was someone Casey was sure he could count on when the chips were down, and now was that time. He was confident he could ask Tex to get him a trade, maybe even to the Cardinals, because they were good friends. Besides, Casey might have even known a little more than he should have about why Dillinger brought in Jacob Riley. Tex had told him a lot of things he wasn't supposed to when he had been drinking.

"Thanks for coming out to dinner with me tonight," Casey said across the table to Klondike after the series finale in Cincinnati. "Hope everything has been good?"

"Well, Case, it's been busy," Tex replied. "We're still trying to get a big trade in to improve the team before the deadline. I probably need to cut out early tonight. Just between us, we have something possibly brewing with the Orioles."

"Well, no one can complain with the job you did this year, Tex. Cubbies finally looking like a playoff contender!"

"Yeah, thanks," Tex answered protectively, knowing Casey wasn't as excited about his team as he might be portraying. "It's been a good year, considering our handicaps."

"Riley, right," Casey answered. "I know that all too well. Now it seems like he's not going anywhere. He's showed enough improvement to not completely suck, and everybody gives him slack because he's not a real ballplayer. To me, that's the big problem! How do you go into a playoff race with a gimmick out there! They can't win like that!"

"Well, Case, if you guys do go to the playoffs, I'm pretty sure Bug will be able to play you whenever he wants. Dillinger's rules on Riley's play was only during the regular season."

"Sure, but what if they don't make the playoffs? Or what if Bug gets pissed enough at me that he actually plays Riley? If that happens, I'll be lucky for any team to sign me next year."

Tex started to understand Casey wasn't there just for pleasure that night. There was something on his mind. He suspected Casey needed his help. Tex might have enjoyed the company of Earl over the years, but he also knew the player's motives and how they weren't always in accordance with the needs of the team.

"Well," Tex said, "you guys are in sixth right now, four games ahead of the eighth spot. It's hard to believe we won't make the playoffs."

The format of the playoffs had changed three years before. With baseball's reputation hurting and its fan base thinning, Major League Baseball decided to increase the amount of playoff teams, hoping to raise the excitement of the fans for a longer period. With over half the teams making the playoffs and having a chance of getting to the World Series, fans could stay tuned in for much longer into the season.

There were still three divisions in each league, with the division winners getting the top three spots and the best records attaining the fourth through eighth spots. The first two series were best of five while the league championship and World Series remained best of seven.

To keep the season from getting too far out of October, all games during each series were back to back, without any off days until that series was over. It had worked well since its introduction and the Cubs were looking to make their first playoffs in over five years.

"I also believe," Tex continued, "that once Bug's hands aren't tied, he'll play the best man in the big games."

"You're probably right, Tex, but I don't know that I want to take that chance," Earl stated clearly.

Tex was now assured of the reason for their meeting. Casey wanted out of Chicago and expected Tex to pull off some magic to get that done. Tex knew an Earl trade wasn't a priority at this point and that nobody in Chicago would be excited about the low-level prospect he might get in return for the veteran second baseman.

He also knew Casey had something on him, and he was sure he would use it if Tex refused, so Tex decided on a different tactic.

"You don't want to be traded now, Casey."

"Like hell I don't, Tex! You see where this is going. It's not looking good for me. I can't stick around here decaying until the playoffs and then roll the dice from there! You can get me to the Cardinals, I know it."

"St. Louis!" Tex replied dejectedly. "I can't send you to a team that's in our division. Cubs fans will hate me for it, especially if you help them win the division. You gotta see how difficult it would be to do what you're asking here."

"Come on, Tex, don't make me do this. You know you can do this for me and we can remain civil through it all."

"I know you're talking about the Riley bet, Case, and it isn't fair for you to bring that up. We were talking in confidence that night and we'd both been drinking. I felt bad for what happened to you and I let the cat out of the bag. Why use that against me? We're friends, and I'll help you get somewhere else, just not St. Louis!"

"I don't want to use it, Tex, but you're leaving me no choice! The Cards need a good right handed bat against lefties and an infield defensive replacement. It also happens they are a playoff contender, and that's all the better for me, right? It makes sense. You're not using me anyway! Don't make me go public with this, Tex. Call them. I'm only asking you to inquire. Please?"

"Oh, all right, Casey, but I can't guarantee anything! I'll call them and see what they think, but that's it! If they aren't interested, it's the end of the conversation. I'm not going to push it and look foolish in a trade that gives us nothing and gives the Cardinals a better playoff team!"

"OK, Tex, I believe you," Earl said with a grin. "Just make sure you go through with it. You don't want to go out of baseball on a bad note, leaking the truth about Dillinger and destroying your reputation amongst the baseball elite while also admitting that you knew something about this awful bet."

Tex took a large sip from his Tom Collins as he pondered the scenario. He knew Earl was right on all accounts, and he didn't want to see his good name soiled right before he was about to retire. On the other hand, it could happen anyway, although not to such an extent, if he pulled off a trade with St. Louis and it helped them win yet another World Series, especially if it was by beating the Chicago Cubs during that playoff run.

He would have to hope the Cardinals weren't interested in Earl and Tex could then get him to a different team, possibly outside the National League. Unfortunately for Tex, his luck had never been that good.

CHAPTER 21

It turned out the Cardinals were very interested in Casey Earl.

They had been thinking he would be good addition to their lineup and knew the Cubs weren't really using him, but they never inquired because they figured the Cubs didn't want to trade him to a division rival. Luckily for Tex, they were willing to part with one of their mid-level relievers, giving the Cubs some depth in their bullpen.

The Chicago papers still disagreed with the trade and wrote that the Cardinals had won out on the deal and now might be even better poised to knock the Cubs out of the playoffs, but Tex still felt the overall damage was less than he had anticipated. He now hoped Earl kept up his part of the bargain and kept his mouth shut about the Jacob Riley issue.

With the back up second baseman traded away and a pitcher going to the disabled list, there was room for a call up from the minors. Cools Perez was chosen immediately.

Cools had learned to be more patient at the plate over his four weeks in Iowa and had reduced his strikeouts while raising his walks and on base percentage. His power had not changed much, but his defense had benefited from his going back to his natural position, second base.

Bug felt Cools could spell Riley at second and also fill in around the rest of the infield when time off was needed. Perez's bat was seen as a boon to the bench as well.

Jake and the Cubs continued to play well, but the teams above them were staying hot, too. The Cubs remained in the sixth playoff spot through August, expanding their lead over the seventh place Giants. The Cardinals continued to be the best team in the Central Division, as well as the National League.

Casey Earl had become a plus to their infield and the Cards increased their lead over the Cincinnati Reds in the Central and over the New York Mets in the league. The Dodgers were the first place team in the West with a small lead over the San Francisco Giants.

The West was the weak division that year, the two playoff contenders barely above .500, but the winner still would hold the third spot in the playoffs, as the Dodgers currently did. Cincinnati was fourth and the Atlanta Braves were fifth.

With only a month left in the season those standings looked solid and besides the tight race in the West for first place, it didn't look like there would be much change by the end of the year unless a team got really hot or cold.

Jake continued his patient hitting and found himself seeing a lot more fastballs early in the count as pitchers had become wary of increasing their pitch count. Jake hit .267 in August, boosting his season average to .211 and his on base percentage rose to .315. He hit two more home runs in August, tripling his amount for the year, and stole ten bases in that month, too, increasing his total to thirty-seven.

His defense was improving as well. He committed only six errors in the month and was now at forty-seven total, still the highest in baseball. He was playing through nine innings almost every day without Earl there to take the last two, but still he took every sixth day off with Cools replacing him.

Three times in the month Bug even let him bat second, knowing Jake's patience at the plate raised pitch counts and forced starters out early. If the Cubs were up against one of the better pitchers in the league, Bug batted Jake early and told him to foul off as many pitches as he could to tire out the starter. Jake did so regularly, to the delight of his manager and the rest of the team. Jake was a weapon now, and Bug used him to the best of his ability.

Jake's comfort level also soared over the second half of the season. He no longer feared baseball. Perhaps it was his increased success combined with the acceptance of his teammates, or maybe even the trade of his biggest adversary to the Cardinals, but whatever the reason, Jake was shining. He was playing almost to the level of his peers and they recognized it and rewarded him for it with friendliness and acceptance.

The amount that Jake had overcome was so great that most players as well as fans couldn't believe it had been possible. There were even theories from the press that Jacob Riley wasn't really some guy off the street and that Big Eddy Dillinger had lied about the whole thing, bringing in a player that had more experience than anyone had first known about.

It was hard for anyone to fathom that Jake could be in the position he was, but the reality trumped the doubt most had and Jake benefited greatly from that.

This benefit wasn't solely in the baseball world, either. Jake's relationship status had taken quite a hit and Jake was defending himself and his family more against Angie. She didn't appreciate Jake's new found self confidence. It was causing her to lose the grip on him she had spent so much time perfecting.

The two fought regularly and Jake found himself realizing more and more that she wasn't right for him and she probably never had been. Angie, on the other hand, felt she had to fight harder to keep her hold on Jake and she was doing everything she could to solidify their relationship. Unfortunately for her, it was pushing Jacob away at an even greater rate than before and she found her life turning upside down.

The greatest damage occurred while Jake and the Cubs were enjoying a ten game home stand at the end of August.

Jake had just gotten home after the Cubs finished a 1:20 pm scheduled game, winning it in extra innings to take two of three from the Reds. It was now 7:30 and Angie had been waiting for him to return so they could get dinner. When Jake walked in the door, she was fully dressed to go out, complete with the look of scorn at the man who had now kept her waiting.

"Oh, hey babe," Jake greeted her, hoping to alleviate some of the tenseness he sensed walking in the door. "You want to go out to grab a bite? We have an off day tomorrow so we can stay out late if you'd like."

"I wanted to go out two hours ago," Angie snapped back, erasing the hope Jake had for any congeniality. "Where have you been?"

"I was at the ballpark!" Jake answered. "We had a game today!"

"You're usually back from your 1:20 games by 5:30. It's past 7:30 now! I've been waiting this whole time!"

"We went into extra innings, Ange, what could I do?"

"Maybe you could've called and let me know?"

"Called in the middle of the game?" Jake answered sarcastically. "I can't do that. I have to focus on my job."

"Yeah, I know where your focus has been lately, Jake," Angie quipped, "and it's not on me!"

"You're one to talk," Jake retorted. "You're saying you didn't even know I was at the ballpark? Weren't you watching the game? Do you ever watch me play?"

"You know I don't care for baseball," Angie answered. "I've never watched it! You can't expect me to now."

"I don't expect you to like baseball or even want to see how the Cubs are doing, but don't you care about how I'm doing? Don't you want to see me play? I would think somebody who cared about her boyfriend would be interested in how he was doing! This is the most exciting thing that has ever happened to me, and I can't even share it with you because you refuse to get involved with it!"

"What is it with this attitude you have, Jake? You never used to talk like this to me. I'm your girlfriend. Doesn't that mean something to you? Show me some respect!"

"Respect is all I've ever given you, Angie. I want you to start returning the favor."

"What, respect you because you're some big shot athlete now? You never earned that. You just got lucky you were in the right place at the right time! I'm not going to get all excited over that!"

"Well, you seem to be excited enough about it to sit back and cash in while I earn all the money. You haven't complained about that!"

"How dare you!" Angie shouted. "Do you think I care about the money when I don't get to see you at all? I'm more upset now than before all this happened. I was satisfied when we had no money and no nice place because I got to see you. Now I sit here in this apartment, lonely, because you can't find the time to keep me happy. This wasn't what I wanted!"

"I'm sorry if that's the case, Angie, but this is where we are now! I have at least another month in the season and we're going to have to get through it whether you like it or not. If you want to say we did this for me, then fine. It was for me. Aren't you glad I'm happy with what I'm doing, that I've accomplished something and have finally felt good about myself? Isn't that important to you, at least because it's important to me?"

"Of course I'm happy when you are, Jake," Angie said carefully after a small pause. "But we both need to be happy, and that's not happening right now. I find it a little selfish of you to ask me to do this for such a long period while you are the only one smiling through it."

"Well, I'm not smiling now, Ange."

Angie sighed deeply and walked up to Jake, giving him a hug and putting her head into his chest.

"Look, Jake, I know I've been testy lately and this has really gotten to me, so a lot of this arguing is my fault. I realize that, and I'm sorry."

Jake couldn't believe Angie was not only taking the blame for this, but apologizing as well. On top of that, she initiated the embrace they were now both enjoying to give him comfort. Jake wondered if his confidence and ability to fight back had finally gotten him somewhere in the relationship.

It was what he wanted, as he knew he loved Angie and was comfortable with her, but he felt it wasn't going to work because he was certain she couldn't change. Now, for a quick moment, she had given him hope.

"You know, Jake, this will all be over soon, and I know we can get back to how we were. You working at the lab, me at the restaurant, spending our evenings together and not worrying about the rest of the world. We have plenty of money stashed away from this whole venture and we'll be able to live comfortably for awhile, maybe even get married. Then we can forget this whole thing ever happened and everything will be just how it was before all this began."

Jake grew uneasy. He hadn't really had time to think about what would happen after the season was over, but the last thing he'd ever imagine would be everything going back to how it had been. Jake had been invigorated by his success and enlivened by his ability. Slumping down in the lab again and cutting himself off from everything in the world except Angie began to frighten him.

It had been all he wanted before baseball and now it scared him to death to go back to it. Jake had finally woken up, and he didn't want to return to his deflating slumber again. Jake loosened their embrace and looked Angie directly in the eyes.

"Angie, I don't want to go back to the lab after all this."

"What do you mean, Jake?"

"I can't go from this to that suffocating lab."

"Well, sure, Jake, that's fine," Angie mustered. "I was just meaning that you could go back to how you were before all this. It doesn't matter what job you take."

"That's just it, Angie, I don't want to go back to who I was. I was scared, frightened of the world and what it held for me. I never realized what I had inside of me. It was trying to get out for so long, and I finally gave it a chance!"

"Gave what a chance, Jake? You're no different than before. Don't try to be someone you're not."

"I've been doing that my whole life, Ange. I'm not some loser, you know."

"I never said you were a loser, Jake!"

"No, Angie, but you acted like it."

"This is ridiculous!" Angie shouted defensively as she pushed Jake's hands away from her. "I'm the one who has always been there for you no matter what! When you were nothing, I stayed right here by your side and got you through it. Now you have this fame from being on the Cubs and you have the audacity to say I've been holding you down? I'm the best thing that's ever happened to you. Can't you see that?"

"Then tell me this, Angie, and be truthful," Jake said, looking directly into her eyes. "Do you think I'm the best thing that's ever happened to you?"

Angie paused, never having considered the question before. She feared the way Jake peered at her and knew he would detect any lie that came from her lips. She never thought Jake was anything but security for her, someone to make her feel better about herself.

He had never been any good, but that was the point. She didn't want someone who was good for her, she wanted someone who was comfortable for her.

Jake, unfortunately, had felt the same way until now.

"That's what I thought, Ange," Jake said with disgust. "You never thought anything of me, and now I am somebody and you can't handle it. Your grip has loosened and it's killing you. Well, I'm glad that for once it's not killing me."

Angie could say nothing. She knew he was right, but she had never expected him to realize it. She was a parasite and her host had suddenly identified it. She knew there was no more to say. Jake was freed from her and she would have to find someone else to live off. She looked down sadly.

"I'm going to my parents," Jake said. "You have until the end of the month to leave here. I'm not paying the rent after that. Take care of yourself, Ange."

Jake walked out on a tearful Angie, but he did not mind. He knew all her sadness was a result of her actions, not his. His confidence allowed him now to be comfortable with who he was and what he had done, not with the results. Angie was temporarily beaten down and defeated, but Jake was only protecting himself from one of the most harmful situations of all, the defeated spirit.

Jacob Riley had freed himself of despair by changing his outlook, and the transparency was leading him to the things he could previously only have dreamed about.

CHAPTER 22

Jake flagged down a cab and headed to his parents' house.

He figured he could stay there until the end of the month and then start looking for an apartment of his own. His parents were always his backup, reaching out to him whenever he was in need. Jake adored them for it and knew they would give him comfort after what had happened with Angie.

After exiting the cab, Jake walked up the familiar sidewalk to his parents' home. It had been his home for years and, secretly, he still considered it so. It was warm and welcoming for him to climb the stairs and open the always unlocked door without needing to knock. The front room was empty but lit, and Jake assumed his mother was in the kitchen and his father in the bedroom.

"Jake? Is that you?" his mother called out from the kitchen.

"Hey mom," he responded.

"Great game today," she stated as she walked into the front room, welcoming him with a kiss on the cheek. "I was so worried you guys wouldn't pull it off, going into extra innings and all. You made a great play in the tenth. It might have saved the game!"

Jake's mom had always been a baseball fan and loved defense. She had preached it while he was younger and Jake had listened. Loretta Riley was probably the reason Jake was now adept on the infield. Jake's father had echoed his mother's sentiment, but he was more of a sucker for a good bat and he often coached Jake on different ways to approach the plate. Because of the Riley's love for baseball and for their son, this had been the most exciting season ever and they never missed a pitch.

"Thanks, mom. It was nice to take the series from Cinci. They've played us well all season. Dad up in bed?"

The answer came from a cry at the top of the stairs and both Jake and his mother turned to the noise.

"Jake? Is that you, son?"

Justin Riley was coming down the stairs via the mechanical chair Jake had bought him four weeks prior. The chair came into view with Mr. Riley on it, frail, pale and gaunt. Every time Jake saw him he was thinner and more sickly. His strength continued to be sapped and Jake felt the changes were so rapid it was as if he could see him dying right before his eyes.

"I hope I didn't wake you, dad," Jake said as he greeted him with a hug at the bottom of the stairs. Jake helped him over to the couch.

"No, I was about to retire when I heard you come in," the elder Riley responded. "Great game tonight, son. You really threw their pitchers off today. It was a big win for the team in general, too. You don't want to fall in the standings now. You guys are on pace to maybe face Los Angeles in the playoffs. I know you can handle them. And from there, who knows?"

"Yeah, things are looking pretty good, at least for the Cubs, right?" Jake answered.

The three of them giggled, knowing how hard it was to be a Cubs fan and how much each opportunity for the playoffs made the city downright giddy. When the Cubs were playing well, you could be sure the whole north side was talking about it excitedly while the whole south side spoke about it nervously and despairingly, professing confidence in the Cubs choking yet another season away.

Jake sat close to his father on the couch, their hips and torsos touching intimately. The view from his mother's arm chair across from the two of them showed her son awkwardly close to his father, yet genuinely comfortable with the situation. Jake knew he didn't have much longer with his father and didn't care how childish he might have appeared.

Jake loved his dad immensely and felt his heart breaking down as quickly as his father's body was. He was going to spend every moment of his time with him, as close to him as possible, in order to never regret consuming their last hours together in a state of spiritless, commonplace apathy.

The truth was Justin Riley adored every minute of his son's tireless affection.

"So, what do we owe the pleasure, Jake?" Loretta Riley questioned. "I thought you and Angie would be enjoying the night, considering you're off tomorrow."

"Yeah," Jake answered hesitantly, "I thought so, too. But it looks like I might need to stay here for a while if it's okay with you two."

"What?" Justin spurted out with surprise. "She threw you out?"

"Well, no," Jake responded clumsily, "I kinda walked out."

His parents couldn't help but widen their eyes in surprise. It was astounding enough to hear that Jake and Angie had broken up, but to hear Jake had initiated it was truly remarkable. Neither of his parents wanted to show any signs of happiness or relief at this point, though. They knew their son was hurting and it would be wrong to seem delighted by his misfortune. They also didn't want to get Jake angry at them during a time when he had come to them for comfort. That kind of behavior could send him back to Angie.

Instead, the two of them just stared at their son in silence, neither wanting to say the wrong thing and both hoping Jake would continue with more details.

Jacob sensed this and he spoke further.

"Look, I know you two don't exactly love Angie, and that's okay."

The two continued to watch their son silently.

"I also know you think she's wrong for me."

"We've never said that, dear," Loretta answered.

"No, but I doubt you'll dispute it, either," Jake said, pausing momentarily to be assured that the verifying silence would continue. "Really, I don't mind your thoughts about us. I never did. Angie is very controlling and I probably wasn't the best person I could be with her. It's funny, but I think it took baseball for me to realize that. Anyway, I think it's time for me to move on in my life and I see Angie holding me back from doing what I need to do to be happy. So it's okay if I stay here?"

"Of course!" the two blurted out in almost perfect unison before they looked at each other and silenced themselves embarrassingly.

"It won't be for too long," Jake started.

"Son, you take as long as you need here," Justin replied. "You know you're not only always welcome, but encouraged to stay with us. We love having you."

"Thanks. It's nice to know I still have a home here."

"Well, now that we know you'll be here a while, don't you think it's time you get to bed, Justin?" Loretta remarked.

"Actually, dear, I was hoping to talk with Jake a little, if you don't mind."

"No, not at all," Loretta said, understanding her men's need for some alone time together. "I'll meet you upstairs."

Loretta kissed her son and again welcomed him home. She let him know his room was still made up and there were towels in his bathroom. She also told him she loved him and was sorry for his loss before she finally said good night and walked upstairs.

"You've really been getting on base a lot, Jake."

"Yeah, I feel I keep getting better at working the counts and I've also gotten better at laying off the bad ones. With more repetition I keep improving my eye. It's really been refreshing to contribute to the team after I held them back for so long."

"Well, it's funny," Justin replied. "These at bats where you work the pitch count have really benefited you because you're seeing more pitches and learning more during each at bat than the other guys. For some, it doesn't matter as much, but for you, being so new at it, I think it benefits you immensely."

"It has, dad. And when I see a good pitch to hit after two strikes, I've been doing some good things. Poking fastballs through the right side of the infield. Hitting the ball up the middle. Pulling the off speed pitches down the left field line. It's been fun."

"I've noticed that on your three home runs you hit pitches early in the count — before you got to two strikes — and had some power behind your swings."

"Well, I can actually hit the ball a long way during batting practice when I know I'm just getting fastballs. My training this last winter strengthened me tremendously, not to mention the great bat speed it gave me. The problem is I'm not at all comfortable enough to swing at most of those early pitches. I feel much better when I choke up on the bat after two strikes and try to place the ball somewhere instead of fully hitting it. It's worked well for me."

"No doubt about it, son. Your ingenuity, as always, has allowed good things to happen for you. But I do fear what will happen when the pitchers start to adapt to it."

"What do you mean, dad?"

"Well, you've become a creature of habit. Everyone knows you're more comfortable after two strikes, and most of the pitchers are throwing fastballs right down the middle until they hit two strikes because they know you're usually going to lay off of them. It's their way of decreasing their pitch count when you're up."

"Well, that's true," Jake conceded, "but what else am I going to do? If I start swinging at the earlier pitches, I have a higher chance of making an out and not raising the pitch count. Bug's depending on me to tire out the pitchers and it's been working great. I'm not going to give up on it now."

"It might hurt you in the future, though. The pitchers will adapt and you might end up right back to where you were at the beginning of the season."

"Dad, there's only a month left. I'm not too worried about how the pitchers will learn my approach for the future. I won't be around by then."

"That's not necessarily true!" Justin argued in defense of his son. "I read an article in the Tribune on how the Cubs might not let you go after this season. They might find a use for you next year, too, with the different style you bring to the team."

"I read that article too, dad, but it's just one writer. Let's face it. I'm lucky to have as much success as I've seen already. I should be happy with that and not worry about next year."

"But you've worked so hard, and you love what you're doing, I can tell! Why not put everything out there for a chance to keep playing ball? It could happen, especially if you get out there and go for it! Think about those homers you hit! You have that potential, too."

"Dad, those were fat pitches I got early in the count and I knew they were coming. All three times I had a 3-1 count…"

"The second homer was on a 2-1 count, son."

Jake paused and laughed quietly to himself. Even in an argument he loved knowing his dad was his biggest fan and knew every play that he was ever involved in and had it memorized to recall at any time he needed it.

"Okay, still," Jake replied, "they were on good counts and I could take a full swing. I can't do that all the time."

"Of course not all the time, but you can do it more often if you took some chances on those early fastballs these pitchers have been tossing to you. Get ahead of them, make the transition before they do and you'll continue to shine. I know you can!"

"I know you think I can, dad, but I'm not cut out for this! I got lucky to find a loophole in the system with something I'm good at is all. That's why I've been better than anyone thought I could be. But let me be happy with that. There's no reason to go thinking about the slim chances of me making the team next year and then getting disappointed by my probable failure. I want this to be remembered as a good part of my life."

"Son, that's not the way a winner thinks. Stop discrediting yourself for your successes. You're the one who found a loophole and you're the one who was smart enough to take advantage of it in a way nobody else has ever done. That's what winners do! You're that person now! Don't feel like you have to settle only because you're afraid to fail."

"I've come a long way, dad, but I have to be realistic! It's not logical to think I can keep doing this. I've been getting lucky and I don't want to keep pushing it."

"You're reasoning things out in order to make it easier on yourself, son, but you know how to use that logic in better ways. You've already used your mind to give yourself an edge. I don't want to see you take that same reasoning skill to bury yourself!"

"I won't be buried, dad. I'll still have all the memories of this and I'll probably be able to go on to graduate school or something like that with all the money I have stored away."

"Why graduate school? Why not medical school? That's what you really want, isn't it?"

"Yeah," Jake conceded again, "but I don't know if I can do that. I don't even know if I can get in."

"Enough of this!" shouted Justin in an angry, raspy voice. "I can't stand hearing you talk this way anymore, Jake! I'm dying. I'm dying soon, and you're what I'm leaving behind. And you're wonderful, more than I could ever believe I deserved. But you don't even know it! You don't believe it or believe in yourself! I was hoping the success you had recently would help you understand how special you are and how powerful you are, but I know that's not always enough. You need to have what it takes to succeed, and I'm not talking about baseball, son, I'm talking about life. About your inner struggles and how you treat the world and more importantly how you let it treat you. You have all the tools, but you still struggle with the mindset. If you can't get over that, I'm going to pass on not knowing if you have what it takes to be that person you desire to be. I see it, Jake, I do! But you have to be willing to take chances and risk the possibility of failure in order to feel the triumph of success. That's what you did at the beginning of the season. You went for it! It was scary for you, I know, but I knew if you worked hard at it and didn't give up you could surprise everybody, and you have! You have to take that chance in every aspect of your life, son. It's not just about swinging at the first fastball you get, but it's a start. You need to live your life consistently, each decision being a positive one that will move you forward, even if you fail and have to be broken down, in order to build yourself up better and stronger than before. You can do that, can't you, Jake?"

"Sure, dad," Jake said defensively, "maybe in important instances in life, but not with every at bat in baseball! I'm faring well with what I'm doing and I'm playing the best odds. It's helped me and it's helped the team. Why would I chance that?"

"Because the bigger the risks, the bigger the rewards, Jake!"

"That's how fools justify losing their life savings at the casino."

"I'm not talking about risking your life on the turn of a wheel or the flip of a card, Jake. I'm talking about betting on yourself. Knowing you can do something that might defy the odds and cause greatness for you or someone else. Sometimes those are the chances you have to take."

"Fine. You're right. But again, that's during important things in life, not baseball."

"When you step up to that plate and represent the Cubs, it's important to every fan out there watching, hoping you can do something good for the team, something that will put a smile on their faces and bring them one step closer to alleviating the pain they have suffered. You say baseball's not important, but I think deep down you feel otherwise."

"Dad, I'm going to do what I need to keep contributing to the team. It's what makes sense and it's what the coaches want me to do anyways! I have to listen to them."

"Remember, Jake, it's about consistency. Every time you make an excuse not to go for it, it makes it easier and easier to back down the next time. Once you start taking those risks, and building yourself up, you'll find it's easier to do the right thing the following time. This is about every aspect in your life, not only when you think it counts. Everything counts! Believe me, I know that now more than I ever have. I look back on my life and realize everything I did mattered, no matter how small. You have to see things that way now, son. At least for me."

"I love you dad," started Jake, feeling defeat, a tear in his eye, "but it's not fair to put that kind of pressure on me right now! I'm going to do what I can, I promise you that! But I need to ease into this. I've made a few big steps, sure, but I still have a ways to go. Let me take it at my own pace."

"Okay, son," Justin said adoringly. "I understand. I don't want to push you too hard, but you know I don't have much time left to say all I need to say. I wanted you to know how special I think you are, and how proud of you I am. That's the most important. But I also want you to know that I know you have what it takes to be anything you want. Please don't shy away from it."

"I won't dad. I won't."

The two hugged on the couch, tears in Jake's eyes.

He hated his father continuing to talk about death. Jake knew his dad had accepted his fate, but it didn't mean his family had. He wanted to make his father happy and he wanted to grant his wishes, but he knew how foolish it was to stray off the course of what he was doing and the success he was having. It might disappoint his father when he continued to play the way he was playing, but he knew his dad's life, and the life of his own baseball career, were both almost over.

He wouldn't have to worry about either one much longer.

CHAPTER 23

Jake stayed at his parents for the remainder of the season.

His mother cooked and cleaned for him and for his father while Jake concentrated on the last month of baseball, possibly for the rest of his life. The elder Riley was continuing to get worse and Jake paid for a sitting nurse to attend to him throughout the day. Both Jake and his mother knew that the time was soon approaching and they were hoping he would be able to last long enough for one more Christmas, even though the doctors did not seem too optimistic about that.

Jake dreaded the last two road trips, both being a week long, because he wasn't able to be around his father. Even with the nurse hired throughout the day, Justin was quite a handful for the family and Jake hated putting that burden on his mother. He was encouraged by Loretta calling frequently before the games to let him know dad would be watching the game and was excited to see him play.

Jake already knew this was the case, but hearing it while he was away made him feel closer to home and he thought about his dad watching him every time he made his way to the plate. The encouragement helped, even though Jake knew his dad was looking for him to start swinging at the earlier fastballs he was given. Jake never found the courage to pull the trigger. Each game and, therefore, each at bat, seemed so important in the playoff hunt.

Jake didn't start off the month of September as hot as he had been in August, but he continued to walk while seeing a multitude of pitches every at bat and causing strain and frustration on the opposing pitchers. The Cubs won their first couple series, but lost their next two on the road, getting swept in the final three games at St. Louis.

The Cubs were having a good year, but they were just 6-11 against the Cardinals, one of the big reasons they remained seven and a half games behind them for the Central Division crown. Jake struggled in the series and got the last day off as Cools Perez took his place at second and went two for five with a two run homer in the loss.

The Cubs were fifteen games from the end of the season, but their mediocre play left them worried about their playoff chances. The feeling was that they might have peaked too soon and now they were hobbling their way into October, a dangerous situation for any team, especially one only in the sixth spot. Since the expansion of the playoffs, no team seeded sixth or lower made the World Series, and only one three seed ever won it. The sample size was low, but it was on the mind of every fan and sports reporter in town, and that led to it being on the mind of every player and coach in the Cub's dugout.

The Cubs had a good team. Their pitching staff was much better than advertised at the beginning of the year. Their top two pitchers were having good years, winning thirty-five games between the two of them to only twelve losses. The bullpen had been outstanding, its 2.89 earned run average the third best in the majors. The young hitting had surprised many people, not so much because they were producing, but that they were doing so that early in their careers.

Bug Wagner had built a team he thought he could mold over time, hoping the young guys would eventually mature into smart, reliable hitters. They had done so at a faster rate than even he expected and now they were leading the Cubs into the playoffs by the likes of Sean Hammel, Bob Oates, Cam Burton, and Brent Gruber. The four offensive heroes had posted big numbers — especially in the realms of clutch hitting — and had led the Cubs to the fifth most runs in the National League, far above anyone's expectations.

Jake, although sapping the team's spirit early in the season, had been a boon the last couple of months, getting on base and wearing down the pitchers for everyone else's advantage. The other players on the team felt they were getting to the bullpen much earlier and therefore getting better match ups leading to more scoring opportunities.

The whole team recognized Jake for that effort and were happy with his production. They might not have seen Jake as positively if he had been brought in from another team with great expectations, but because most had expected him to absolutely destroy their team, they were pleasantly surprised and they even expressed that now.

Jake was now batting .214 with a .324 on base percentage, and the money was in the bag for his boss, Big Eddy Dillinger. The Cub's owner had been delighted by Jacob Riley throughout August, taunting Stan Maverick with text messages every time Jake's average went up. Now that Jake would have to pretty much not get a hit in the final fifteen games of the season, Dillinger saw him as the greatest thing in the world. Tex Klondike went from hating hearing the sob stories about the young second baseman to hating hearing the gloating on the same subject.

Klondike was reminded often of the dangerous move he had made trading Casey Earl to the Cardinals during the Cub's last series with them. Earl played great defense and had a game-winning hit for the redbirds, causing the media to again put down Klondike for the move. Tex didn't care about what the media said. He was more worried about Earl spilling his secret and causing Klondike to look like a fool.

Klondike hadn't been happy about what he had to do — he truly wanted the Cubs to be successful and for Earl to be a part of that — but the thought of his whole career being tarnished was more in the front of his brain. Now that Earl was off in St. Louis, though, Tex couldn't keep an eye on his friend and he was afraid as time went on apart, their closeness would dissipate and that might lead to Earl's full confession.

The last fifteen games for the Cubs ended up being about the same as the rest of September. They went one game over .500 on the stretch and solidified their spot as the sixth seed while the Los Angeles Dodgers won a one game playoff against the San Francisco Giants to take the National League West title and the third seed in the playoffs. The Giants ended up the seventh seed.

The Cardinals were still the first seed with the Mets taking the second spot. The National League Central had four teams in the playoffs, with the Reds taking the fourth spot and the Pittsburgh Pirates getting the eighth seed with a 79-83 record. The fifth spot was held by the Atlanta Braves.

The playoffs were seeded in such a way that no matter who won each round, there was no change in the seedings. What that meant was that if the Cubs could beat the Dodgers in the first round, they would most likely have to face the New York Mets in the second and the St. Louis Cardinals in the third, all the division winning teams that year. They could hope for an upset of the Mets or Cardinals, but they didn't have to worry about the other series. They needed to be focused on their own.

The Cubs finished the last month of the season with just a 12-14 record, second worst by any National League playoff team. Momentum was not with them, although history had never showed that momentum mattered much. Once in the playoffs, any team could win, and the Cubs were certainly one of those teams. They hoped to get their swagger back and they leaned heavily on their top two pitchers to get them through the first round.

In Chicago the big question going into the series was whether or not Jacob Riley was going to be starting at second base. In the beginning of the year, everyone would have said no, but now he was a nifty player for manager Bug Wagner. His OBP was above the norm, and his batting average during the second half was almost .250. He tormented pitchers on the base paths right after he had done so at the plate. He was also seeing the most pitches per at bat in all of baseball at 5.2, almost a full pitch more than the next best hitter.

His defense was still not close to that of Cools Perez, but he wasn't making that many errors anymore and he could even make some sharp plays at times. He ended the year with forty-eight errors, the most in the league by eleven, but he was far off the overall record of one hundred twenty-two while still close to the modern day record of fifty-one.

Chicago was split on the decision. Many fans had warmed up to their new second baseman and wanted him to be part of the playoff run. These fans liked his approach at the plate and his hustle on the base paths. They saw Jake as a hard-working, middle class ball player who received the chance of a lifetime and made the best of it. Coming from that angle, it was hard not to like him.

The national baseball media always lauded his play by the time September came. They were fascinated by his quick maturation and ability to open up a facet of the game nobody else had seen before. There were hundreds of full length articles about his stance both before and after two strikes, his eye at the plate, and his ability to make the other team continue to have to throw extra pitches. The metrics also showed how much he did for the Cub's daily chances on the field.

Those who were rooting for Cools Perez to get the starts couldn't be blamed. Cools was a great defender and after his demotion at the all-star break he had become a much more patient, and therefore improved, hitter. He was able to drive the ball to the alleys and hit the long ball and his potential was as enormous as they came. His at bats in the playoffs could be game changers and the possibility of Perez helping the Cubs in the playoffs was hard to pass up.

Those who argued for Cools didn't necessarily mind Jake, though. Most people now respected his play and it was easy for the fans to think sensibly about Riley's role for the Cubs now that they were in the playoffs and he was playing so much better. It was understood that Jake had been given a rare opportunity and that anyone in his shoes would have done the same, but there were still many who blamed Dillinger for the move and claimed that the Cubs would have had a chance at winning the Central if Earl had been their everyday player.

These people had a good point, one that Jake could never argue with, but the reality of the current situation still loomed. Jacob Riley was now an asset to the team and could easily be seen as the starting second baseman come playoff time.

While the city was split, the manager of the Chicago Cubs was not. Bug Wagner was sticking with Jacob Riley. He had many reasons for this, but the one he usually gave was that the Cubs had gotten to this point with him in the lineup and it made sense to stick with it. Bug liked the spark Jake gave to the other players by getting on base and leaving the opponents flustered.

Bug also was happy with the resiliency his second baseman showed. There weren't many people who could overcome what Jake had at the beginning of the season, and that could be a real asset in postseason play.

The real reason, though, that the Cubs' manager loved Riley was that he reminded him of himself, a gritty player who battled every time he was at the plate and who valued the importance of getting on base. Jake not only did this, but he found a new way to do so with skills Bug had never seen before. The kid was special, and although he might not be the best talent he had at second base, he was the best producer.

That was enough for Bug Wagner.

The Dodgers would not answer the questions from the media when asked who they would rather face at second base, at least not directly. They gave conservative answers such as 'each player has his own positives,' 'we feel we're ready for either possibility,' or 'it's really more about how we play, not them.'

The truth was that all of major league baseball outside of Chicago still hated Jake and hoped he was done for good. Not only was his route to get to the majors an abomination to the game, but Riley had even showed some success while doing what nobody thought he could. Almost every pitcher in the league had at least one infuriating Jacob Riley at bat where Jake spoiled pitch after pitch, raising the pitch count and sometimes ending the at bat with a soft single to right or a free pass. The pitchers couldn't stand being shown up by an amateur and Jake had a knack for being able to do just that.

The Dodgers and every other team in the league were secretly rooting for Cools Perez and an early exit for the insurrectionary Chicago Cubs.

The announcement of Jake's starting at second base for game one of the series came on October 4th, one day before the first game. This gave the media twenty-four hours to debate the move in the newspaper, on talk radio, and online. Fans were at it, too, each one thinking they had an unparalleled reason for one side or the other. The decision had the city in an argumentative state, but the solidarity of the Cubs over the Dodgers of Los Angeles still held strong. The series would be one the whole country would remember for a long time.

CHAPTER 24

The five game set opened in L.A.

There would be two games there, then two in Chicago, and, if necessary, the rubber game back in Los Angeles.

Dodger's fans had been worried about their team for a while. They had finished at 83-79 and could easily be the underdog in the series, but there were some bright spots for the California team as well. They had beaten the Giants in a three game set and then in a one game playoff to claim the NL West title. That gave them excitement and momentum.

Besides, the Cubs weren't playing their best baseball as of late. The sixth seed would have to win a five game series while playing as many as three games in Los Angeles, all in five days. That meant they could only start Vance Clary twice. He was 18-5 with a 2.68 earned run average, and they would have to rely on their third and fourth pitchers — average at best — in their two home games. The Dodgers had the advantage in pitching and home field, but nobody was counting out the Cubbies.

It was the evening of October fifth, and the Cubs were warming up at Dodger stadium. The young team, although not willing to admit it, were slightly anxious about the series. Only one starter had played in a playoff game before, setting a National League record. Each player had a good idea of what they needed to do in the game and the series, but preparing for a game and carrying out the plan were two different things.

Bug Wagner hoped he had taught his team enough to play loose and forget about the anxiety of playoff baseball, but he was pretty sure it would take a few innings to get to that point. He was relying on his ace, Vance Clary, to keep the score down and give his team a chance to scratch across a run or two in order to get the lead. Hopefully, that would put his players at ease. Clary was just the guy to do it as the one starter who had played in a playoff game and had a 3-2 record in such a situation with a 3.18 ERA.

Jake might have been nervous about the game, but it was offset by his being ecstatic by his home life. His father had done better than anyone thought, and although very sick and fragile, he was still around to enjoy seeing his son play in the playoffs. When Jake left his home the night before, his parents couldn't erase the smiles from their faces and they beamed because of their son and his accomplishments. Jake thought it was sweet but somewhat ridiculous until he realized he couldn't stop grinning, either. The game would be broadcast at 8:05 Chicago time, and the two elder Rileys assured their son they would be watching every second.

Jake was worried about his role on the team, especially when he saw that he would be batting second against the Dodger ace, Kyle Reider. Bug had used this strategy quite a few times, hoping Jake could run the pitch count up against the other team's ace in order to get to the bullpen early and have a greater chance of scoring more runs against inferior pitchers. Because of all the games being played on consecutive days, it was even more important to try to get the starting pitchers out early in order to wear out the bullpen and force them to be less effective in the final games.

Jake held some anxiety about having this responsibility in such an important situation, but he had performed well against such pitchers in the past. Bug knew Jake already had many experiences with apprehensive at bats as all of them had been this way for him in the beginning of the season.

The first inning came quickly, and Jake was in the on deck circle when he saw Hammel strike out on four pitches. Reider looked good already. His breaking ball was sharp and his fastball had great movement on it. From the first four pitches Jake could see the Cubs were going to have a hard time scoring as long as Reider was in the game. The second baseman approached the plate knowing what he had to do.

The first pitch was a ninety-seven mile per hour fastball on the outer edge of the plate for strike one. The second pitch was a befuddling curve that started out at Jake's eyes but landed right in the middle of the plate for strike two. Jake shook his head, knowing this was going to be difficult.

The third pitch was a change up that Jake saw coming right out of Reider's hands. The ball was high and Jake let it go. Even Reider was surprised when he saw the umpire call strike three on a pitch far out of the zone. Jake thought he had seen the pitch well, but went back to the bench, out on three pitches. Reider smiled, knowing he dodged a bullet with Jake's ability to run up pitch counts.

After a quick one-two-three inning, Jake ran out to second to field his position in the home half of the inning. Vance Clary looked as good as Reider had throughout the first three batters, striking out the first two on nine pitches before getting a ground ball from the Dodger's third batter.

Unfortunately, the grounder wasn't as routine as everyone would have liked.

The ball was an easy three hopper to Jake, and he only had to move one step to his right for it. He got in front of the grounder well, but as he timed the third hop, he pulled his glove up too quickly and the ball hit off the webbing of his glove. The ball fell in front of him with enough time to still get the runner, but Jake bobbled it again as he tried to swiftly make up for the misjudgment and pick the ball up with his hand.

Jake hadn't realized it until then, but his nerves were getting the better of him. He felt choppy in his approach to the easy grounder, something he hadn't felt in months, and it cost him and the Cubs. After the next batter doubled in the unearned run, the game went into the second with the Cubs down 1-0 and manager Bug Wagner's game plan unraveling early.

The next two innings were mundane, the Dodgers getting a cheap infield single which was wiped out by a double play, and the Cubs getting a two out walk who remained stranded at first. Reider had gone through three innings without surrendering a hit and having struck out five Cub batters.

Clary had looked almost equally impressive, but the run scoring double was the difference between the two pitchers and the two teams at this point.

Jake led off the fourth inning and was looking for redemption for his quick strike out and costly error. Jake was now feeling more nervous than he had before the game had started and he was looking for a way to break his anxiety. There was no better place than in the batter's box, where Jake was able to completely focus on each pitch that approached him and funnel out the clamor surrounding him.

The first pitch came in exactly as it had in his first at bat, a fastball on the outer half of the plate for strike one. Jake remembered that Reider had given him a perfect curve on the second pitch of his last at bat, and thought he might see the same thing. Sure enough, Jake saw a pitch coming in around the eyes with quick downward movement. Reider had been throwing that pitch for a perfect strike in the first three innings, and Jake recognized it immediately. He knew the ball would fall right into the middle of the strike zone, so he decided to take a swing at it.

When he connected with it perfectly, he smiled widely while running to first base, the ball getting right in between the shortstop and third baseman for the Cub's first hit of the night.

Jake was on with no outs, and he wanted to make it count. Reider had a good move to first and was quick to the plate, but the Dodger's catcher was not particularly good at throwing out base runners. Jake took a good sized lead, big enough to warrant a throw from Reider. The pitcher's toss over to first was a weak one, and Jake got back easily, but was not fooled. He knew Reider was setting him up for his good move, trying to give Jake a false sense of security in order to catch him leaning the wrong way.

For that reason Jake took a half step more on his next lead, waiting for the pitcher's move. At Reider's first movement, Jake broke back for the bag, now playing a game of his own. Jake took a chance on Reider attempting a pickoff, and when the throw came over, Jake was easily back to the bag, giving Reider the feeling that he wasn't going to be able to get the runner at first and Jake hoped he would allow for that same big lead the next time.

Jake again led off, this time with the intention of running. Reider went home with the ball, and by the time the catcher was throwing down to second, Jake was already sliding in easily with his first postseason stolen base.

Cam Burton was at the plate and knew what he had to do. Runs were at a premium with the tough pitching match-up, so the batter's job was to get the runner to third with only one out in hopes of him being able to score without the benefit of a hit.

Unfortunately, Reider was pitching so well he quickly got Burton into a 1-2 count. Jake was at second with a good lead and was pretty sure he knew what pitch was coming next. Four out of Reider's five strike outs had come by a breaking ball in the dirt. The pitch was a good one, starting in the zone and falling fast to where the hitter couldn't get to it.

Jake also knew how hard it was to field that pitch as a catcher and the

Dodger's backstop had dropped a few of them already. As soon as Jake saw Reider release the ball, he knew he was right with the pitch. The ball started at Burton's knees and fell to the left and into the dirt. Jake had taken a couple extra quick steps as soon as Reider had gone into his wind-up and then broke for third when he saw the catcher fall to his knees.

Burton couldn't hold up and swung, striking out for the first out, but Jake slid safely into third without a throw because the catcher could only knock down the filthy pitch from Reider.

The Cubs were set up to tie the game.

Bob Oates was the next batter, and Jake knew that he was looking for that first pitch fastball that could be hit into the outfield, hopefully deep enough to score a run. Jake was also ready for a ground ball, as the infield played in, but at a depth where Jake was running on contact in order to score the Cub's first run of the night.

Reider instead threw a change up and Oates crushed it four-hundred feet foul. The next pitch was a good fast ball and Oates was fooled by it. He took a weak swing as the ball moved toward the outside of the plate and the ball dribbled down the first base line.

Jake took off for the plate as soon as contact had been made and the first baseman of the Dodgers ran up the line to field it. The throw was to home, but just tardy enough for the speedy Riley to score and Jake had manufactured the Cub's first run of the postseason.

The Cubs players were filled with life, breaking through on the Dodger's ace and injecting hope into every Chicagoan. The whole team saw their second baseman take the top of the fourth into his own hands and tie the game. The Dodger pitcher was perturbed, but still masterful, and got out of the fourth and went through the fifth without any more runs. Clary matched his effort and the score remained tied in the top of the sixth when the Cubs came to bat.

The Cub's seventh hitter, center fielder Mike Otter, popped weakly out to third to start the inning, but the Cub's catcher, Ross Davidson, followed with a sharp single to center. After Clary successfully sacrificed his catcher to second, the All-Star Shawn Hammel had a chance to provide some two-out offense.

Shawn didn't get much to hit. Reider knew he'd much rather face Riley, and Shawn walked on five pitches. Jake came to the plate with runners on first and second with two outs.

Reider had been very good, only giving up the one run through five and two-thirds innings and up to this point he'd struck out nine Cubs. His strikeouts, though, had built up the pitch count to a higher rate than expected for a pitcher who had only faced nineteen batters through almost six innings.

At eighty-four pitches, Reider still had a chance to pitch two more innings if he could get out Riley quickly and have a one-two-three seventh. If he got caught up in Jake's web, however, he'd be lucky to finish six. The Dodger ace knew he would have to coax Riley to swing at an early one.

The first pitch was a fastball on the outer half of the plate and was a strike, exactly as it had been the last two at bats for Jake. The second pitch came in eye high and was off speed. It looked like the same curve ball Jake had seen on the second pitch of the previous two at bats. Jake waited for it to fall into the strike zone while Reider waited for the batter to swing at it like he had last time for a hit.

Jake wasn't going to swing, though. He had decided to run the pitch count up and was surprised when the ball stayed high through the zone and was called for ball one. Reider had tried to fool Jake into thinking he'd throw that same curve ball, but instead had thrown a high change up. Reider was irritated that Jake hadn't taken the bait and popped a ball up to the infield.

The third pitch was another fastball around the center of the plate and Jake took it for strike two. Reider cringed when he saw Jake choke up the bat and get into his two-strike stance. There was a fight coming, and Reider wanted to win it early so he could keep his pitch count low, but at the same time he didn't want to give Jake anything juicy enough that he could poke through the infield for an RBI single.

Reider threw the same high change up that the umpire had rung Riley up on in the first at bat. Jake wasn't going to let that happen again and he swung weakly, fouling it straight back. The fourth pitch was a breaking ball that dipped out of the zone, but Jake got a piece of that one, too, keeping the count at 1-2. The fifth pitch was a fastball on the inner half of the plate and Jake fouled it straight back, as he often did with balls in that location.

Reider stepped off the mound and wiped his brow while taking a deep breath. He had already thrown five pitches to Riley. It seemed like he couldn't get him out. He knew he had to continue throwing good pitches hoping that Jake would get himself out on one of them.

The sixth pitch was a fastball that was barely off the outside corner, but too close to take, so Jake poked it out of play. The seventh pitch was a low fast ball that Jake tipped just behind the plate. The eighth pitch was an inside change up that Jake chopped foul down the third base line. The ninth pitch was a fastball that came right at Jake's head. Jake hit the dirt immediately as the ball sailed over him at ninety-six miles per hour.

The umpire immediately ran halfway out to the mound and pointed to Reider and to both benches. Warnings were issued because the ump knew the throw was intentional. The next pitch from either team which hit a batter or came close to hitting one — in the umpiring crew's estimation — would result in an ejection of the pitcher.

Reider yelled sourly to the ump that the ball had slipped. At the same time the Dodger manager came out to argue briefly with the ump. Cubs players were at the railing of their dugout, yelling out at Reider for his dirty play.

When things settled down, Jake stepped back into the box with a 2-2 count and Reider's pitch count up to ninety-three. Jake was unfazed by the bean ball. He was in his zone now and nothing could pull him from it.

He knew what he had to keep doing and he intended to foul off pitches for the next hour if he needed to.

The tenth pitch was a fastball on the outside corner and Jake lined it into the right field stands purposefully. The eleventh pitch was a good breaking ball that fell into the dirt and Jake laid off it for ball three. The twelfth pitch was a high change up that Jake fouled straight back. The thirteenth pitch was a low fastball that Jake lined off to the right side. The fourteenth pitch was a fastball that landed squarely between Jake's eighth and ninth ribs and sent him to the ground again.

The umpire ejected Reider as Jake got to his feet.

The Dodger pitcher did not argue and was walking back to his dugout with his head bowed, screaming out expletives as he threw down his glove. The Cub's dugout was halfway out onto the field, angry with the throw, but the coaching staff was able to keep them from charging the Dodger team.

Jake calmly walked to first base. He put his foot on the bag and dusted himself off as if nothing happened.

The Dodgers tried to hold on to their composure, but after Cam Burton hit a base-clearing double off of Reider's replacement, they couldn't come back. The Cubs won game one of the series 5-2 and had a huge edge now on the Los Angeles team.

With the loss, the Dodgers would now have to win three out four games against the Cubs with two of those games played in Chicago. Reider knew he had lost his cool and maybe even the game for his team. Jacob Riley had gotten the better of him. He swore he would make up for it come game five when he was next scheduled to pitch, but he never got that chance.

The statistics had shown time and again there was no definitive evidence that raising pitch counts led to more runs or higher chances to win, but it categorically gave the Cubs a huge edge in game one and simultaneously in the series.

After the game, Jake received an unexpected guest to his hotel room, Cam Burton. Cam had given him the most trouble about being an outsider and a sub-par ballplayer, and he had done so since the two met at breakfast the first day of spring training. Cam's comments were usually poking fun at Jake's abilities and his cracks were perceived by Jake as oblivious comments, as if Cam didn't even know how insensitive he was being.

Jake usually brushed off those kinds of quips as he had gotten so used to inflammatory remarks all around him. However, it was always harder to have those comments come from your own teammates, and Jake knew Cam's, in particular, had stung more poignantly than the rest.

"Hey, Cam," Jake greeted as he opened his hotel door with surprise. "Nice game tonight. What's up?"

"Hey, Riley, I was hoping I could come in and have a word?"

"Sure, come in," Jake answered as he opened the door wider and sat down on the sofa, leaving the chair open for Cam.

Cam closed the door behind him and sat down. Jake didn't think of offering him anything because Cam was holding a can of soda. Cam seemed uneasy and didn't immediately look Jake in the eye even though his companion looked directly at him.

"Look, Riley," Cam started hesitantly, "I know I've given you a lot of shit this year for being an amateur and all that. I even know I probably made things a lot harder for you, too. I'm not trying to make excuses, but I really didn't want you here, and I think that not being able to blame you for taking the position as you did made it even harder for me. I was really angry at Dillinger, but it was much easier to be a dick to you. It probably wasn't fair, and I'm sorry for it."

"That's okay, Cam," Jake replied after a pause.

"Wait, I'm not done. I know people kinda look at me as a stupid jock, a guy who just clowns around and doesn't take anything seriously, but that's not true. Not all of it, at least. I really want to win, and I really take my playing seriously. I know I was lucky enough to be born with the talents I have, but I work hard — much harder than people think — to get even better. But the big thing here is that I know I need guys around me who are going to produce in order to win games. That's why I was so pissed when I heard you were going to be playing for our team. Casey Earl isn't the greatest teammate, but he was solid at second. It was hard to see him replaced for a guy who had never played before, you know? That was on the minds of all of us, but I was the one who really let it show. Now I realize that not only was it mean to you, but unprofessional as well. I'll tell you something, I know you would have never done what I did. By your actions you've taught me a lot about being a professional, not only on the field, but off of it. You don't realize how much that affects your teammates, Jake. You've done some real good here."

"Thanks, Cam," Jake said with a warm smile. "That really means a lot."

"Well, I really wanted to say thanks to you. For that double, I mean."

Jake glanced at him with a confused look.

"You know," Cam tried to explain, "my base-clearing double today? You're the one that allowed that to happen. You completely changed the game when you got Reider ejected. That at-bat was classic! Even before he hit you, I knew we had him and the Dodgers because of what you did to his psyche. I don't know if you noticed, but after you got hit, almost the whole team was on its feet, yelling at Reider. But not me."

"No?"

"Nope," Cam answered absolutely. "I knew it wasn't what you would do. It wasn't professional. This was too important of an at bat for me to lose my cool, so I kept to my warm up swings and kept my head. I knew we had the momentum so I did what I could to keep it. Sure enough, I got a first pitch fastball right over the heart of the plate and I crushed it. It felt great! And the whole time I was thinking, 'Riley set me up for that. I better thank him'. You helped me help the team, and you want to know what else?"

"What?"

"When Bug said that you were going to start the game over Cools, I knew it was the right call. And when you were batting second, I knew you were going to do something to help us tonight. I can't explain it, Jake, but you're that kind of player, and the whole team has learned from it being so close to you this season. You've helped us get to this point, and I'm hoping you can help us get even further. And that leads to why I'm really here."

Jake looked at him as if he should continue.

"From now on, you're part of our family. Anything that happens to you, happens to us. We've got your back now, and you deserve it. You're like my brother, and the whole team feels the same. That's what happens on a real team, Jake, and that's why so many of us treated you like an outsider, because you were. You broke up our family and we got protective. Forgive us for that and try to understand it wasn't personal."

Jake was touched by Cam's words and tried hard to hold back tears. The words meant so much to a man who had so many months of heartache on a team who hadn't accepted him and from players who didn't want him there at the same time the city was practically calling for his execution. The words Cam uttered made sense and were healing to the aching and damaged soul Jake had been lugging around for months.

Jake stood up as Cam did and reached out his arm for a handshake, but Cam instead pulled his friend in for an affirmative hug.

"From here on out, we'll be there for you," Cam stated as he exited the hotel room. "I just hope we get the opportunity to prove it."

Neither of the two Chicago Cubs realized how quickly that moment would come.

CHAPTER 25

The second game of the series started off well for the Cubbies as well as for Jacob Riley.

They batted first, being on the road, and wanted to take advantage of the Dodger's second best pitcher, Cliff Lozenge. They already had a 1-0 lead in the series and hoped to make it next to impossible for L.A. by beating them in a second straight game on the road.

Jake was again batting second for Chicago, and he stepped up to the plate with a man on first and nobody out. He was ready to work some Jacob Riley magic.

The first pitch came in hard and at the knees for a called strike. The second pitch was a mirror image of the first, and Jake took it for a 0-2 count. He then shifted his grip on the bat and his stance to get into protective mode. The third pitch was a breaking ball that started up high and dipped down into the strike zone.

It was a beautiful pitch and Jake stuck his bat out into the strike zone to foul it off. The bat hit a little more squarely than he expected, though, and the ball dribbled weakly out onto the field of play towards the Dodger's shortstop.

Jake's training had served him well all year in the majors. His first days with Sid in the simulated cages had taught him all the essentials of the game while his experience over the last six months had helped him work some of the bugs out, but one of the best things he had engrained into his routine was a quick release from the batter's box and hustling out every ball.

He had definitely turned some outs into hits over the season, but that wasn't even the greatest benefit of his effort, at least in terms of his contributions to the team. Every infielder in the National League knew of Riley's quickness out of the box and therefore they'd hurry even the most routine plays in order to make sure they got him out.

That led to many rushed efforts and multiple errors that sometimes opened up into big innings. Little did Jake know at the time of his training how important that attribute would be, even in the playoffs.

Jake was moving quickly down the line as the Dodger's shortstop decided to barehand the ball and sidearm it over to first. The ball beat Jake, but unfortunately for Los Angeles it was inside the bag and high. As the first baseman reached in for the ball, he hit Jake's shoulder with his glove, knocking his glove off and sending the ball sailing past both of them.

The ball headed right for the Cub's dugout, hit a metal pole and ricocheted back out into right field. Jake turned the corner and got to second while Hammel reached third.

After that, a sacrifice fly, a walk and a three-run bomb by Gruber put the Cubs up four before L.A. could stop to breathe. Jake's hustle once again opened things up for the Cub's offense, and manager Bug Wagner was looking like a genius.

Chicago continued to dominate with good pitching and fielding. A few good defensive plays — including a slick double play turn by Hammel and Riley — kept the four run lead for the Cubs through five innings. After a Riley walk and a stolen base by him and a Burton RBI single, the Cubs extended their lead to five and were looking pretty good in the seventh, up 6-1, when an odd phone call changed everything for Jacob Riley, the Chicago Cubs, and even Major League Baseball.

The phone call came in from Chicago and went to the Cub's travel secretary. None of the players were allowed to keep their phones on them or in the dugout during the games in order to keep any distractions away for the few hours a day they were on the clock. Therefore, all calls had to go through the team, and they were only brought to the attention of the manager if deemed important enough. After some debate and discussion of the matter, the secretary brought the call to manager Bug Wagner in between innings.

The skipper knew exactly what to do as soon as he heard the news. He walked up to Jake immediately after the second baseman had sat down on the bench at the end of the seventh.

"Jake," Bug explained meekly to his player, "there's a phone call for you. I think you should take it."

"For me? Now?" Jake asked with surprise.

The look in Bug's face was a somber, yet serious one, and Jake suddenly became aware of the quickening of his own heartbeat and a lump that grew in the middle of his throat.

"Oh," Jake responded heavily, aware of the possible situation. "Okay, coach. Back in the clubhouse, I'm guessing?"

The manager nodded grimly at Jake and watched his player stand up slowly and move towards the dugout's back entrance like a man walking down the hall to his execution. Bug took a deep breath as Jake turned the corner and noticed the rest of his teammates were starting to surround him, looking to their coach for answers.

Bug had to tell them something.

Jake took the phone call just outside the dugout from a phone that was attached to the wall, as it probably had been for decades. Jake faced the wall as he picked up the receiver and hit the blinking light. All he said was hello, and then listened for about three minutes to the story he knew was coming.

His mother did most of the talking. Jake listened on the other end with his head down. He was so engrossed in what his mother had to say that he had no idea his teammates had started filing into the small room behind him, eavesdropping anxiously.

"Okay, mom, I'll be home as soon as possible," Jake stated dejectedly. "I love you, too."

Jake hung up and drearily turned around, hardly flinching when he saw the rest of the Cubs looking at him compassionately. No one said a word, but everybody's face was screaming for Jake to let them into his mournful world.

"Look, guys, it was my mother," Jake started, knowing they yearned for the news. "My father was brought to the hospital today with chest pain. He had a heart attack and died before he got to the ER. My mother wasn't even with him when it happened."

Jake started trailing off as he uttered the end of his explanation. The rest of the team, with Bug, Sean, Cam, and Cools in front, saw his eyes growing heavy and wet. They started to huddle closer, giving their second baseman, and friend, some comfort in his despair.

Jake felt it and was uncomfortable at first.

"Look, guys, I'm okay. Really," Jake tried to explain.

"No, you're not, Jake," Cam interrupted. "I'm sorry you're not home for all this. We all are. But we're you're family, too. I'm hurting right now. So is Cools, so is Bug, so are all the guys in this room. We know this has been so tough for you, and now it's at its worst. We're here for you, Jake. We love you, and we love your pops, too."

It was too much for Jake.

He was trying to control himself, but the emotions began to flood. Tears streamed from his eyes and he put his head down, feeling embarrassed, but at ease, too. He felt Cool's arm around his left shoulder and Bug's hand on his right arm. Everybody was there to console him and Jake was amazed at how the solidarity strengthened him internally and even allowed him to feel better about the tears that continued to flow.

"I don't know what to say," Jake muttered.

"Neither do we," Shawn answered.

"Thank you," was all Jake could utter.

The players almost forgot they were in the middle of a playoff game when they heard some commotion behind them. It was the umpiring crew, wondering what the hold up was.

"Hey!" the home plate ump exclaimed. "What's the deal here? We have a game to play. If you guys don't get out onto the field in the next thirty seconds, I'll call this game!"

One of the coaches in the back interrupted the umpire's disciplinary speech and started to whisper something into his ear. The umps all listened attentively, looking up at Jake as they took in the mournful story.

The head umpire appeared put in his place and humbled. Silent at first, he then uttered something to the team.

"Oh, okay. You guys take as much time as you need. I'll let the Dodgers know you'll be out in a minute. Sorry for your loss, kid."

Jake gave a weak smile in the direction of the umpiring crew as they walked out of the overcrowded room. The rest of the team backed off from their mourning teammate slowly and now gave him some space.

"Jake, go home," Cools spoke out calmly, breaking the silence. "We got this, and you'll be back whenever you feel comfortable. We need you, but your family needs you more right now, and you need to say goodbye to somebody. We've got you, bud."

"Thanks, Cools. Thanks to everyone. Coach, you okay with me finding a flight back home right now?"

"Jake, we'll see you in Chicago," the manager answered.

The Cubs won the game easily, holding their lead and making the Dodger's deficit 2-0 before going back to Chicago.

Jake listened to the rest of the game while waiting for his flight to take off, and afterward contemplated his place in the world during his three and a half hour flight back to his hometown.

He was in a good place with his teammates, better than he could have ever imagined. He was thankful for such a turnaround in their demeanor, especially knowing it was in response to the results of his hard work. That kind of respect had not even been considered in Jake's mind during the early parts of the season, and now it was coming so naturally.

His father had died, but his plight was such a difficult one that the culmination was almost a relief to Jake. He felt terrible about not being there, but knew his father, a devout Cubs fan, wanted it this way. There was probably no other way that his father could have been happier about his exit from this world than watching his son play a prominent role in the Cubs beating the Dodgers in game two of the playoffs.

Jake actually smiled when he thought of it. He had given his father more than he could ever have imagined.

Jake thought about his mother, too, and how hard it had been on her with his dad's sickness and poor prognosis for so long. She must be grieving, but Jake was also happy it hadn't been more painful for both her and her husband.

Jake even thought about Angie and what she was doing now. He hadn't heard from her for two months, and he assumed she was over him and already moved on to another man she was trying to control. Jake smiled, knowing it wasn't him.

Thinking about Angie led him to think about himself and the changes he had undergone over the short baseball season. He had gained confidence, and by doing so had gained perspective. His life was much more ordered now and he realized he was the one in control. It was such an odd feeling for him that, so suddenly realizing it, he hardly believed it was true.

The gradual access of his inner self had been powerful, but almost undetectable. It was as if he finally had time to step out of his chaotic life and see what was happening in it. He liked the view. He not only saw things working out better for him, but he knew that he was the one responsible. Jake had been letting Angie control so much of his life that he had only been hoping it would turn out alright. Now he could see it really had been up to him, not chance.

He thought again about how proud his father had been of him, and right now that was most important.

Jake did know there was still some room for him to grow, and although he didn't yet suspect it, he would have to take those next steps soon if he wanted to help the Cubs continue in their quest.

CHAPTER 26

While Jake had mourned with his family in Chicago, the Cubs easily beat Los Angeles 8-2 in game three.

Cools filled in nicely for Jake with three hits and three RBI in the contest, wrapping up the series for the playoff victory. Jake also watched the Mets easily handle the Giants with a 3-0 series win. The Reds and Cardinals each won their series 3-1 and the whole National League had a few days of rest before they played again.

Jake welcomed this for the extra time it gave him with his family. His mother was mourning and Jake was comforting. The rest of the family gave condolences and took pity on these two Rileys who had lost an intimate part of themselves.

When the Cubs traveled to New York to face the Mets, Jake was back in the starting lineup batting 2nd. The team welcomed him with warmth and comfort, making his transition back to baseball an easy one. Jake wasn't sure how he would perform after the loss of his father, but having the support of his teammates helped tremendously.

The Cubs played loose baseball in New York and Jake followed. He had four hits in the two games in New York and he played spotless defense. The Cubs took the first game easily, 6-2, but dropped the second in a nail-biter after leaving the bases loaded in the ninth inning and losing 3-2.

The split was a good one for the Cubs, who now had home field advantage. They hoped to win the next two games in Wrigley in order to prevent their having to travel back to New York for a do-or-die game five.

Their prayers were not answered. They won game three by a score of 5-3 but lost game four, 7-5. Cools started the second game at Wrigley and played well for Jake, but he left two men on in the ninth inning to send the team back to New York. Now the Cubs had a must-win situation, and it would be in New York at Citibank Field instead of the friendly confines of

Wrigley.

Vance Clary got the start for Chicago after having pitched well in the playoffs up to that point. His seven inning, two earned runs, effort in game one of the series one week prior was strong enough to give him confidence in game five. The Mets opposed Clary with Steve Turnout, a big lefty with a great fastball and an even better change-up.

The gambling community was giving the Mets a small advantage.

The game started off with a 1-2-3 inning for both teams, Jake having struck out on seven pitches. The next few innings only saw two hits from the Cubs and one hit from the Mets, without either team getting a man into scoring position. The pitcher's duel was an exciting one, and the stadium, not to mention the millions watching on TV, all held their breath with each pitch, knowing one run could be the difference in who was going to the National League Championship Series and who was going home for a long, unsatisfying winter.

The Cardinals had already beaten the Cincinnati Reds three games to one, so whichever team won this game would be traveling to St. Louis for game one of a seven game series against the league's best team. Neither the Mets nor the Cubs were thinking about that at the moment, though, as each team was trying to find a way to keep their opponent scoreless and push out a run or two to give them the victory.

The Mets would strike first.

With two outs in the sixth, the Mets's second batter, Eduardo Hernandez, hit a soft liner to the opposite field between second and first. Jake was playing him up the middle and had to travel to get to the slowly hit ball after its first bounce. He dove to his left and the ball hit his glove, but spin on the ball made it difficult to grasp it and transfer it to his throwing hand while he positioned himself on his knees. The ball fell and hit the ground and the speedy Hernandez was safe at first.

The next batter, Domingo King, stepped to the plate. His large stature and calm, relaxed stance put fear into any pitcher, even the usually unflappable Vance Clary. Clary also had to be concerned with the possibility of Hernandez stealing a base and getting into scoring position for King. The Cub's pitcher knew one run could win the game and wanted to be careful with the base runner.

Unfortunately, his concern for Hernandez took too much away from his attention on the hitter, and on a 2-1 pitch King hit a monstrous shot deep into the left field bleachers. The fans at Citibank cheered in excitement while Clary looked down at his spikes in disgust.

The score stayed 2-0 until the top of the eighth, when Clary was lifted for pinch-hitter Cools Perez. The at-bat was intense, Cools working a 3-2 count and fouling off three good pitches before watching a breaking ball miss low. He trotted to first with a smile on his face and his teammates cheered on the great at-bat from the dugout. They saw an opportunity.

Hammel followed with a hard line drive to right field and the speedy Perez got to third on the play.

The Mets were not about to let Turnout face Jake. The starting pitcher had already thrown ninety-seven pitches and was showing signs of fatigue. The Mets's manager knew Jake could work the count to his advantage and drive up Turnout's pitch count further, possibly drawing a walk to load the bases with no outs for the Cubs's big hitters.

Instead the manager turned to the veteran right hander Michael Roberts, a pitcher with excellent control who threw to contact. The Mets wanted to put their money on Jake getting an out by hitting the ball rather than having the chance to work a deep count and eventually walk.

Roberts threw some good pitches to Jake, getting him to an early 1-2 count, but that's when Jacob Riley's talents came into play. He fouled off three straight pitches and watched the seventh pitch come in low for ball two. Roberts was not going to let Riley get on base with a walk and Jake knew it.

The next few pitches were all on the outside corner, and Jake fouled them off to the right. The next pitch, however, caught a little too much of the plate and Jake reached out and lined the ball over the first baseman's head, landing inches inside the line.

Jake hurried into second with a stand-up double and watched Hammel slide safely into home for the tying run. Jake couldn't help but smile as he adjusted his helmet and watched his teammates cheering him from the dugout.

Two batters later, Cam Burton hit a sharp, two-out single into center, scoring Jake from second base. The Cubs relief staff would hold down the

Mets for the final two innings with the Cubs winning the game and the series 3-2.

The city of Chicago celebrated as they anticipated the next series in St. Louis against Casey Earl and the hated Cardinals. Jake slept well that night knowing he was one of the reasons the Cubs were playing on.

CHAPTER 27

St. Louis was ready and the Cubs knew it.

On their way from the airport to the hotel the Cubs got their first glimpse of the Missouri city's excitement about playing the underdogs from Chicago. The city streets were filled with red and Cardinals caps, sweatshirts, and jackets were worn by waves of citizens while banners and billboards displayed Cardinals players, slogans, and colors. There was even a billboard that read, "Beat the Cubbies back to Chicago!"

Jake had been a Cubs fan his whole life and knew how heated the rivalry was between both sides. Unfortunately, St. Louis usually seemed to have the last laugh and they had multiple World Series Championships to prove it.

Even so, Jake loved the atmosphere.

The other Cubs players were not intimidated by it either. Maybe it was Bug's teachings or the way he prepared them for the game. Maybe it was even that the Cubs were so young they didn't know any better to be nervous. Either way, they had been playing good ball as of late and were confident in their ability.

They had beaten a good Mets team and were ready to keep fighting their way to the top. They knew they had to beat the best to be the best, and they were now getting their chance.

The first game didn't go well.

The Cubs gave up two first inning runs and three third inning runs and were quickly looking at a 5-1 deficit. The pitching regained it's exposure to hold the Cards to just one run over the next five innings, but the offense could only push two more across the plate—both on a two out single by their pitcher in the fifth—and were doubled up in game one 6-3.

On the bright side for the Cubs, this was not as much of a concern in a seven game series. Bug reassured them that it was only one game, and if they could win game two, they would take home field advantage and take the momentum away from the Cardinals heading back to Chicago. The Cubs were not looking to win both of the first two games in St. Louis, but instead to split the series and take their chances in Chicago when they would be able to throw Vance Clary in game three.

Their plan was a good one and the Cubs rallied back in the series with a game two victory. Although their pitching wasn't pristine, the offense took over to lead the team to a win. A two home run day for Bob Oates and another dinger from Cam Burton gave the Cubs a total of eight runs on the night and propelled them to an 8-5 victory.

The Cubs had tied the dreaded St. Louis Cardinals and were able to go back to Chicago feeling good about their chances.

The next game was not a good one for the Cubs. The Midwest was buzzing about the two teams and their dreaded rivalry and the Cardinal's fans had the upper hand as usual because of their team's history of winning. This year was a little different, however, because St. Louis had developed some trepidation over the Cubs' recent success and now their home field advantage.

The Cardinal's players were discussing their strategies amongst each other while revealing their anxiety over their next few games against the Cubs. This St. Louis team was a young one, and although they had been brought up in the Cardinal's farm system and been taught success, most of them had not yet experienced it. They were looking to the veterans for calmness and confidence.

One of their players was more outspoken than the others, and many were ready to listen to someone who had known the Cubs better than anyone else. Casey Earl.

The morning of the first practice was an easy one for the Cards, and some of the players had begun talking among themselves. Casey Earl was pontificating about the weaknesses of the Cub's team, and he focused on Jacob Riley. Earl's dislike for Jake had only worsened when the two became rival second basemen in the NLCS. On top of that, Jake had one more hit than Casey in the series, a stat only Casey himself was aware of as it ate away at him.

Casey was looking for any reason to undermine the one who had stolen his position from him and he was happy to talk about how terrible a player Jake was to any Cardinal who would listen.

Unfortunately for Earl, most of his teammates didn't care about his hatred for Riley. They didn't like Jake, either, but they couldn't deny the success he had brought the Cubbies. Instead, the other Cardinal's players would attempt to change the subject to something more pertinent to them winning the series, and each time they did, Earl became more and more perturbed.

Casey Earl had been holding in the secret that Tex Klondike had made him aware of for a few months now. The only reason it had not yet been revealed was because Casey promised Tex to keep it to himself, but it was getting harder and harder for him to do that. Earl knew that the information that Jake was merely a wager among some rich owners was juicy gossip and it would further tarnish Riley's reputation considerably.

Earl was not having success badmouthing Jake any other way, and eventually he decided to use the ace up his sleeve.

As most exciting news does, the gossip about Big Eddy Dillinger's wager quickly got around once it left Casey Earl's lips. Within three hours the internet sports news was lit up with the information and Major League Baseball had already decided to investigate the matter.

Both Big Eddy and Tex were beside themselves with anxiety over what was about to occur once everything was confirmed. There was no denying what had happened. Too many people knew and it made too much sense to lie about.

Jake was not surprised by any of it. He had suspected something sinister since the first day he met Dillinger. Bug also was unfazed. He couldn't understand why Dillinger had insisted upon Jake playing, but the new information was like a piece of the puzzle that finally revealed everything. The Cub's team was surprised, but not all that upset. Jake was their teammate and part of the family and they were going to defend him at all costs.

Jake was questioned by the MLB twice that afternoon and once the morning after. The press and the MLB big shots hanging around the field were a distraction for both teams, but especially for the Cubs.

By the time game three had began, every player on the field wanted to forget about the scandal.

Luckily for the Cubs, Dillinger and Klondike were honest about the accusations and they completely exonerated their second baseman. Most of the public believed that Jake knew nothing of the bet and it didn't change their minds about his character.

It did, however, change the public's minds about the Cubs. Fans were quick to criticize a team owned by such a scoundrel as Dillinger. Everything they had accomplished on the field seemed to be tarnished by the selfish bet of its owner. It didn't matter that Dillinger took accountability — and rather humbly — for the scandal, it only mattered that he initiated it and stained the reputation of baseball.

People would not forgive him for it nor would they look favorably upon the Cubs for the rest of the playoffs.

The only bright side to the fiasco was the loyalty of the fan base. The Chicago Cubs fans were quick to defend their team even though they were also calling for Dillinger's head. In the mind of the fans, what Dillinger did was villainous, but it didn't change what was happening to the Chicago Cubs presently. Despite the handicap that their owner placed upon the team, the Cubs were still in the NLCS and fighting hard to beat their rivals over the next five games.

The fans of the lovable losers now fought passionately for their team despite the enormous hatred that surrounded them. The Cubs were close to the World Series, and nothing would stop the city from believing in them.

The Cubbies fought hard that night in an electric Wrigley Field for game three. Vance Clary pitched seven strong innings, giving up one run on three hits. The Cubs countered with two runs in those seven innings, both manufactured by good base running, timely hitting, a sacrifice fly and a suicide squeeze. After the relief staff gave up a run to tie the game in the top of the eighth, the Cubs put together four hits and three walks in the bottom half of the inning.

They brought home four runs and a 6-2 victory for the series lead.

Game Four was equally successful for the North Siders. The Cardinals managed only two runs on three hits for the game while the Cubs, bolstered by an early three run first inning, were able to easily win 7-2. The Cubs were now up 3-1 in the series and had only one game to win to get back to the World Series. Chicago fans, despite the news still circulating about the Dillinger scandal, were on the edge of their seats for game five while they anticipated their team's triumph over the Cardinals and a trip to the World Series.

The stadium seemed to fill within the first few minutes the gates opened and fans flooded the stands as quickly as they could while zealous

Cubs supporters lined the streets outside. The players could barely get through the entrance as fans called out and cheered them from every angle before the big game. ESPN blanketed Wrigleyville, both inside and outside the stadium, interviewing any player, coach, or fan they could for a potential story.

The Cubs were huge news again, and everyone wanted a piece of the action.

The game was a tight one, too, and left every onlooker standing for almost the entire nine innings. The Cardinals hit a first inning home run to take the lead and the wind out of the Cub's sails. The home team struck back in the bottom of the first with a run of their own on an RBI single by Oates which brought in Riley from second. Fans again were bolstered by their hope of a possible World Series showing for their beloved Cubbies, and they hung on to every pitch thrown.

After the Cardinals scored two runs in the top of the third, the Cubs answered with a solo home run in the bottom half of the inning and a Shawn Hammel RBI triple in the fourth. The Cards scored again in the sixth, chasing the Cub's starter, but the men in blue tied it up in the bottom of the seventh with Jake hitting an RBI single to center. The top of the ninth saw the Cardinals fight hard for their lives as they manufactured two runs after a Bob Oates error.

It was now the bottom of the ninth, and the Cubs would have to rally if they wanted to wrap up the series in Chicago.

The inning started off well as the bottom of the order produced for the first time that night. After a one-out single, Cools Perez lined a ball down the left field line that produced a puff of chalk as it landed and left the Cubs down only one run with Perez now hugging second. Hammel got fooled by a change-up, though, and with two outs Jacob Riley stepped up to the plate.

Jake was unexpectedly calm for such a situation, and saw himself take the first two pitches for balls. The next two, however, were right down the middle and Jake never lifted the bat off his shoulder. After three more good pitches that Jake was able to foul off as he usually did, the Cardinal's closer became agitated. He had thrown nineteen pitches before Jake came to the plate and knew that the seven he had already tossed over to the scrappy second baseman could increase dramatically if he had let them.

The next pitch came in right at Jake's left thigh and there was no escaping it. Jake hobbled a bit as he moved towards first base, the home crowd booing. Jake was not disturbed, though. He had done what he wanted to do, which was to get on base.

He felt even more rewarded for it when Cam Burton belted a game winning three-run homer into the left field bleachers for the series win.

Jake trotted around the bases happily, jumping up and down as his teammates waited for him and Burton at home plate. The crowd was pouring onto the field, security having no more authority over them. The Cubs were huddled around home plate laughing and screaming at their success.

The Cubbies were going back to the World Series.

CHAPTER 28

The World Series. On the north side of Chicago. Cubs fans could barely contain themselves.

The team, for the most part, couldn't get caught up in the hype surrounding their unprecedented success. These "kids" hadn't known the struggles of the Cubs over the years nor had they felt the multiple opportunities that had been destroyed in heartbreaking fashion. They hadn't experienced the Ron Santo black cat, or the Leon Durham missed ground ball, or even the Steve Bartman NLCS disaster. Most only remembered the one year of glory, 2016, and that was enough for them.

There was a disconnect between the team and the fans in this regard. None of the members of the team had even grown up in Chicago or rooted for the Cubs or knew the disastrous history of the team. Except for one.

Jake knew everything about his team.

He had felt the disappointments of the Cubs and had heard all the stories of the bad luck of the franchise so many times it was as if he had experienced it all himself, all the terrible last place finishes over the years, all the good years that ended in first round playoff sweeps, and all the times when the baseball gods again laughed at the Cubbies as they pulled the rug out from under their feet. The one successful season, 2016, seemed like an aberration, and the city needed reassurance that they wouldn't have to wait another one hundred years for the next celebration. These were all parts of Jake's soul. He knew how important this was and what it meant to millions of people like him.

The sports world was in an uproar over the Cub's success. Not only did the Cubbies break their playoff draught, but they now would be going up against one of the most hated teams in baseball, the New York Yankees. While the Yankees had a great following, their success had left many angry with the team and had kept many baseball fans rooting against them.

New York had won two World Series over the past six years, adding to their already dominant number of rings. This meant not only were there millions of people outside of Chicago who were interested in the series, but they were all hoping to see the Cubs win. This year's increased incentive was sure to give a much needed boost to the number of viewers of the series, which had steadily been decreasing over the decade.

It seemed like the only place in the country that wanted to see the Cubs lose was Chicago. Sure, New York really wanted to see their Yankees win, but there were many Mets fans who also hated the Yankees and were pulling for the Cubs. It was similar in Chicago because White Sox fans were also rooting for the Yankees, hoping to see the suffering of their hated counterparts continue. The rivalry had been going on for years, the White Sox having bested the North Siders in 2005 by winning the first World Series for Chicago in almost ninety years with a team even Cubs fans were jealous of. The 2016 Cubs evened the score, but now White Sox fans were calling the season a fluke and the Cubs were eager to prove them wrong.

Now the Cubs had a chance to repay the favor, and the fans on either side were excited about each prospect, their winning or their losing.

The Cubs had the advantage, though. There was no denying that. Despite the Yankees having a better overall team, four of the seven games would be held in Chicago, and a large part of that benefit fell on the shoulders of Shawn Hammel who had played so well in the All Star game. The odds makers were giving the Cubs a little more than the Yankees, but betting on the Cubs was still seen at more than four to one. Excited Cubs fans were flooding the sports books.

The young Cubbies would be opening up the series at Wrigley Field, and all of baseball couldn't be more excited about it.

The first game was a dandy for all the viewers. The Cubs were able to reset their rotation and they now had Vance Clary facing the Yankee's ace, Cy Young finalist Mark Shooster. Shooster had a fastball in the upper nineties and a wicked breaking ball that made many great hitters look like they needed to go back to the minors. His change up was also useful because of the velocity of his fastball and he could use all three of his pitches effectively to get batters out. The Cub's hitters knew they were in for a tough game at the plate, even after the excessive amount of film they watched to prepare for the game.

The first few innings were what many expected, a pitcher's duel. Clary started the game off by striking out the first two Yankees and getting the third to pop out to Jake at second. The Cubs went down one-two-three as well in their half of the inning, Jake with a good nine pitch at bat that ended with a sharp line out to second.

Both pitchers managed to face the minimum going into the fourth. After Clary got out of a jam in the top half of the inning by getting the Yankee cleanup hitter to ground into a 4-6-3 double play, the Cubs started their only rally of the game. Hammel shot a line drive into center and Jake coaxed an eleven pitch walk. After a dramatic double steal succeeded, the Cubs were able to hit two straight sac flies which scored two runs and put the Cubs ahead.

Little offense was seen in the rest of the game besides a two out solo homer by the Yankees in the eighth to make the Cubs victorious by the slimmest of margins. The Cubs were up 1-0 in the series and looking to make the Yanks desperate by taking the first two before going to New York.

The Yankees had other ideas, though.

The second game went the Cubs way early as they scored single runs in the first three innings. Jake scored the first run after walking and stealing second. The Yankees countered with a two-run, two-out double in the top of the fourth and a manufactured run in the fifth to tie the game.

Oates hit a long home run for the Cubs in the bottom of the seventh, but the Yankees number eight batter did the same in the top of the eighth to tie it up again. After a passed ball and a wild pitch led to a Yankee run in the top of the ninth, the Cubs saw themselves trailing for the first time in the series. They needed at least one run to keep their chances alive.

The bottom of the ninth was upon them, with Jake batting fourth. He didn't realize how much that at bat would change his life.

After a lead-off strikeout by the eighth batter, Cools Perez came in to pinch hit. After three straight balls, the second baseman took a called strike. The next pitch was a fastball in on the hands of Cools, and his powerful stroke had just enough on it to fist a ball over the second baseman's head for a one-out single.

Hammel batted next but could only hit a weak ground ball to first, getting himself out but moving the base runner to second. It was time for

Jake to bat with two out and the tying run on second. He was ready for it.

Jake stepped up to the plate coolly. Far behind him were his moments of shame and anxiety. He was much more confident now, or at least he knew how to fake it. He didn't look at all intimidated as he dug in and stared down at the Yankee's big, overpowering reliever. Jake was ready for anything, even from one of the best closers in the game.

Matthew Bostis was a mammoth of a pitcher, standing 6'7" and weighing 280 pounds, but the success of the big right-hander wasn't with his size as much as it was with his smarts. Bostis knew the game well and the hitters even better. He was a master of studying film and looking for weaknesses he could exploit in hitters. Whatever the Achilles' heel of the batter, he was sure to see it exposed.

All the Cubs knew this and had tried to prepare for him. However, as most other teams had discovered, his skills were difficult to overcome.

Jake was sure Bostis knew him inside and out, even though this was the first time the two had ever faced each other. Jake assumed he would see some inside fastballs and high change-ups, the two pitches Jake had struggled with the whole year, but Jake was ready for whatever Bostis was going to throw at him, and he stood in the batter's box calmly.

The first pitch was an outside fastball, and Jake took it for a ball. The second was an inside fastball that barely hit the corner, making the count 1-1. Jake saw another inside fastball just miss the plate and a breaking ball hit the dirt in front of him to give him an advantageous 3-1 count. Jake knew that the tying run was on second, and that he represented the winning run.

He wanted to get on base by any means possible.

The fifth pitch was supposed to be an inside fastball, but Bostis made a mistake and the ball sailed almost directly down the middle. The closer, as well as all of Yankee nation, was relieved when Jake let it go by him for strike two. Jake then took a low and outside breaking ball for a free pass, and trotted down to first as the winning run.

Unfortunately, Oates popped up on the first pitch to end the game and even the series at one. Jake shook his head as he jogged off the field.

As soon as he entered the clubhouse, Jake saw Bug waiting for him. The Cub's skipper seemed solemn, as was expected. Jake sensed, though, that his manager was upset at him.

"Jake," Bug began, "tell me what you were thinking when you stepped up to the plate in the ninth."

"Well," Jake answered, confused, "I guess I was just trying to get on base. I knew I was the winning run and I was sure I could coerce a walk..."

"That's enough," Bug interrupted. "You looked so calm up there, so confident."

"I was!"

"But you didn't feel you could tie that ballgame up?"

Jake was stunned. He had faced arguably the best reliever in baseball in the World Series and coaxed a walk as the potential winning run, and his manager seemed to be giving him a hard time about it. Jake had done what he did best, and had felt good about it, at least up to this point.

"Well, I guess I could've, but I was looking to get Oates a chance to win it for us."

"That's right, Jake, you were. You were so wrapped up in a walk that you didn't see a golden opportunity come right down the middle. You didn't even appear to be looking for it."

Jake realized what Bug meant. The 3-1 fastball that was right over the plate. Jake had to admit it was a good pitch to hit. Perhaps he could have tried to hit that somewhere, but it seemed better to put those odds in the hands of a better hitter, and Jake had thought that through before he even had stepped up to the plate.

"I wanted to give Bob a chance..."

"Jake," Bug interrupted again. "Do you know what Bostis was thinking after you let that pitch go? Did you see his face after he made one of the biggest mistakes of the year and you let it sail past you for a called strike? He was relieved! Thanking God, right there on the mound, that you didn't pound that ball up the middle for a game tying hit or even worse, over everyone's heads for a home run!"

"But I'm not the guy..."

"Do you really think that, Jake? You're not the guy? Did you notice the way Bostis pitched to you? He wanted no piece of you. He wasn't interested in throwing fifteen pitches to you to eventually end up in a walk or to give you anything to hit to bring in Perez. But he went right after Oates and got him on the first pitch. He was pitching around you to get to Oates."

Jake looked at his manager in disbelief, not knowing what to say. He couldn't believe that anyone would pitch around measly little Jacob Riley to get to a great hitter like Bob Oates. But remembering the at bat, it did seem like he got on rather easily. It still appeared too crazy to be true.

Was Bostis afraid of him? Jake couldn't believe it.

"You know another thing, Jake?" his manager started again, realizing his second baseman was too dumbfounded to answer. "I was looking to you for that hit, not Oates. I knew you were the one who could tie that game up. I was disappointed when I saw Bostis pitching around you, but more disappointed when I saw you let him get away with it."

Jake looked down, not wanting to keep eye contact with his manager. It all hit him at once. Even as he realized what had happened, what he had done for years and what he was continuing to do, his manager spelled it out for him anyway.

"Not everyone has what it takes to play baseball, Jake. Somehow, by some one in a million shot, Eddie Dillinger found you in a crummy restaurant and brought you to where you needed to be. I don't know how the hell it happened, but it did. Some people would grab that opportunity and squeeze every ounce of excitement from it even though they would most likely go down in flames. They wouldn't care about the outcome so much as the opportunity. But you, you came in scared, despite your abilities and despite your success. And that's okay. It was a scary thing for you. But that's over now. You're here, and we're here, in the World Series, because some no-name at second base has lit a fire under a young, talented team looking for something to rally around. You are the one I want at the plate when the game's at stake, and you have to start believing in yourself and what you've done! This isn't just about baseball, Jake, but about you! Some people want to give someone else a chance to win the game, but the true champions want it to come down to them. You have to show the world you've got what it takes to be that winner, but first off, you have to convince yourself of it. Look, I'm an MLB manager who's been around this game for a long time, and I see it in you. Isn't that enough?"

Jake was almost looking through his manager now, listening to every word but lost in thought. He was dismayed about his situation and knew Bug was right. He had always been the one to want someone else to be the hero, and he had proved it tonight. He had made so much progress, and he thought that was enough, but it wasn't.

It wasn't enough for his father, either. A tear formed in his eye that threw Bug backpedaling.

"Look, Jake, I didn't mean..."

"No." Now it was Jake's turn to interrupt.

"No, what?"

"No, Bug, it's not enough for you to have faith in me," Jake said with meaning and self-conviction. "People have had faith in me my whole life, but I never acknowledged it. Now one of them is gone, and my biggest fan will never see me fulfill his expectations. It's about time I had faith in myself. No one will be disappointed in me like that again."

Jake walked away from his manager, not waiting for a reply. Bug cocked his head in approval and pride as he watched his star rookie walk away.

Things had been set right, and both men could feel it.

CHAPTER 29

The series was tied 1-1 and headed to New York.

Yankees fans cheered triumphantly when their home team clobbered the Cubs 8-2 in game three. The Cubs were pushed against elimination after losing a close one in game four, 4-3. Behind another strong World Series outing by Vance Clary, the Cubs managed to send the series back to Chicago with a 5-1 victory and now trailed 3-2 overall. The Cubs had to win both games, but now they had home field advantage.

Backed by two Jake Riley walks followed by Bob Oates homers, the Cubs were able to win game six 8-4. They had won two games in a row and with that momentum were able to play a winner takes all game seven at home. The city of Chicago was buzzing about their team and the Cubs players were excited about their chances.

Jake had done well over the series, playing solid defense while collecting a few big hits. The sting of Bug's words from game two still hurt, though. Jake knew that although he had made strides he never thought possible in the game of baseball, it hadn't really changed the way he lived his life. He had made a few friends along the way and had shed the clinging and corrosive Angie, but he still was conducting himself the way someone who didn't believe in himself did.

Jake knew his father was never proud of this behavior and had expected much more from his son. Now he had done something in baseball nobody thought possible. Maybe his father was right to expect such things.

Jake realized it was time for him to start feeling the same.

Game seven was talked about all over the country. Every Chicago fan had gotten up early that day and had already filled the establishments of Wrigleyville. They were anxious and excited at the same time for the outcome that would either cause a widespread celebration or a heartache worse than any felt before, even for Cubs fans. The sportscasters were all around Wrigley, interviewing fans about their feelings going into the evening and about their guesses on the conclusion of such a tumultuous season.

The players, though, had remained relatively calm. The initial anxiety of playoffs and the World Series now seemed to be past them. The team was in the locker room and on the field early, preparing for the contest and attempting to do a little extra in hopes it would pay off come game time.

Jake was going through his usual routine of meals, stretching, batting and fielding practice, knowing that although this was going to be a night unlike any other, it didn't change the approach. Jake, and the Cubs, had been well prepared for every game this year and there was no reason to change things now.

When game time did arrive, 7:05 central time, the seats were full of fans, many already with hoarse voices from cheering on anything they found appropriate. The analysts were peppered all over the television channels, each with his own predictions of how the game would turn out and who would be the heroes and the underachievers.

Nothing could deter the excitement or the anticipation of the first chance the Cubs had of winning the World Series at Wrigley Field, and the first inning didn't disappoint.

The Yankees first three batters had two singles and a walk, loading the bases for their cleanup hitter. On a tough ball in the hole between short and third, Shawn Hammel made a nice pick and throw to second while Jake made a nice turn to finish the double play and keep the Yanks to only one run.

The bottom half of the inning featured three hits including a majestic Cam Burton homer to give the Cubs a 3-1 lead. Jake watched all the action from the bench after he struck out swinging.

The second inning was rather quiet, both teams going three and out on relatively few pitches. This was a relief to both sides as nobody wanted to have to go to their bullpen early to decide the outcome of the biggest game of the year.

The third inning, however, was disastrous for the home team. An error by the catcher on a sacrifice bunt led to runners at second and third with no outs. Three batters later the Yankees had fully capitalized and made it 3-3. Worse, the next two batters hit back to back homeruns, giving the Yankees four runs on the inning and a 5-3 lead and chasing the Cubs' starter early.

A pinch hitter in the bottom of the inning meant a change in the pitcher, and everyone saw Vance Clary warming up in the bullpen and hoped their ace could come in and limit the damage from the opposing team on only two days rest.

Unfortunately, the stress was tough on Clary and he tried to do too much. There were multiple walks and the Yankees were able to run up the score.

After five innings the home team was looking at a 7-3 deficit with time running out to come back. Fans were starting to lose hope that this would be a year of celebration on the north side of the city.

Another walk and a wild pitch in the top of the sixth made things even more grim, the Yankees going up 8-3. Hearts were breaking and spirits were melting in the Cub faithful. The stadium was quiet, appearing anxious and solemn all at once. The fans in the street were stagnant, nervously shifting from one side of their body to the other, the only movements noticeable from above.

Even some of the players had started wondering if the deficit was insurmountable.

Before the bottom of the sixth, Bug approached Jake, the leadoff hitter for the inning.

"We really need base runners," he told his young infielder, looking into his eyes almost in desperation.

"I know, coach," Jake answered back confidently as if he wasn't even aware of the score. Bug looked back intently, attempting to draw some inspiration from his player until he realized it should be the other way around.

Jake stepped up to face the Yankees starter who had already thrown eighty pitches throughout the first five innings. Jake watched the first pitch go right down the heart of the strike zone. The second wasn't much different. Jake watched patiently as he went down in the count 0-2. Jake choked up on his bat and stood in the stance familiar to all in the park. It was time to waste pitches, as many as he could, in order to get on base, run up the pitch count, and hopefully frustrate the Yankees.

As usual, Jake was able to do just that. He ruined a great slider, fouling it off to the right. The next pitch was another fast ball that Jake was able to foul straight back. The fifth pitch in the sequence was a breaking ball that landed in the dirt, Jake coaxing his first ball. Three more pitches came in close enough to the zone that Jake weakly offered at them, sending them out of play.

It was eight pitches in and the Yankee's starter saw no end in sight. He knew where this was going, but what could he do? The last thing he wanted was to give up base runners while up five runs. He decided to groove a couple fastballs and hoped Jake would put a ball in play and get himself out.

Jake wasn't looking to chance that. Foul ball after foul ball heightened the nerves of the pitcher and the patience of the Yankee's manager.

After fourteen pitches, pitch number 94 overall, the count was full at 3-2. The pitcher finally gave in and threw the next pitch way outside, conceding that he had lost to Riley and put him on first base.

The crowd started to cheer, hoping this would cause some momentum to shift back over towards the home team. Sure enough, the Yankees starter was now fatigued and irritated, and the Cubs were able to take advantage.

Oates ripped a double down the line, scoring Jake from first. Burton then cut the deficit by dropping a ball into the basket in left field, just enough muscle to make the score 8-6. The Yankees pulled their starter and were now into their bullpen, feeling their once safe lead was quickly disappearing.

Both bullpens fared well over the next couple innings, and the Cubs found themselves still down two going into the bottom of the ninth. The jolt that Jake had sent into Cubs nation was starting to turn back to nervous anticipation. A pinch hitter was due up for the pitcher's spot and then the top of the order with Hammel and Riley would be the three bats that everyone was depending on.

They would be facing their biggest obstacle yet.

The behemoth of a man Matt Bostis was warming up and was ready to take down the Cubbies once again, this time for good. He was an unbelievable pitcher even when he had to protect a one run lead. Now he had a two run cushion. He was fresh, too, not having pitched since game five. He looked sharp on the mound during his warm-up tosses with each pitch hitting its spot with a dramatic boom in the catcher's mitt.

After every pitch Bostis would glare at the on deck circle for his first victim. Cools Perez stood there waving his bat for warm-ups, unfazed by the pitcher's attempts.

Jake walked up to Cools to make sure his teammate was prepared for what was coming. Cools looked at him as if they were talking in the clubhouse without the World Series on the line.

"What's up, Jake?"

"Cools, you know what we need here, right?" Jake asked, more for reassurance than to question him.

"Yeah, bud. Base runners," Cools answered calmly. "I hope Jake Riley knows what we need when he sees me on base in a few minutes."

Jake grinned at his friend's understanding. Cools smiled back.

"Now get back to the dugout. I'm up first, not you. Wait your turn!"

Jake walked down the steps with his bat, watching Cools approach the plate. This was it. Would it be enough?

Cools stood in the box and watched Bostis' first pitch hit the outside corner at 99 miles per hour. Down one strike, Cools saw the next pitch come in low, evening the count 1-1. The next pitch was again on the outside corner for strike two. The fourth pitch was a nasty breaking ball that fell to the dirt and Cools was able to hold off to again even the count, now at 2-2.

The fifth pitch was another fast ball on the outside corner, and Cools flung his bat out, weakly fouling it off to the right. The sixth pitch was a curve ball on the outside corner, placed perfectly, and Cools again fouled it off. The seventh pitch came inside, and it was close enough that Cools again had to foul it off to stay alive. The eighth pitch was an elevated fastball that was taken to make the count full.

The next three pitches were all fastballs in the strike zone, and Cools weakly made contact on all three of them, fouling them straight back to keep the at bat going.

It was eleven pitches in, and Bostis hadn't even gotten an out yet. He was used to throwing only 15-20 pitches at a time, and he knew he would have to try to get rid of Cools Perez as quickly as possible. After two more pitches were fouled off, Bostis began to see what Perez was doing, and it infuriated the Yankee's closer.

Bostis glared at Perez angrily and threw a fastball right down the middle of the plate. Perez fouled it back weakly. Bostis had had enough.

"What's the matter, Perez? Afraid to hit the ball?" Bostis barked toward the plate as he caught the catcher's return throw. Cools stood in the box calmly, waving his bat as he had done before.

"You trying to be like your boy Riley? That kid's a joke! And so are you!"

Cools continued to wait the next pitch, not uttering a word.

Bostis was steaming now. His next pitch was way off the mark, a fastball high and tight at 101 miles per hour. Cools jumped back and then smiled as he tossed his bat to the side and trotted to first base with a lead-off walk.

Bostis turned his massive body in disgust, trying to calm down before the next batter.

Hammel stepped to the plate and took two strikes that were almost right down the middle of the plate, quickly going down 0-2. Then the whole stadium saw Hammel choke up on his bat and await the next pitch. Bostis saw his intent and snorted in disgust.

Wrigley Field got louder and louder as Hammel fouled off pitch after pitch, finally evening the count at 2-2. The next pitch was again right down the middle of the plate and Hammel played pepper with it, hitting it right back up the middle for a clean single, sending Perez to second.

The Cubs now had runners on first and second with no outs, the winning run coming to the plate, and Bostis already having thrown 24 pitches.

Hope spread from Wrigley Field to O'Hare airport and all the way over to Joliet. Cubs fans could feel it.

Bostis felt it, too, and it made him nervous. He was already frustrated and he knew what the Cubs were trying to do to him. It was working, and now Riley would be coming up to the plate to do the same. He couldn't let Riley reach with a walk, as it would put the tying runs in scoring position and the winning run on first with the power hitters coming up. Bostis knew he had to get ahead of Jake early and find a way to get him out before he found himself having thrown forty pitches in the inning.

Jake stepped up to the plate, ready for what was to come. He saw Cools look at him from second and nod. Jake looked over at first and saw Hammel smiling at him, and that caused Jake to grin, too.

Jake looked at Bostis and saw fear. This was the time for Jake to break through. This wasn't self-sacrifice time, or playing it safe time. This was hero time and Jake was ready for his transformation.

Jake took his warm-up swings in the box as Bostis looked down at his catcher for the sign. Jake was not going to be choking up. His hands were at the bottom of the handle and his bat was held back ready for authority. As expected, Bostis came to Jake with a fastball right down the middle of the plate, but Jake had been well set up by his teammates' patience at the plate before him.

As the ball traveled right into the heart of the zone, Jake stepped his left foot forward and twisted his back powerfully. He swung his bat out through the middle of the zone, his arms fully extended and his eyes focused on the ball.

As soon as he started his swing, Bostis' eyes grew wide in fear. He knew he had been set up before the bat even hit the ball.

The crack of contact filled the stadium, previously silent with anticipating Cubs fans. The ball ricocheted violently off Jake's bat and headed for the left field bleachers. The ball buzzed out of Wrigley in a hurry and sailed over the seats and to the left of the video board.

Everyone was on their feet in excited disbelief. Jake, for the first time all year, stood in the box and watched his majestic shot clear the stadium. It was the most beautiful thing he had ever seen.

Jake began to run the bases, the whole crowd having erupted over what they had witnessed. The Yankees were walking off the field, and Bostis' head hung down in disgust. The Cubs were flooding the field and crowding around home plate as they welcomed their teammates in one by one. Jake saw fans coming out onto the field and a couple of them made it past security and patted Jake on the back as he was rounding second.

Jake ran the bases in a state of tranquility.

He was able to drown out the noise and excitement of the moment and focus on what he had done. His home run was one that freed the captive north side of Chicago from possibly experiencing another drought incomprehensible to the rest of the world. Jake had given the win to the city of Chicago, and they would be grateful for the rest of his life.

But this was about more than baseball. Jake had not only realized what he needed to do to become the man he needed to be, he had gone out and done it. And in dramatic fashion! Swinging at that first pitch, knowing what was coming and delivering the dagger was something he never would have done in the past. Suddenly it seemed as natural as could be. Jake was who he wanted to be, and the Cubbie Blue was thankful he was.

What broke through the peace Jake had felt as he rounded the bases was the sight when he rounded third—his whole team, his new family, all waiting there for him with smiles and excitement, waiting to congratulate him and celebrate with him something they had all built together and he, Jacob Riley, had completed.

For a second Jake looked away embarrassed, but a smile came to his face as his teammates jumped up and down, clapping and chanting his name. Jake jumped onto home plate as they all swarmed him aggressively with what seemed like the rest of the city soon to follow.

The Cubs had won the World Series. Suffering had been eradicated. A hero had been born.

It was time to celebrate.

CHAPTER 30

The celebration lasted for over a week.

There were parades, banquets, and parties, all to congratulate the Chicago Cubs on their championship. The players rejoiced and the fans reveled. No one was able to talk about anything else.

Big Eddy Dillinger was reprimanded by the League. He was told to find a buyer for his now profitable baseball team within one year and he was banned from ever being affiliated with baseball again. He was also fined, an appropriate amount of ten million dollars, erasing his winnings from the infamous bet that would go down in the folklore of Chicago sports as one of the greatest disasters—or was it, some fans wondered—ever.

None of that stopped Dillinger from doing one thing he had hoped to do before he got out of baseball. With the fans backing him all the way, Dillinger signed Jacob Riley to a one year contract worth three million dollars. The team had hoped to sign Riley for at least two years, but the hero second baseman wouldn't let them.

Jake spent most of the off season training and spending time with his mother, knowing she needed him desperately after the death of his father. Loretta Riley would remind her son that his dad was excited about the Cubs, but even more thrilled about his son's new found success.

Jake would also find time to hang out with his new friends from the team. They were like brothers now, always bringing up different moments of the season just as if they were all sitting around the dinner table while growing up. Jake enjoyed his new coterie far more than he could have ever imagined after first meeting them not even a year earlier.

The companionship made it easy for him to move on with his life happily while easily resisting multiple attempts by Angie to rekindle an old broken romance.

But baseball was not the center of Jake's life. It never had been, and he knew it never should be. Baseball was a game — a great one — that gave him what he needed to succeed, but it wasn't more powerful than life itself.

Jake applied for medical school, was accepted and would enter it the following year. He would also have plenty of money to pay for it after signing his one year contract. Baseball had given him so much, and now it would pay his way through school and give him enough money, and popularity, to be able to live his life comfortably.

That next season Jake batted .261 with an on base percentage of .381. He hit six home runs, scored 107 runs while collecting 57 RBI and watched his Cubs fall to the Atlanta Braves 3-2 in the second round of the playoffs.

Overall it had been a successful year, though, and Jake knew his teammate Cools Perez was in line to take over the spot he would abandon. The year had been a good one for Jake, too, but nothing compared to the next eight he spent in medical school, residency, and fellowship.

Jake became a pulmonologist and he worked hard in the prevention of cancer and smoking related disease states. He was a great physician and well known throughout the city for his medical prowess, not just for his hero status as a member of the magical '25 Cubs.

He was able to live his life the way he wanted — with him in charge— and he taught his children to do the same. Jake's success in life gave him the opportunity to touch others' lives, and he was always well appreciated.

Jake, even years after the famous World Series championship, remembered that period of his life as the time he was able change from a boy to a man. He remembered his father well for his help in the transformation and Jake was often sad that his father was never able to see the result of his son's maturation. Jake also credited Bug for his success and he continued to meet with him as old friends, or family, often would.

Baseball is baseball, but life is paramount. There was a time when Jake wasn't so sure of that, but it had become crystal clear. Jake would always look fondly on his time in a Chicago Cubs uniform, but he knew it was transient next to what that time had done for his future. Nothing could take that away from him now. His new found confidence was too cherished to ever let it wander again.

Jake was happy with the man he had become, and baseball was happy with the man it had created.

The world was fortunate for both.